Sleuthing in Stilettos

By Debra Sennefelder

Food Blogger Mysteries
THE UNINVITED CORPSE
THE HIDDEN CORPSE
THREE WIDOWS AND A CORPSE
THE CORPSE WHO KNEW TOO MUCH
THE CORPSE IN THE GAZEBO

Resale Boutique Mysteries
MURDER WEARS A LITTLE BLACK DRESS
SILENCED IN SEQUINS
WHAT NOT TO WEAR TO A GRAVEYARD
HOW TO FRAME A FASHIONISTA
BEAUTY AND THE DECEASED
SLEUTHING IN STILETTOS

Sleuthing in Stilettos

By Debra Sennefelder

LYRICAL UNDERGROUND
Kensington Publishing Corp.
www.kensingtonbooks.com

LYRICAL UNDERGROUND BOOKS are published by

Kensington Publishing Corp.
119 West 40th Street
New York, NY 10018

All Kensington titles, imprints, and distributed lines are available at special quantity discounts for bulk purchases for sales promotion, premiums, fund-raising, educational, or institutional use.

Special book excerpts or customized printings can also be created to fit specific needs. For details, write or phone the office of the Kensington Sales Manager: Kensington Publishing Corp., 119 West 40th Street, New York, NY 10018. Attn. Sales Department. Phone: 1-800-221-2647.

Lyrical Underground and Lyrical Underground logo Reg. U.S. Pat. & TM Off.

First Electronic Edition: December 2022
ISBN: 978-1-5161-1102-2

First Print Edition: December 2022
ISBN: 978-1-5161-1104-6

Printed in the United States of America

For my cousin Debbie Mulach.

Chapter 1

Kelly Quinn eyed the closet of tunics and blouses before stepping forward and flicking through each one. She quickly appraised what could sell at her consignment shop, the Lucky Cove Resale Boutique. Annabeth Travis had been a frugal woman before her death six months ago, and it showed in her wardrobe. Her daughter, Courtney Johnson, had told Kelly her mom preferred not to spend money on frivolous things. Fashionably speaking, there certainly was nothing frivolous about Annabeth's clothing. Not even a ruffle in sight.

"Well? What do you think? There are also clothes in the dresser. And in the hall, there's a coat closet." Courtney had led Kelly through the modest home into the bedroom minutes earlier. Her shoulders had slumped with the weight of grief and responsibility. Kelly understood how her friend felt. She remembered how much work it had been when she inherited her granny's business and home.

"Your mom preferred the minimalist look, didn't she?" Kelly reached for the sleeve of a V-neck mixed-stitch tunic. She inspected the finish on the sleeve and the underarm area. Unfortunately, visible signs of wear and laundering meant it wouldn't sell at the boutique. However, the item had a little life left and could be donated.

Courtney chuckled. "If by minimalist you mean frugal, then yes, she was."

Kelly's gaze landed on a pair of knit black bootcut pants. She pulled the hanger out and slipped the pants off. "These look brand new."

While Kelly had gone to work looking for consignable clothing, Courtney had gone back to her task of packing. She looked up from the box of knickknacks she'd just taped closed.

"They are. I bought those pants for Mom just before she..." Her voice choked, and she lowered her head. "I'm sorry."

Kelly set the pants on the bed. Her heart ached for her friend. Annabeth's death had been sudden, leaving Courtney to deal with the loss while tending to all the details of her mom's estate. The modest estate consisted of the home her parents purchased fifteen years ago—a simple ranch home on a cul-de-sac with a Sold sign on the front lawn. The house sale had been quick, which meant Courtney had only days to clear out everything before the closing. She'd asked Kelly to come by to see what could be consigned, while antique dealer Walt Hanover sorted through the furnishings to see what he could sell at his antique shop.

"There's no need to apologize. I understand. I really do." Kelly couldn't let her thoughts go any further on the subject, or she'd dissolve in a puddle of tears.

Courtney gave a small, knowing smile. Kelly knew they both felt raw with emotion and were treading carefully so as not to completely break down.

"I hope this gets easier and soon. I really do." Courtney pushed the box off to the side with her foot and then lifted another box off the floor and set it on the bed.

Kelly folded the pants and set them to the side. She noticed a hardcover book on the nightstand and moved closer. The title caught her attention: *Danger Next Door*. True crime. She hadn't read one of those in ages. Instead, she'd been living it. She lifted the book and flipped it over to read the blurb on the back.

"My mom was obsessed with true crime. She always had one on the nightstand. So, I have no idea how she slept at night." Courtney reached her arm out over the double bed for the book. "How have you managed to sleep soundly at night?"

Kelly handed over the hardcover and pressed her lips together. The question was a valid one. She had found herself tangled up in one too many murder investigations since returning to her hometown of Lucky Cove, New York. Unfortunately, the one that caused the most sleep deprivation had been the murder of her cousin, Becky Quinn, over the summer. She was tempted to shrug off Courtney's question and give a glib answer so they could move on with their tasks at hand. But she wasn't feeling that glib.

"It's not easy. But knowing that justice was served helps. Like it must have for Adriana Barr's family." It had taken a little time searching her memory before Kelly finally remembered. The Manorville resident written about in *Danger Next Door* had become the obsession of a neighbor, which ultimately led to her death.

Courtney nodded thoughtfully. "It was so sad. Her family was devastated, and his family was…well, he really didn't care about anyone but her."

"They never do."

Courtney set the book down and propped her hands on her hips. Her gaze swept around the room. "I don't know how I'm going to get the entire house packed in time for the closing."

"I know it seems overwhelming, but you'll get it done. You have Walt going through the furniture, and I'm going through the clothes." Kelly flashed her most hopeful smile, and it worked. She got a small smile from her friend. "I'll help you pack."

Kelly would be grateful for another task to add to her to-do list. Keeping busy seemed to be the only way she could not think about Becky's death 24/7, though her therapist had said doing what she was doing was unhealthy. Perhaps Dr. McMahon had been right. Possibly stopping the sessions hadn't been the smartest thing Kelly had done. Heck, it was just another bad decision in a long list of bad decisions over the years.

Kelly snapped out of her thoughts and refocused on the here and now. She walked around the bed, on her way to the dresser to check out its contents, when she stopped at an opened box on the floor. Stuffed inside were photographs, file folders, and magazines. Definitely a hodgepodge of things Courtney would need to make decisions on at some point.

"I appreciate the offer, and I'll probably take you up on it," Courtney said. "Not only do I have to sort through all the furniture and knickknacks, but I also have to sort through boxes my parents packed decades ago."

She hoisted one such box up to the bed. Scrawled in black marker on the side was a date. It had been packed twenty years ago.

The stack of photographs in the box drew Kelly's interest. She peeked at the top one—a group of people on the beach. It looked like a bonfire.

"This one plus two others were up in the attic." Courtney blew out a breath, and her wispy cinnamon-colored bangs fluttered. She closed the box and carried it to the corner of the room where three others had been stacked. "I have to figure out what's important and what isn't, but that can wait until after I hand over the keys. Between all this and the shop, I swear I need an extra ten hours a day."

Courtney owned the gift shop Courtney's Treasures. It was a few shops down from Kelly's boutique. Courtney had been one of the first shop owners to welcome Kelly into the Main Street business community. Not too long after, Kelly eagerly joined the chamber of commerce.

"You have Zoe to help you. Speaking of work, I need to get back to it and see what else I think will sell." There wasn't a lot Kelly could work with, but the bright side was that Courtney would be able to make a sizable donation to the church's clothing drive. She dove back into the closet and started sorting clothing, and twenty minutes later, she had an armful of clothes to take back to the boutique. And Courtney had three full bags of clothes to drop off at church later in the day.

"I have to get going to open the boutique. I'll come back later to look into the coat closet and dresser, okay?" Kelly asked as she reached the doorway. "Don't forget about the chamber of commerce meeting."

While volunteering for the chamber had been out of necessity to keep herself busy, Kelly had come to enjoy taking on a more active role in the business community. It made her feel more grounded and connected to Lucky Cove. She'd turned her back on her hometown ten years ago. Maybe this was her way of trying to make amends for her mistake.

Courtney groaned. "Another meeting?"

"Don't be like that. It's a luncheon meeting at the Lucky Cove Inn. They have great food." Kelly's mouth watered at the thought of the inn's fettucine Alfredo. She wondered if it would be on the menu.

"They do set up a nice buffet. So, I guess I can squeeze it into my schedule. And it would be nice just to sit for an hour."

"That's one way to look at it. It's crucial all the members attend this meeting. We're going to discuss plans for the holiday season. We want to promote Shop Small Saturday. Lucky Covers should be spending their disposable income right here on Main Street, not in Manhattan."

Shop Small Business Saturday was a national shopping day sandwiched between Black Friday and Cyber Monday. The day encouraged consumers to shop and support their local businesses. Last year, Kelly had been too overwhelmed with her first holiday season to participate in the event. So she intended to make up for it this year.

"It's hard to compete with the city," Courtney said.

"Well, they do that Christmas show, and they have all those amazing shops and that giant tree." A hint of wistfulness worked its way into Kelly's voice. She loved strolling along Fifth Avenue, shopping bags from countless stores in hand, with the brisk air wafting the fragrance of roasted chestnuts and the chorus of ringing of bells by sidewalk Santa Clauses. The memory was beloved, but her hometown was where her heart was now. While Lucky Cove had a tremendous amount of charm and tradition, it could up its game when it came to decking itself all out for the holiday shopping season.

"Perhaps we can get the Town Players to whip up a Christmas musical." Courtney laughed, and Kelly joined in, happy to see some lightness in her friend again. "And a taller tree!"

"I might just suggest that at the luncheon. Oh, I'll invite the newest shop owner on Main Street to join us," Kelly said.

The lightness in Courtney dimmed as quickly as it had appeared. "Miranda Farrell?"

Kelly nodded. "I haven't had a chance to meet her yet. Though, the shoes she has displayed in the shop window are killer."

"Well, Miranda isn't much for joining things." Courtney moved toward the chest of drawers and removed the framed photos set on top to the bed.

"You know her?"

Courtney shrugged. "Not really. She lived here a long time ago."

The silence that fell between them was thick. It was clear to Kelly that Courtney hadn't wanted to talk about Miranda, which piqued her curiosity about the woman.

"I…I should get going." Kelly hoped Courtney would say more about Miranda, but she hadn't. Just silence. Okay, then. "I'll be in touch about the rest of the clothes." She gave a final glance at the room and then turned to leave. She traveled along the hall and when she reached the living room, she glanced in.

Walt Hanover stood at the claw-foot coffee table with his hands propped on his hips and an exasperated expression on his face. His employee, Bud Cavanaugh, was leaning against the fireplace mantel and texting on his phone.

"Would you get off that darn thing?" Walt snapped. "Go on into the dining room and get the chairs out to the truck."

Bud slipped the phone into his back pocket and moped out of the room, passing Kelly, and he flashed a sheepish smile.

"Good morning, Kelly." Walt looked up from the coffee table. The piece of furniture looked old but in good condition. His interest indicated that it was an antique. The salt-and-peppered, reed-thin sexagenarian had a deep appreciation for all things old. "He's worse than a teenager with that phone. But I think it's because he's lovesick."

Kelly chuckled. First, Walt's use of the word "lovesick" seemed as ancient as the antiques he coveted. Second, hearing that a man in his early forties behaved like a teenager with a cell phone just seemed so funny. Though she was happy to hear that Bud probably had a new girlfriend. The last one broke his heart.

"You think you can sell that coffee table?" Kelly didn't want to gossip about Bud's personal relationships, so she steered the conversation back to the coffee table.

Walt straightened up and grinned. "This is a mahogany Chippendale coffee table circa 1930. I have at least two clients who would jump at this. You think you can sell what you have there?"

Kelly glanced at the clothes draped over her arm. "In a New York minute. So I'd better get going. Have a good day, Walt."

She stepped out into the chilly morning air. Early October was a fickle month in the northeast, especially on Long Island. The temperatures could range from the low fifties to balmy nineties and anywhere in between. That morning was an in-between morning and had her reaching for her newest purchase—a camel-colored coatigan. Officially, the longline garment was a sweater. But its weight and style lent itself to being a coat when it was too chilly for just a cardigan, and you didn't want to pull out a heavier outerwear garment just yet. The day promised to warm up as the sun broke through the clouds. Kelly wasn't overly excited about that forecast. She loved autumn in all its pumpkin spice goodness and coziness of sweaters with tall boots.

When she reached her Jeep, which technically wasn't hers, the cargo door opened with a click of her key fob. The vehicle was on loan from her friend and employee, Pepper Donovan. Pepper and her husband had graciously handed over the keys after Kelly returned to Lucky Cove when she inherited the boutique. Having lived in New York City since her college days, Kelly hadn't needed a vehicle. She'd had taxis at the wave of her hand or an Uber at the tap of her cell phone. Lucky Cove didn't have reliable public transport, and she'd go broke with rideshares. So, she was grateful for the loan of the car.

Kelly set the clothing inside. She was confident what she pulled out from Annabeth's closet would sell quickly. The garments were good quality, season appropriate, and in the size many of her customers wore.

With the cargo door closed, Kelly dashed around the vehicle and slipped in behind the steering wheel. After starting the ignition, she navigated around Walt's box truck and pulled out of the driveway onto Moor Cove Road. Within a few minutes, she was turning right onto Main Street.

She checked the dashboard clock and saw she had time to make a quick trip. After parking behind the boutique, she hurried to Doug's Variety Store for a coffee. This autumn, Doug changed his seasonal coffee flavor from the tried-and-true pumpkin spice to apple cider donut. Hesitant at first, Kelly had been converted. Minutes later, she exited the shop, sipping her large coffee.

Main Street was waking up for the day. While faithful runners paced themselves as they traveled along the sidewalk, shop owners were busy tidying in front of their stores, setting up displays, and inspecting their windows. Passing her fellow chamber of commerce members, Kelly nodded and greeted but didn't stop to engage in conversation because she was enjoying her coffee so much. That was until she reached Miranda & James, the new shoe store on the block.

Only a few weeks ago, it had been an empty storefront after Gem Jewelry closed, leaving papered windows and a closed sign hanging on the door. Now there was a striking display of fall footwear that stopped Kelly in her tracks. She got so close to the glass, her nose was almost pressing against it, while her gaze locked on a pair of black suede D'Orsay pumps.

"Hello, lover." She couldn't resist the iconic line from her favorite television series as she took in the beautiful work of art in front of her. Four-inch stiletto heels with cut-out sides, delicate ankle straps, and pointed vamps. Sophisticated. Chic. And expensive. She sighed. Why did she always fall in love with high-three-digit-priced shoes?

"See something you like?"

The unexpected voice had Kelly pulling her gaze from the shoes and to the woman standing beside her.

Where had she come from?

The woman, tall and slender, was dressed in a classic wrap dress. Her long, sleek dark hair fell below her shoulders, and her wide hazel eyes held a glint of amusement.

"Ah…yes…those shoes!" Kelly pointed to the pumps. "Gorgeous."

"They are indeed. And I think I have your size if you'd like to try them on."

Kelly pressed her lips together. She'd love to try them on, but she knew they were out of her price range. Way out of her price range.

"Thank you for the offer, but I have to get to my boutique to open." Kelly dragged her focus from the shoes and extended her hand. "I'm Kelly Quinn, owner of the Lucky Cove Resale Boutique. You must be Miranda Farrell."

Miranda's handshake was firm. "Nice to meet you."

"I'm actually glad I bumped into you; it'll save me a trip later."

Miranda took back her hand and tilted her head. "We could talk while you try on those marvelous shoes. You know, D'Orsay pumps are classic."

Kelly chewed on her lower lip. The temptation was hard to resist, and so was Miranda's hard selling. But she couldn't fault the gal for trying to make a sale, even though it wasn't Kelly's style.

"To be honest, they're out of my budget. However, that designer is on my wish list." She glanced back at the shoes again, and her heart gave a pitter-patter. No. She'd remain strong and not give in to such an expensive impulse buy. She'd done that too many times over the summer, and now her credit card was on a time-out.

"The reason I wanted to speak with you is to invite you to the chamber of commerce luncheon tomorrow. We're going to be talking about what we can do for Shop Small Saturday."

Miranda's gaze darted for a moment, and then she tucked a lock of hair behind her ear. "Well…I appreciate the invite."

Kelly was surprised that Miranda seemed hesitant. She didn't strike Kelly as shy. "Since you're a new shop owner, it's a great way to meet fellow business owners and network. And the Lucky Cove Inn has amazing food. No rubber chicken." She flashed what she hoped was an encouraging smile.

"You're right about the food at the inn. Yes, I'd like to go. Especially now, since I have a friend."

Friend? That was fast. If that's what got Miranda participating in the business community, then so be it. *Having another friend would be a wonderful thing,* Kelly thought.

"Great. All the info is on the chamber's website, and I'll meet you there."

"Sounds good." Miranda stepped away but stopped. "Hey, do you know anyone who's looking for a job? I need at least one more salesperson."

"Poaching Breena wasn't enough?" Kelly laughed, making light of the situation.

Breena Collins had come to work for Kelly after quitting her waitress job at the Thirsty Turtle, a local bar with a questionable reputation. Until the past summer, she supplemented her income by working part-time at Doug's Variety Store. Putting herself through college and raising her daughter wasn't cheap. So even though she now had full-time hours at the boutique, she needed a little bit more money to save for Christmas gifts. Her daughter, Tori, had already started her list for Santa.

Miranda joined in on the laughter. "She's a very hard worker. I promise—" The ringing of her cell phone interrupted her. When she glanced at the phone's caller ID, her forehead creased with annoyance, and she huffed. "I should get back inside. See you at the luncheon."

Before Kelly could say bye, Miranda had reached the door. Her exit was abrupt, and Kelly couldn't help thinking it had something to do with the call. But, whoever it was, wasn't any of her business.

For the final quarter of the year, she had decided to change things up not only with her wardrobe but also with her not-so-flattering flaw—nosiness.

She wanted to tone down exaggerated sleeves, embrace more pastel colors, and not get involved with other people's drama or murder. She was 100 percent confident she could achieve her fashion goals. Staying clear of drama or murder…well, that was a hard one.

Especially since she'd already been dragged into her uncle's deep, dark secret. The one that turned her relationship with Ariel Barnes upside down. She wasn't sure their friendship could overcome another obstacle. But she did her best to remain hopeful.

Kelly pivoted and walked along Main Street toward her boutique. Staying clear of another murder should be easy to do since she was determined not to find another dead body. Ever.

* * * *

Back at the boutique and ready to start the workday, Kelly flipped over the closed sign and unlocked the front door. Then, she spun around and took a sweeping glance over the sales floor.

The transition to fall clothing was complete—mannequins decked out in layers, gloves and scarves displayed on the old farmhouse table, end-of-season garments marked down on sales racks.

She was about to celebrate her first year as proprietor of the Lucky Cove Resale Boutique. She'd hoped she'd have been able to restructure the first floor of the two-story building by now. The downstairs layout was choppy because her grandmother, Martha Blake, hadn't had the funds to take down walls in the once single-family home. When she became a widow with two children to raise, she had to work with what she had. And a majority of her money went to converting the upstairs bedrooms into an apartment.

This wasn't the only disappointment Kelly was dealing with. Her earlier thought of Ariel had sent her checking her phone for a message. There was none. Since July, she'd been trying to talk to her friend, but somehow Ariel had become skilled in avoiding Kelly. The few times Kelly had gone to the library, where Ariel worked, to talk, Ariel always managed to be busy. This wedge between them was growing and breaking Kelly's heart.

She walked to the counter and lifted her phone to check yet again for a message. None. She sighed. Then she noticed the time and realized that Pepper was late.

Pepper was never late.

Kelly tapped on her contacts app and scrolled through the list just as Pepper rushed in from the back of the boutique. She looked unusually frazzled, which set off alarm bells in Kelly.

"I was just about to call you. Is everything okay?" Kelly set her phone down and walked around the counter. She'd already filled the cash register and now tidied up the space. Pepper had set a mini farm truck with faux pumpkins on the counter. It was her tradition to decorate with a bit of tchotchke each season. Kelly wasn't sure that the truck fit the boutique, but it made Pepper happy.

"Not really. Well, maybe. It's okay." Pepper's indecisiveness in answering a simple question had Kelly stop her wipe-down of the counter and look at the older woman with concern.

"It's Gabe. He was in an accident overnight."

Kelly's eyes widened as her brain processed what she had just heard. Gabe, her childhood friend and now one of Lucky Cove's police officers, had been in an accident.

"Is he okay? What happened?" Kelly discarded the wipe and moved to the end of the counter.

Pepper approached and leaned forward, resting her forearms on the glass surface. Close up, her eyes were hooded, fatigue and worry dulled her usually bright complexion, and her shoulder-length blond hair hung limp.

"He was on duty when it happened. Clive and I got the call around two, and we rushed to the emergency room. Thankfully, he wasn't badly injured. Though, he does have a concussion. The doctor's orders are for him to stay home for the next few days."

"Why don't you take the day off. I can handle the boutique on my own." It wouldn't be the first time Kelly went solo, and since most of the summer people had returned to the city, she didn't expect to have a crush of customers.

"Thanks. But Clive is staying with Gabe today, and I could use the distraction of work." Pepper busied herself adjusting the mini farm truck. She'd been an employee at the boutique since it opened. Through the years, Pepper had been a loyal friend to Kelly's granny, and because of that, she was protective of the boutique. She hadn't liked the changes Kelly made when she inherited the boutique. It almost caused Pepper to quit. Luckily, they'd worked through their differences, and now they worked harmoniously together. Which was a good thing because Pepper was more than just an employee to Kelly. She was like a mother.

"How did the sort go over at Courtney's mother's house?" Pepper stepped away from the counter and walked to a rack of blouses.

"I got a few items. There was a lot I knew wouldn't sell. But Walt Hanover found an antique."

"Good old Walt." Pepper chuckled. "He always uncovers something."

"I also met Miranda Farrell; she owns the new shoe boutique. Courtney mentioned she lived in Lucky Cove a long time ago."

Pepper looked up from the blouses, and her gaze drifted off as if she was searching for a memory. "Huh. There was a Miranda about twenty years ago. Well, I'll be.... She came back?"

"You knew her? Why did she leave? Where did she go? Why did she come back?" Even Kelly surprised herself with her rapid-fire questions. She reminded herself of her Q4 goal to tone down her nosiness.

A tiny smile twitched on Pepper's lips. "Remember what curiosity did to the cat. Anyway, Miranda left town after her husband died. I have no idea where she went after leaving Lucky Cove. I'm surprised she came back after everything."

"What are you talking about? What happened?" Okay, so she was a work in progress. Kelly knew she couldn't change overnight.

The bell over the front door jingled, and Enid Millerton burst in and declared, "Fashion emergency! I need a dress ASAP."

Pepper moved from the blouses and hurried to Enid's side. She then guided the customer toward the rack filled with dresses.

While Enid chatted about the cause of her fashion emergency, Kelly couldn't help but wonder what the deal was with Miranda. What had happened before she left town and what had caused her to return to Lucky Cove?

Chapter 2

The following afternoon, Kelly checked her lipstick in her mirrored compact. Maplefrost. The shade was a medium-intensity brownish color with a glimmer. Perfect for autumn. The lipstick was part of the Autumn Daze collection from Define Beauty, the cosmetics company her late cousin had started. The fall collection was the last one Becky had worked on before her death. Kelly inhaled a deep breath and shut the compact, dropping it into her smooth black shoulder bag. It had been an investment, but nothing like a Chanel or Dior would have been, but it was the purse she grabbed for when she wanted to look polished and competent.

"Don't worry about rushing back. We've got it covered." Breena stirred oat milk into her coffee at the kitchen counter. The kitchenette was one of the three spaces the staff room had been divided into. The round dining table served double use as the meeting area, while the office section consisted of Kelly's desk, a small safe, an ancient filing cabinet, and a clothing rail where merchandise waited to be put into inventory.

"Thanks. I've been looking forward to this meeting. Can you believe we're weeks out from Shop Small Saturday?" Kelly adjusted the purse's strap on her shoulder. In retail, you always worked weeks, if not months, ahead of the new season. She was already looking at the trends for spring/summer next year.

Breena shuddered. "I don't want to think about the bitterly cold weather. It's too soon. Besides, Shop Small Saturday is in November, and we're barely into October. So cool your PSL, boot-loving, leaf-peeper self down a bit."

Kelly laughed. "I haven't had a pumpkin spice latte yet."

Breena's eyes bulged. "You are depressed!" she blurted out and then clamped her hand over her mouth while regret flashed in her eyes. "I am so sorry. I shouldn't have said that."

Kelly's smile waned, and her chin tilted downward. "It's okay. Don't worry about it."

Breena lowered her hand. "No, it's not okay. That was thoughtless of me to say. I apologize."

"Apology accepted." Her friend's concern felt like a warm hug to Kelly. She wasn't sure how she would have survived the summer without Breena.

"Good." Breena sipped her coffee. "I have the next quarter's marketing plan ready to go over when you have the chance." Her college major was marketing, and she happily took on the task for the boutique. "I know I just told you to cool your jets about fall and winter, and here I am thinking about the start of next year."

"The nature of retailing. Let's set up a time when I get back to review it," Kelly said.

"Well, the way you're stuffing your calendar with things to do, is there any spare time to review the plan?" Breena stared at Kelly over the rim of her mug.

"Ha, ha. If you're trying to say I'm doing too much..."

Breena gave a hapless shrug.

This wasn't the first time Breena had suggested that Kelly's to-do list overflowed. Pepper had also shared the same sentiment. As had Gabe, her best friend Liv, and Nate Barber, her boyfriend...sort of. He was an extraordinary guy who had superhuman powers that chipped away at the wall she'd erected after her breakup last spring.

"There's plenty of time in the day to do all the things I want to do."

Kelly turned and moved from her desk to the oval mirror hung beside the coat-tree. After slipping into her faux-leather moto jacket she gave herself a once-over. Her short-sleeved black top was tucked into her ruffle-trimmed leopard-print wrap skirt. Yes, it was a mouthful, but the skirt was to die for, and she'd clicked on it immediately during a late-night shopping spree. Heartbreak, grief, and too much wine was a recipe for a maxed-out credit card. But, hey, she might be broke, but she looked darn cute.

"Love that skirt. Too bad we're not the same size." Breena was a few inches shorter than Kelly and curvier. "Looks like I'll have to buy my own. Then we could be twinning."

Kelly chuckled as she turned back to face her friend.

"I'd say we could go out to a club or something, but you've already got a new man. How is Detective Nate doing?"

"He's fine. He's been working a lot." Not much good had happened over the summer for Kelly. Though, there had been one bright spot. Nate, who she'd met months earlier when he took over the investigation of Tawny Lee's murder, reappeared in her life after Becky died. He'd come to check on her, see how she was doing. One thing led to another, and by late summer, they went out on a date. Kelly hadn't expected to find love again, and to be honest, she still wasn't sure if she had. She liked Nate. A lot. And she tried not to overthink things and just go with the flow. She'd fallen too fast and hard for Mark Lambert when she'd met him. Lesson learned. Because she wasn't sure if she'd be able to get back up if she fell for Nate too quickly and her heart got broken.

Kelly glanced at her watch. "I better get going. Call if you need anything." She left the boutique through the back door, stepping out into crisp fall air. Unabashedly, she was a boot-loving leaf peeper who embraced the change of season. It couldn't happen fast enough for her. Kelly hurried to her Jeep and got in. She pulled out of the boutique's parking lot and drove along Main Street toward the Lucky Cove Inn.

A few minutes later, she arrived at her destination and parked in the lot beside the impressive Victorian. She followed the paved path to the front entrance and entered the lobby. She paused a moment, looking for Miranda. And didn't see her. Stepping farther into the welcoming space, she passed the comfortable seating area for guests. She spotted Aaron Mitchell, the inn's manager, with Paul Sloan chatting on the sofa. Both men held coffee cups and looked like they were swapping stories. The fragrance of freshly baked chocolate chip cookies had Kelly's nose wriggling and her attention drifting from the two men. She spun around and found Renata McPherson holding a tray of warm cookies.

"Good afternoon, Kelly. Here for the luncheon?" Renata asked. She'd been working at the inn since high school and worked her way up to management.

"I am. And I'm going to do my best to resist those." Kelly pointed at the tray. Those cookies and the inn's waffles were famous up and down Long Island.

"Don't fret. We're serving cookies as the dessert." Renata winked as she stepped away to greet a couple entering the lobby.

Kelly continued through to the dining room. She stopped when she spotted her uncle, Ralph Blake, talking with another man in the room's doorway. They looked in good spirits.

Ralph slapped the man's back; then they each gave a hearty laugh and walked into the dining room. It was good to see her uncle there. Maybe she'd have a chance to talk to him in private. He, like Ariel, had become skilled in avoiding her.

"Kelly!"

At the sound of her name, she looked over her shoulder and saw Miranda walking toward her. She wore a stylish navy pantsuit and carried a British tan tote. Her hair was pulled back in a ponytail, and large textured golden earrings caught the light from overhead and glinted.

"I'm so glad you came. Come on, let's get a table, and I'll introduce you to my friends." Kelly led Miranda into the spacious room set up for the luncheon. She caught the eye of her friend Liv Moretti. Liv's family owned a bakery on Main Street, and she served as the chamber's secretary. She also noticed a few stares as she and Miranda walked through the room toward a table. A definite chill had settled in there. She looked over to Miranda, who had initially looked apprehensive and now looked empowered. In place of her soft smile was a grin. Okay, Kelly was now officially weirded out. What was going on?

"Hey there, Kelly." Walt Hanover passed by, giving a nod to Miranda.

"About time you got here." Frankie Blake, Kelly's cousin and owner of Frankie's Seafood Shack, breezed by, giving her arm a squeeze. "Talk later."

"That was Walt, he owns an antique shop, and my cousin Frankie, he owns a restaurant," Kelly said to Miranda. She then considered she might have misread the room. Walt and Frankie seemed fine.

"I remember Walt," Miranda said with a note of affection, but it vanished quickly. "Just like I remember him."

"Who?" As soon as Kelly asked, she saw Ricky van Johnson approaching. He owned Gregorio's Specialty Shop, Lucky Cove's premier gourmet food shop. It was pricey, but it was well worth it for hardcore foodies.

"Good to see you, Kelly." Towering over Kelly by a good six inches, his bulky frame came from good eating. He regularly gave cooking demonstrations at his shop, and his recipes were to die for. Then, his attention shifted toward Miranda. "I didn't think I'd see you here." His tone had changed to tense and cool. Which wasn't like Ricky. He was more of a bear-hug type of guy.

Liv shuffled over and grabbed Kelly's arm. "Come on, lunch is being served, and the meeting is about to start."

"We'll catch up later," Miranda told Ricky as she stepped away with Kelly and Liv. They walked to their table; Liv had chosen one up front by the podium. Kelly set her purse on a chair and then headed to the buffet. She lifted a plate, picked up utensils, and surveyed the offerings. The chicken piccata looked delicious, so she added it to her dish.

"Everything looks so good." Miranda piled a large serving of salad greens on her plate and then drizzled a little balsamic vinaigrette on top. She followed Kelly along the line and paused to scoop fruit onto her plate.

Kelly glanced at her chicken piccata and generous portion of rice. She considered ditching the plate for a nanosecond and starting over more healthfully like Miranda. And in an instant, that thought was gone. Summer was over, and she had a considerable collection of Spanx collecting dust. It would be a waste not to use the costly shapewear.

"I'm starving," Liv said as she filled her plate with the chicken, rice, and a heaping spoonful of mac and cheese.

Kelly couldn't help but gape at the amount of food on her best friend's plate. Liv was long and lithe and could wear leggings without worrying about tush coverage. The gal worked in a bakery, for goodness' sake, and was surrounded by cakes, cupcakes, and bread all day long. So how did she not gain an ounce?

"Ricky still owns Gregorio's?" Miranda asked as she walked with Kelly and Liv back to their table.

"He does," Kelly said. "If you don't mind me asking, why did you decide to come back to Lucky Cove?"

Liv pulled out her chair and sat. "You lived here before?"

"Yes, I did. Looks like you've done your homework, Kelly." Miranda's voice was neutral, and Kelly couldn't decipher if Miranda was offended or impressed.

"Not really. Courtney Johnson, she owns Courtney's Treasures, mentioned it. And Pepper Donovan, who works at my boutique, said you left after your husband passed away."

"Actually, both of my husbands died." Miranda reached for her water glass.

Kelly's mouth gaped open again. Two husbands?

"Good afternoon, everyone. Welcome to our monthly meeting." Ernie Baldwin had taken his place at the podium and flashed a broad, cheerful smile. The bank manager always had that winning attitude he reinforced with a smile or thumbs-up. "Today on our agenda, after Liv reads the minutes from last month's meeting, is the discussion on our upcoming Shop Small Saturday event. We all know how important this time of the year is to our bottom lines. We're forming a committee to oversee this event. We have a lot to talk about. But first, if you haven't gotten your lunch yet, please do so and enjoy your meal over good conversation with your fellow business owners." After another flash of his smile, he walked from the podium toward his table.

"Well, he worked his way up the ladder at the bank," Miranda said before sipping her water.

"I'm sorry, did I hear you correctly when you said you had two husbands who died?" Kelly asked as she pierced a piece of chicken with her fork.

Miranda nodded as she set her glass down. "Yes, you did. Daniel and Nolen. May they rest in peace."

"I'm sorry for your loss," Kelly said before eating her bite of chicken. As she chewed, she processed this new information and the reaction from Ricky and others toward Miranda. Her idle curiosity was now in full-blown overdrive. She had to know why Miranda came back to Lucky Cove. And what happened to her husbands. So much for her goal of not being nosy. Her spidey senses were tingling up a storm, and that was never a good thing.

Miranda swallowed her helping of salad. "Thank you. If you don't mind, I'd rather not discuss it." She wiped her mouth with the linen napkin and then placed it back on her lap. "I have to say, the vinaigrette is superb. I'd forgotten how good the food is here."

The three of them sat in awkward silence for a moment until Liv set down her glass and asked, "What are your marketing plans for the shoe shop this holiday season?"

Within seconds, the three of them fell into an in-depth conversation about promotion and marketing while they finished their meals. Liv's head swiveled. "Oh…look, they're putting the cookies out now. I'll get us some."

Kelly wiped her mouth and then dropped her napkin on the table. She'd eaten every bit of her food but managed to save a little room for a chocolate chip cookie.

"Miranda Farrell." Kelly's uncle swaggered toward the table. "Looks like history is repeating itself. Worming your way into someplace you don't belong yet again."

"Dear, dear Ralph. I'm a Lucky Cove business owner, which means I most certainly belong here at this meeting." Miranda's lips curved upward as she shifted in her seat. "I was so pleased when your *niece* invited me."

Kelly stiffened when she heard the emphasis on "niece." Suddenly, she felt like a pawn in a game she knew nothing about.

"Would one of you like to tell me what's going on?" Kelly asked.

Ralph huffed out a breath. "You need to stay out of this, Kelly."

"Still telling people what to do?" Miranda rose from her chair and propped her hands on her slender hips, staring daggers at Ralph. Challenging him. She waited a beat before continuing. "Guess some things don't change."

"Let's make this simple. You don't like me, and I don't like you, but we both can make a smart business decision." Ralph's whole life revolved around business. He'd worked his way up in real estate from an agent in his twenties to now a successful developer. He had projects up and down Long Island and a reputation for getting what he wanted when he wanted it. It seemed that Miranda had something he wanted.

"Nice try. But I'm not giving up my lease," Miranda said.

Kelly nodded. Now she was up to speed. She'd heard he'd been interested in the two-story brick building that housed Miranda's shop and an art gallery. But that was months ago, before Becky's murder. Since then, Kelly had lost track of some things. Like her uncle's business affairs.

Miranda cocked her head sideways. "I love my shop's location, and there's no amount of money you can offer that will make me leave it. I have no intention of doing you any favors."

"Favors?" Kelly's gaze darted between Miranda and her uncle. "You want to take over her lease? Why? Did you buy the building, Uncle Ralph?"

"He did, and now he wants me out so he can jack up the rent," Miranda said.

"Is that true?" Kelly asked her uncle.

"Nothing unusual about it. It's business," Ralph said.

"He already got the art gallery to agree to move into the empty storefront by Michelangelo's Restaurant," Miranda said. "But I'm not going to help you out. Before I left Lucky Cove, I told you you'd regret leading the witch hunt after Daniel died."

"It wasn't a witch hunt." Ralph jabbed his finger in the air. "Everyone knew you weren't as innocent as you claimed."

Kelly raised her palm. "This isn't the time nor the place to do this."

"You're wasting your time trying to talk sense into this man." Miranda squared her shoulders and then swept past Ralph, heading to the exit as Kelly lowered her hand, expelling an aggravated breath.

"Did you really have to do that now?" she asked her uncle.

"There's never a bad time to talk about business."

"It seems there was more to that conversation than just business. You knew her husband, Daniel?"

"We were friends."

"What did she mean by you leading a witch hunt against her?"

"Ralph!" a bald, chubby man called out as he approached with a glass in his hand and a wide grin on his face. "We need to discuss your new property."

Ralph chuckled as he slapped the guy on the back. "Let's see what you can do for me." Ralph broke away from Kelly.

"Hey, we're not finished," she said.

"Yes, we are." Ralph walked with his buddy to a table across the room.

"He is impossible," she muttered as she stood and went to find Miranda. Out in the carpeted corridor, she looked in both directions. To her right were the restrooms, and she figured Miranda might have slipped in there.

At the restroom door, she heard a raised voice.

"No one has forgotten what happened twenty years ago!"

The female voice sounded familiar, and when Kelly pushed open the door, the woman's identity was confirmed. Erica Booth had Miranda pinned against the sleek countertop. Her neck was corded, and her cheeks were flame red. What on earth had the bookseller so upset?

Miranda's arms were folded, and she had a smirk on her face. She looked unfazed by the volume of Erica's voice or her anger. Quite the contrary. It appeared she enjoyed Erica's outburst.

"What is going on in here?" Kelly entered the room, giving the stalls a quick glance. They appeared empty. "I heard you outside, Erica."

"We were just catching up. Weren't we, Erica?" Miranda's tone was far from friendly.

Erica backed away and composed herself, though her tight expression remained in place on her plump face. She tucked a lock of her shoulder-length auburn hair behind her ear and pushed her oversized glasses up the bridge of her nose.

"We have nothing to catch up on. You should have never come back to Lucky Cove."

Miranda gave a simple, nonchalant shrug as she turned to face the mirror. Then, leaning forward, she inspected her makeup, letting Erica stew for a moment. And it worked. Finally, Erica huffed and swung around. Kelly barely had enough time to get out of Erica's way, or she would have been knocked into the wall as the bookseller marched out of the room. Kelly couldn't remember the last time she saw Erica so angry.

Well, the incident when Erica tossed her cheating husband out of their historic home on Main Street came to mind. And the other time when she chased after a shoplifter last Christmas. Come to think of it, Erica had a temper.

Now Kelly was curious about what Miranda had done twenty years ago to set off Erica's temper that day.

"Are you okay?" Kelly asked.

"I'm good. Never once did I think coming back to Lucky Cove would be easy." Miranda pulled back from the mirror and looked at Kelly. "Don't look so worried. Those little lines between your eyes will only get deeper."

Kelly was pushing thirty, and she didn't want premature lines, so she immediately relaxed her face.

"I think they all just need to get whatever they're feeling out of their systems."

"All? How many people are you talking about?" Kelly asked. "From what I've seen so far, I think what they're feeling is anger."

"You're absolutely right. Come on, let's get back to the meeting." Miranda's mood certainly brightened despite the unpleasant run-ins. She held the door open for Kelly and followed her out into the hall. Together, they walked toward the open doorway of the banquet room but were stopped by Ricky van Johnson. He had a scowl on his long face. He often reminded Kelly of a hound dog with sagging jowls and big brown eyes.

"We're on our way back to our table," Kelly said in hopes of defusing another confrontation.

"Mark my word, Miranda, you'll regret coming back." And with that, he stalked off, heading toward the lobby.

Kelly watched him until he disappeared, and then her gaze returned to Miranda. Now she was sure. Inviting her to the meeting had been a mistake. Probably just like Miranda returning to Lucky Cove.

Ernie Baldwin came out of the dining room, holding his cell phone to his ear. Passing, he gave Miranda a look that left Kelly speechless. The chill that had come off his stare had been arctic. Miranda continued walking, but Kelly lingered, looking at the bank manager as he came to a halt several feet away and talked on his phone.

"Come on, Kell!" Liv popped out of the dining room and waved. "We're starting to talk about Shop Small Saturday."

When she arrived for the luncheon, she'd been excited about the Shop Small campaign. Now Kelly had too many questions about Miranda and her past to concentrate on the business at hand. Luckily, she didn't need a refresh on the minutes from the last meeting, and she hoped Liv wouldn't notice her not paying attention. When Liv finished reading the minutes, she introduced the chamber's vice president. Jay laid out the objectives for the upcoming holiday season. He concluded his presentation with a call for a volunteer to lead the Shop Small Lucky Cove campaign. Kelly's hand shot up, and it earned her a concerned look from Liv.

There was no doubt in her mind she'd be on the receiving end of a lecture from Liv.

You're juggling too much, you're fragile, and one overcommitment from cracking.

While Liv would be lecturing, Jay was beaming. He had a live one and wouldn't have to worry about overseeing the committee himself.

"Thank you, Kelly, for volunteering." Jay's appreciation was followed by a round of applause from her peers.

The remainder of the meeting proceeded without any incident. Of course, it helped that Miranda had snuck out before the meeting officially ended. She claimed she needed to get back to the shop for an interview.

Kelly was relieved and vowed not to invite Miranda back to another chamber meeting. In fact, she thought it would be a good idea to keep her distance from the woman. Something wasn't right, and she didn't like feeling like a pawn in some weird game going on between Miranda and the people from her past. Especially her uncle.

Kelly finished her water and then slipped the strap of her purse over her shoulder. She waited while Liv gathered her files, and together, they walked toward the dining room door.

"Do you really think you can handle the committee on top of everything else you're doing?" Liv waited and let Kelly exit the dining room ahead of her.

Even though she expected her friend to ask the question, it still irritated her. She wasn't a fragile flower that needed to stay secluded in her apartment until her heart mended. Who knew how long that would take? She was over Mark Lambert, lawyer and jerk extraordinaire, but her heart was still shattered by Becky's murder. Maybe her friends and family had a right to be concerned. Maybe she was doing too much to keep her mind off her cousin. Maybe she'd never fully recover from Becky's death. Then again, she'd heard a lot of talk about closure. Surely, she'd get some. Maybe?

"Are you okay? You're not jumping down my throat about what I just said," Liv asked.

"When have I jumped down your throat?"

"Umm…last week. And the week before that." Liv pulled out a tube of lip balm from her purse.

Kelly shrugged. "Guess I'm used to being lectured once a week."

Liv flashed a smile. "Okay, that's better."

It was time to change the subject. "You won't believe this. I found Erica Booth yelling at Miranda in the restroom."

"Erica?" Liv sounded as surprised as Kelly had felt when she'd entered the bathroom. "Why? What did she say?"

As they walked through the lobby, Kelly recounted what she'd walked in on, and it left Liv with a puzzled look on her face.

"Wow. Sounds like Miranda pushed Erica's buttons," Liv said as they exited the inn.

"It wasn't just Erica. Ricky also got in her face, saying pretty much the same thing. And my uncle. Oh, and the look Ernie shot her…" Kelly shook her head. "I don't get it. She seemed nice when I met her."

"You better than anyone should know people aren't always what they seem," Liv said.

"Point taken." Kelly had been surprised by people she thought were innocent of murder. It looked like she'd forgotten that life lesson momentarily. "Maybe Pepper knows more than she told me about what happened twenty years ago with Miranda."

"Really? You're going to add something else to your to-do list?" Liv asked. "Look, it's probably better that you stay out of Miranda's personal business and let her sort out things with the people from her past."

"How will that help ease my curiosity?"

"It won't." Liv chuckled and then broke away, heading for her car.

Kelly sighed. Perhaps, in this case, she probably should listen to Liv. Still, the more she thought about Miranda's interactions with Ralph, Erica, and Ricky, the more she wanted to know. It was official—she'd be able to keep her goals when it came to fashion. But, as far as her nosiness was concerned, she had to face the fact that she was a curious person. She should accept it, and so should everyone else in her life, even though her curiosity had put her in some precarious situations.

Chapter 3

When Kelly arrived back at the boutique, she ducked into the staff room to write her weekly newsletter since Pepper and Breena were working on the sales floor. She settled at her desk with a cup of coffee and her laptop computer. In that week's edition, she shared five tips for stylish fall dressing on a budget, plus tips for caring for sweaters. She wrapped up the newsletter with a call to action to click reply and ask a fashion question. Feeling accomplished by finishing the task, she was about to take a celebratory drink of her coffee when she realized the cup was empty. She frowned. Time for a refill.

Or so she thought. On her way across the room to the kitchenette, she remembered she had wanted to take another look at the window display. She'd changed it out yesterday before closing and wasn't sure she was happy with the floral midi dress on the mannequin. It might have been too dark to grab the attention of passersby. She dashed back to the desk and grabbed her cell phone before heading outside.

Standing on the curb with her hands on her hips, Kelly studied the boutique's window with a discerning eye. She'd been right. The midi dress was too dark. She did a mental inventory of what she could replace the dress with. There was an above-the-knee burnt-orange dress that would pair amazingly with the animal-print scarf consigned two days ago by Mrs. Williamson. "Yes!" Kelly loved it when inspiration struck.

"Hey," Courtney called out as she approached with Liv beside her. "This is a beautiful afternoon, isn't it?"

Kelly nodded in agreement. The extra-chilly morning had warmed slightly but not too much to take away the feeling of autumn. She gazed upward. The sun peeked through the still full trees that were now striking shades of gold and crimson.

"I stepped out of the bakery for a break and found myself walking." Liv laughed.

"I did the same thing," Courtney confessed. "But I should get back."

"Good afternoon, ladies. Gorgeous weather." Walt Hanover approached, carrying a large coffee from Doug's. The variety store that sold everything from sandwiches to newspapers to cartons of milk kept things simple with their hot beverages—small, medium, or large.

"We were just talking about it," Kelly said.

Walt started to speak but stopped when a loud disturbance interrupted him. "What's going on over there?"

Liv and Courtney turned in the direction of the loud voices. Kelly's head turned and huffed at the sight of her uncle and Miranda. "What on earth is going on between those two?"

"It goes way back. I thought that ancient history would stay exactly that," Walt said. "I should get back to my shop." He tipped his head and then stepped off the curb and waited for a break in traffic before crossing.

"People are staring, Kell." Liv made a face, and it was clear to Kelly that she should intervene before the situation got out of hand.

"I better try to break it up. See you two later." Kelly walked toward the bickering duo. When she arrived, they didn't notice. However, two middle-aged women standing a few feet away had, and they looked on with curiosity. She cleared her throat, hoping to gain her uncle's and Miranda's attention. No such luck.

"You may own this building, but you have no right to come in and create a scene in front of my customers. You cost me a sale," Miranda said through gritted teeth.

"I most certainly have a right to enter my own property," Ralph shot back.

"Would you both cool it," Kelly said as she stepped forward, wedging herself between them. "You're both causing a scene now. People are staring."

"If this harassment continues, I'll call the police and have you charged with stalking!" Miranda swung around and stomped back into her shop.

"Did you really cause her customer to leave?" Kelly asked.

Ralph grunted.

She took that as a yes.

"You're going to have to find a different tactic, because this one isn't working for you. Do you really need her to give up her lease? Why not just wait it out?"

Ralph, dressed in an expertly tailored gray suit that was a size too small on his chunky frame, rubbed the bridge of his nose. Clearly, the exercise and diet plan his third wife, Summer, had put him on after his heart attack a few months back wasn't working. "I don't need any business advice from you."

Kelly quickly counted to ten to stop herself from exploding. Her uncle could be infuriating at times because he was thickheaded and stubborn. He never considered someone else could have a worthy point or a smart piece of advice. Nope. It was Ralph Blake's way or the highway.

Feeling a little Zen by the time she reached the number ten, she sucked in a cleansing breath and decided to change the subject. She wasn't sure if it was a smart move or not.

"Have you talked to Ariel?" Kelly's friendship with Ariel had been complicated, and it only became more complex because of Ralph's secret. A year ago, she and Ariel had begun to rebuild their relationship after a ten-year break. What had started out as a fun summer night at a friend's beach house had ended in tragedy. Kelly had snuck off with a boy, leaving Ariel with a group of girls. Ariel wanted to go at some point but couldn't find Kelly, her ride home. So, she accepted a ride from Melanie Grover, who had been drunk. They weren't far from the house when Melanie crashed the car, and Ariel's injuries left her paralyzed.

Even though Melanie had been driving drunk, a hefty dose of blame had been dropped on Kelly's shoulders for abandoning Ariel at the party.

Looking back, Kelly had come to realize that it probably was easier for everyone to channel their anger at the situation onto her. Melanie had been sentenced to several years in prison; she wasn't around every day to blame. Kelly still lived and went to school in Lucky Cove. That made her an easy target for people to unload on.

Ralph shook his head.

The look of disappointment on his face surprised Kelly. Had he finally come around to wanting a relationship with his daughter? The one he kept a secret her whole life at the behest of Ariel's mother?

Kelly had learned about the brief affair between Ralph and Ariel's mom last spring during a massive argument with her uncle. Then, out of nowhere, he blurted out the secret that he was Ariel's biological father. That he'd dated Ariel's mom when she was separated from her husband. After the couple got back together, she learned she was pregnant with Ralph's baby. They had agreed to keep the secret for the sake of their families.

It was a mess that only got worse when Frankie, Ralph's son, took a DNA test, as Ariel also had. With the swab of a cheek, everyone's life got turned upside down.

"I'm guessing you haven't either," Ralph said.

"She's still not returning my calls and avoids me when I go into the library." Kelly understood her friend's anger toward the whole situation. Still, blaming Kelly for not revealing the secret Ralph had dumped on her seemed unfair. Kelly hadn't asked to know about the private lives of her uncle or Ariel's mother. Since it hadn't been her secret to share, she had kept quiet. Now it looked like that decision had cost her a friendship. A friendship she had waited a decade to repair. And one she would miss tremendously.

Ralph's phone buzzed, and he pulled it from his pocket. He checked the caller ID and, without looking up, he said, "I gotta take this call." He turned and walked away, just like that.

"Nice talking to you too." Before heading back to the boutique, she looked inside the shoe shop and saw Miranda on the telephone. She debated whether to go inside and check on her. Perhaps it would be wise to stay out of the problem that was between her and Ralph.

Her phone chimed, and she tapped the screen to open Nate's text message.

Hey, how are you doing?

She smiled as she typed her reply.

Better now. Still on for dinner?

The ellipsis bounced, and she waited impatiently for his reply like a silly teenager who was smitten by a boy.

Yep. Looking forward to seeing you.

Kelly pulled the phone to her chest and smiled. Oh, goodness, she was smitten with Nate Barber.

The remainder of the day flew by as Kelly worked the sales floor. Breena had left to take her daughter to an appointment, and Pepper dashed out early to make and then deliver dinner to Gabe. Late in the afternoon, Kelly had found time to give him a call and check on him. He said he was sore but feeling good and should be back to work in a few days. Of course he would be. He loved his job as a police officer.

When it was finally time to close the boutique, Kelly headed upstairs to her one-bedroom apartment. At the door, she was greeted by Howard, the orange cat she inherited along with everything else from her granny. He slinked around her ankles and meowed loudly. Since she'd never had a pet before, it had taken a while to understand what his vocal cues meant.

Turns out, they were pretty simple. He had cues for food, play, and rest. She patted him on the head. What a simple life he had.

She set her purse on the table between the front door and hall closet and then made her way into the kitchen to prepare Howard's meal. The vocal cue he had been emitting was clearly for dinner. As she dished out the tuna pâté and refilled his water bowl, she turned over ideas of what to wear to dinner. Since Gio's wasn't a fancy restaurant, a pair of faux-leather leggings and a cozy tunic should be okay. Casual dressy. She liked that phrase and made a mental note to use it in an upcoming newsletter.

Howard had perched on the top of the trash can, overseeing Kelly. His tail flicked back and forth. She felt immense pressure from the feline.

"How can you be so hungry? You probably slept all day." Kelly placed both bowls on Howard's mat and stepped out of the way. The cat leaped from the trash can and trotted to his dinner.

While the cat dined, Kelly tidied up the counter and then hurried to her bedroom to change. By the time she was dressed for dinner with her shoulder-length blond hair swept up with wisps framing her face, Howard had finished eating and was now on the sofa washing his face.

She said goodbye to her furry companion and quickly changed from the professional purse to a dumpling clutch that was a dupe for an outrageously expensive designer bag. The supple faux leather and cute design made it a must-have for Kelly. She wasn't sure how long the trend would last, but knowing she spent less than fifty dollars on it would make saying buh-bye to it somewhat easy.

* * * *

The early night air was seasonable, not too warm or too cold, so she opted to walk to the restaurant. Along the way to Gio's, she passed Erica Booth's bookshop, Turn the Page. She glanced in the front window and saw a group of customers seated in a circle. It looked like there was an author visiting. Then, she spotted Erica standing off to the side. She dawdled just long enough for Erica to notice her, and they locked eyes. And Erica's hadn't looked friendly, so Kelly resumed walking to the restaurant, her pace quickened.

Within a few minutes, she reached the restaurant, and inside, the hostess showed her to the table where Nate sat reading on his phone. He looked up as she got closer, flashing a smile that sent her heart fluttering.

He set his phone down and then stood. He gave her a kiss on the cheek and pulled out her chair.

"You look amazing," he whispered into her ear.

Her body tingled at his warm breath on her skin. *Oh, gosh, every time I see him, I feel like a teenager.*

"You don't look so bad yourself." Kelly peeled her gaze off him and settled on her chair, setting her clutch on the table as Nate returned to his seat.

Their server appeared with a warm welcome and recited the daily specials. Kelly ordered Milanese chicken while Nate asked for lasagna. Over a glass of wine, while waiting for their meals, Kelly filled him in on what happened at the chamber's luncheon between Miranda and the others.

"I never imagined chamber of commerce meetings could be so interesting." Nate lifted his glass and sipped his wine.

"Neither did I. Who knew?" Kelly swirled her wine before sipping. "You know, what was really shocking was that both her husbands died."

"Don't go there, Kell." An edge had crept into his voice.

Kelly's mouth dropped open. "I'm not. I'm just saying that it's curious both her husbands died shortly after marrying her." She leaned forward. "Could she be one of those black widows?"

Nate set his glass down and then reached for Kelly's hand, covering it with his. "Kelly, sometimes people die unexpectedly. It happens."

"Aren't you supposed to be the cynical one? Jaded by years in law enforcement? Suspicious of coincidences?"

"No, that's you." Nate chuckled as he pulled back his hand.

"I'm not jaded! Maybe a little suspicious and perhaps a smidge stressed." She took a long drink of her wine.

"You have a lot on your plate. And now you're leading that new committee. Do you think it's a good idea to take on such a big project while you'll have your hands full with your own holiday marketing?"

Kelly shrugged. "It helps me not think about Becky all the time." She lowered her gaze.

Her therapist had said she needed to acknowledge the pain to heal from it. Okay, she admitted it. So why did her insides still feel like they'd been shredded, leaving jagged edges that cut every time she took a breath?

"Kelly, what you're doing is running from it, and believe me when I tell you it's going to catch up with you. And it's going to win."

She lifted her gaze, and before she could say anything, their server arrived with their meals. Happy to change topics, Kelly wasted no time tasting her Milanese chicken and declaring it delicious.

Their conversation continued from there with no more mentions about the chamber of commerce or Becky. An hour had passed before she realized it, and her belly was full from the tasty entrée and the decadent dessert. She'd ordered a slice of chocolate torte while Nate had a piece of apple pie. Tomorrow she'd definitely have to wear something loose fitting.

After the dinner bill was paid, Kelly and Nate strolled along Main Street hand in hand until they reached the boutique, and he pulled her close to his chest. Up close, the musky scent of Nate's cologne was intoxicating, and it had Kelly thinking about things that curled her toes. He dipped his head and leaned down for a kiss. Yes, that was one of the things she'd been thinking about. But he pulled back before she was ready to let go.

"I have to be in court tomorrow morning," Nate said with regret in his eyes.

"How early?"

"Too early to stay." He kissed her forehead. "Sorry."

Kelly sighed. *Not as sorry as I am.*

"I'll make it up to you." His thick brows waggled with mischief. "Promise."

"You better." Stepping back, Kelly pulled her key holder from her clutch. She caught a glimpse of Bud Cavanaugh walking out of the florist shop carrying a bouquet of roses.

"Well, well, it looks like he does have a new girlfriend."

"Who?" Nate asked.

"Bud Cavanaugh. He works for Walt Hanover. Yesterday Walt mentioned Bud has been texting up a storm. Maybe because of a girlfriend. And look, he bought roses. He has a new one," she said with confidence.

"You have superb intel skills on the happenings on Main Street." Nate chuckled.

Kelly playfully slapped his chest. "Go ahead. Mock me." A flash of light had her gaze drifting to the curb, but she quickly returned her attention back to Nate.

"Never!" He leaned in for one last kiss before escorting Kelly around the back of the building. He made sure she got inside safely before saying good night.

Kelly locked the door and then kicked off her shoes, carrying them upstairs. Inside her apartment, she dropped her shoes on the floor and her clutch on the hall table. Her cell phone chimed. She pulled it out of the purse, expecting a text from Nate. It wasn't.

Don't forget Pilates tomorrow morning.

Kelly groaned at Liv's text. She had been looking forward to sleeping in tomorrow. Now she couldn't. Not with a practically before-dawn class. She'd signed up for the classes in late August at the suggestion of her therapist. Since moving back to Lucky Cove, her main exercise had been running. Primarily because the biggest expense was a new pair of sneakers every few months. But she missed how her body felt after a Pilates class, though her checking account hadn't.

To fit the classes into her budget, she finally accepted Uncle Ralph's wife's family discount. A model turned Pilates instructor, Summer wasn't the easiest person for Kelly to get along with. She'd had hopes that since they were close in age and both loved fashion, there would have been an instant friendship. Well, there wasn't. She learned that Summer placed a high emphasis on status and moved within the right social circles. Her love for fashion didn't extend to secondhand clothes.

Kelly typed her reply to Liv. They went to the same class in the morning before both their businesses opened.

How could I forget? See you then.

Kelly had totally forgotten, but she couldn't tell Liv that. Liv loved the classes and even upgraded her membership for one reformer session a week.

She padded into the living room and dropped onto the sofa, earning a glare from Howard, who shifted and curled tighter into a ball. She made an apologetic face and then shrugged. Sometimes it felt like their relationship was all about him. Then again, he was a cat, and they tended to have that outlook on life. She refocused on her phone. This time, she opened the browser and searched for Miranda Farrell.

A bunch of hits came up, and she scrolled, stopping when she came across an article posted on the *Lucky Cove Weekly* newspaper website. She tapped on the link, and the archived article opened.

She read about the death of Miranda's first husband, Daniel Parnell. According to the article, he died from a heart attack after he'd been arraigned on several counts of embezzlement and fraud.

Kelly's eyes nearly popped out of their sockets. Miranda's husband had stolen money from his financial clients. Most of the article was about his alleged crimes, and there were only a few mentions of Miranda. There were some other quotes from the people who claimed to have lost their life savings because of Daniel.

"Why on earth would she want to come back here?"

Kelly finished reading the article, and it left a bad taste in her mouth. How could someone do something so heinous as to steal from people's retirement? Steal life savings that had been hard earned? Betray the trust of a client?

A notification came up on her phone. It was a reminder that it was time to get ready for bed. Another one of her therapist's suggestions had been for

Kelly to start using a sleep app so that her slumber would be more restful. The app reminded her to put down her electronic devices at least thirty minutes before bedtime. Despite wanting to know more about Miranda and her husbands, she closed the browser and then turned off her phone. All the information would be there in the morning.

Chapter 4

With her yoga mat slung over her shoulder and desperate for coffee, Kelly yanked open the Pilates studio's door and stepped out onto Main Street. She inhaled a deep breath of the crisp morning air, grateful to be done with her class.

Summer had worked her abs and buns to the max. It amazed Kelly how the moves appeared so simple, but they took a lot of precision and control. It had only been a few weeks of mat classes, but she was already feeling the shift in her body and posture.

Another benefit of the classes was the cute outfits she got to wear. Like the heather-blue leggings with matching tank top she had on beneath a long duster. The cozy fleece fabric had a relaxed fit, perfect for barre or brunch. At least that's what the ad copy said. And under the influence of a frozen pizza and a generous glass of wine at midnight, the thought of living such a chic, healthy lifestyle, of going from barre class to brunch in a cozy duster, had her one-click buying the garment. The impulse purchase had depleted her bank account three digits and had her looking for a way to justify the purchase. Hence, the Pilates classes.

"Want to get coffee at Doug's?" Kelly knew it was too early for brunch, so she'd settle for an apple cider donut coffee to go with Liv.

When there was no answer, she looked over her shoulder and found her friend was nowhere in sight.

"Where the heck…" She looked through the glass door and saw Liv at the counter with Joanie, the perky receptionist. Liv was probably checking the date for her next reformer class. Kelly wasn't that into Pilates…yet. She was satisfied with the mat classes for now. They were a perfect supplement to her morning runs. Together, those activities had helped her feel calmer and steadier…most days.

She turned and took a step from the door. Then, absentmindedly, she lifted her hand to take a drink of water. Except there wasn't a water bottle in her hand. She'd left it inside.

"Good thing your head is attached to your shoulders, Kell," she muttered as she swiveled around and bumped into someone.

"Whoa!"

The unexpected voice and collision snapped her out of her thoughts about her forgetfulness.

"Sorry, Kelly," Paul Sloan said.

Where had he come from? He wasn't there on the sidewalk a moment ago. Or had he been? "It was my fault. I should have been looking where I was going."

He'd grabbed her arms, helping to keep her from tipping over. Even in retirement, the cop in him still looked out to protect others. He released her and gave a quick smile.

"Well, no harm. Have a good day." With that, Paul hurried off.

The studio's door opened, and Liv exited. "Thanks for waiting. Here's your water bottle." She handed it to Kelly.

Kelly's gaze pulled from the retreating Paul Sloan. "Huh? Thanks. All set with your schedule?"

"Yes, I am. But, you know if we take a reformer class together, it'll be cheaper."

"Thanks, but the mat is good for now. Come on, let's get coffee." Kelly bumped Liv's shoulder and smiled. Maybe it was more than just the Pilates workout that had her feeling calmer and steadier. Maybe spending forty-five minutes with her best friend three mornings a week had more to do with it than those dreaded One Hundreds. Whatever it was, she was grateful.

"How's the presentation coming along for Shop Small Saturday?" Liv fell into step with Kelly and they walked to Doug's. "You know, Jay was thrilled when you volunteered. He was worried he'd have to oversee the committee. Even though I think you've taken on too much, you have saved me a lot of grief since I won't have to listen to him complain. So thank you."

Inside Doug's, they ordered their caffeine fix and batted ideas back and forth about what their businesses could do on that upcoming Saturday. Outside, they continued walking along Lucky Cove's main hub, which was starting to come alive for the day.

Up ahead, they saw Lulu setting out buckets of fresh flowers in front of her floral shop. Petite yet sturdy, the gray-haired woman had owned the shop for nearly thirty years. She'd left nursing to pursue her passion for flowers. Over the past year, she'd become a role model for Kelly. Not only in business, but in life. Lulu had overcome a lot of heartache and disappointment, and she was a reminder that most things could be overcome.

"I have to show you the most gorgeous pair of shoes. Ever." Kelly hurried ahead like a child eager to show her parents a must-have toy for Christmas. "Come on, hurry up!"

"Speaking of shoes, how's it working with Breena splitting her time between you and Miranda?" Liv asked.

Kelly shrugged. "Okay, so far." She looked past the flower shop and saw Breena standing outside the shoe boutique. Her nylon backpack was slung over her shoulder, and she held an insulated cup. And she looked confused.

"Good morning, Breena!" Liv waved when Breena looked in her direction.

"Is everything okay?" Kelly asked.

"I'm not sure. The front door is open. See." Breena pointed at the shop entrance. "But it's not opening time yet. Miranda told me to open today."

"Do you think we should call the police?" Liv asked as she peered into the shop through the glass door, which was ajar.

"She probably just forgot, or she had something to do first thing this morning," Kelly said. "But just to be safe, let's all go in together."

"Safety in numbers. I like that." Breena pulled the door open, and all three entered. "Looks normal." She took a few more steps forward. "Miranda? Are you here?"

No longer concerned about an intruder, Kelly drifted away toward the window display and frowned. "Did she sell those D'Orsay pumps?"

Breena set her backpack and coffee cup on the sales counter. "That's why she came in. She changed out the window display. Duh!" She giggled.

Kelly spun around. "I'm serious. Did she sell them? Is there another pair?" Since she was practically in debt for the comfy yet chic duster she had on, why not throw in the fantastic shoes that had her drooling the other day?

"I'll check to see if there's a pair of those D'Orsays in your size. Maybe I'll even let you use my employee discount. Miranda!" Breena called out as she headed toward the back room, which was separated from the sales floor by a curtain. She swiped the curtain out of the way and entered the room, briefly disappearing.

"These are gorge!" Liv had found a pair of suede ankle boots and was stroking them.

"I'm not sure what Miranda's deal is with her past, but the woman has amazing taste in shoes," Kelly said. "Who knows—" Her words were cut short by a scream.

The hairs on the back of Kelly's neck prickled, and her head swung in the direction of the back room Breena had disappeared into. Then, she darted to the curtain and swept it back, not wasting a moment.

Her gaze first landed on Breena, whose hands covered her mouth. Next, she noticed her uncle Ralph standing a few feet from Breena.

What is he doing here?

None of this made sense. Breena's screaming and the look of horror plastered on her uncle's face. Well, not until Liv squeezed her arm and asked, "Is she dead?"

That's when Kelly's gaze traveled down to the floor, and there was Miranda, sprawled out on the tile flooring.

Lying faceup, her long dark hair was a tangled mess beneath her head, and her hazel eyes seemed to stare off into space in a lifeless sort of way.

Kelly gulped. And then summoned every ounce of fortitude she had in her and walked to Miranda. Up close, she noticed discolored lines ringing Miranda's neck. Had she been strangled? The reason why Miranda was on the floor wasn't the big concern at the moment. Finding out if she was alive was the priority. Even though just looking at her… Still, Kelly squatted beside Miranda and felt for her carotid pulse.

There was none.

Kelly looked up to her uncle and announced, "She's dead."

"I swear, I found her like this," Ralph said as he took a step forward.

"Stay back!" Breena held out her hand. "Don't you move! You killed her!"

Chapter 5

"Can you walk me through what happened?" Nate, seated across from Kelly, had his notepad open, ready to jot down details she provided. He'd arrived after two uniformed officers responded to Breena's 9-1-1 call. They'd cleared out the back room when they entered the shop and separated Ralph from Kelly and her friends.

Kelly had expected another detective to show up instead of Nate. Marcy Wolman always seemed to be working when Kelly found dead bodies. She was also the sister of Kelly's ex-boyfriend, Mark Lambert. That dynamic made situations, like crime scenes, even more awkward.

So when Nate showed up, Kelly had been relieved for a couple of reasons.

With Wolman, Kelly found it difficult to maintain boundaries. She wanted to be helpful but somehow ended up more involved in the detective's cases than she bargained for. And those few times almost got her arrested for interfering with a police investigation.

The other reason Kelly was grateful to have Nate on the case was that she believed he had enough common sense to know her uncle wasn't a murderer, despite what Breena had blurted out earlier.

How could Breena utter such an accusation?

Kelly sucked in a breath. She glanced at her hands—shaky and sweaty—and then clasped them together on her lap. She'd taken a seat beside a display table of shoes. The assortment showcased the perennial favorite material of fall—suede. She'd been mesmerized by the fine stitching of the patent toe cap flat. Its craftsmanship was reflected in the price tag. But, since she couldn't afford to purchase them, she settled for admiring them. They were a welcome distraction from the ugliness she'd just seen.

"Kelly…did you hear me?" Nate leaned forward and rested his hand on her leg.

She nodded, not looking away from the shoes. "I can walk you through what happened."

"Okay. Take your time."

"Liv and I were at Summer's studio for a Pilates class. Then we went to Doug's to get coffee. When we left, we found Breena standing outside the shop. She was confused."

"About what?"

"The front door was open." Kelly lifted her head and pointed. "She said that she was supposed to open this morning. Liv and I came in with her. I noticed that the shoes in the window the other day were gone, and then Breena realized that the window display had been switched out. It all made sense then. Miranda decided to come in early and do that."

What didn't make sense was Miranda's murder. Having some time to think about what she'd seen, Kelly was confident that Miranda had been strangled.

"Then what happened?"

Kelly looked at Nate. His features had softened since he first arrived on the scene. When he first walked in, he was in full cop mode, only wanting the facts from the uniformed officer who met him at the door and gave him a recap of what happened.

"Breena went in the back room to see Miranda while Liv and I stood out here…browsing." Gosh, she'd been looking at footwear while her friend was discovering a dead body. *Not cool, Kell.* She sucked in another breath and continued. "Then we heard Breena scream and went running to her. That's when we…I saw Miranda on the floor and Ralph standing there." She squeezed her eyes shut. She didn't want to see her uncle standing over a dead woman's body, but the image was seared into her brain.

"It's okay. Take your time." Nate removed his hand from her leg, leaving that spot of her thigh cold. All she wanted to do was to curl up in his arms and bury her head in his chest and forget what had just happened.

"I checked Miranda's pulse. There wasn't any. She was dead."

"Did your uncle say anything?"

"Yes, he did. He told us, 'I swear, I found her like this.' That's all he said. Breena called 9-1-1, and I told him not to say anything else. He looked as surprised as we must have."

While she and her uncle had their differences and were currently in a very challenging situation regarding Ariel, she didn't want to testify against him. Whatever he would have said at that moment would have been used against him if the police considered him a suspect. Because he and Miranda had been battling over the shop, an argument could have been made that he had a motive for killing her.

A chill skittered down her spine at the thought.

"Even with the shock of finding Miranda Farrell's body, you still had the wherewithal to caution your uncle from saying anything that could incriminate him." Nate's tone was neutral, so Kelly couldn't tell if he was impressed or disappointed.

"He's my family. I thought it was the prudent thing to do. You know, Uncle Ralph is a lot of things, but he's no killer."

Nate closed his notepad. "What makes you think Miranda was murdered?"

Kelly leaned back and crossed her legs. She felt better, less unnerved and able to think more clearly now. "Well, there appeared to have been a struggle in the back room. And there were bruises on her neck. Like she'd been strangled."

Nate's brows arched.

"Also, it didn't register at first because of where Miranda's body was, but I noticed the loose papers on the floor that most likely came off the desk and the shattered vase. Also, the roses that had been in the vase had been stomped on. That's odd, right? Why would someone do that?"

"No theories?"

Kelly shook her head. She only had questions. Then her thoughts turned to the person who had given Miranda those roses. "Poor Bud."

"Bud Cavanaugh?"

"Will you tell him about Miranda?"

Nate nodded. "Yes, I'll make the notification. What can you tell me about your uncle's relationship with Ms. Farrell?"

"Not much. I didn't know until yesterday that they knew each other from years ago or that he owned this building." Kelly shifted in her seat. "You don't suspect my uncle of having something to do with her death, do you?"

"I'm sorry, I can't comment on an open investigation."

"But he's my uncle, and I'm your..."

"Detective Barber," an officer called from the back room.

Nate looked over his shoulder, indicated he'd be right there, and then turned back to Kelly. "All the more reason for me not to comment on this case. You're free to go."

"What about Uncle Ralph?"

Nate stood. "Not quite yet." He turned and headed for the back room.

Kelly sprang up from her seat. "Nate! You can't be serious."

He stopped and looked back at her. "Go home, Kelly. It's for the best." He continued into the back room with the officer.

Kelly huffed.

Go home, Kelly. It's for the best.

Best for whom?

Maybe she'd been wrong about Nate. Based on his demeanor and questions regarding Ralph, maybe he didn't have that much common sense if he believed Ralph could murder someone.

Liv stood from her seat across the shop and walked to Kelly. "He's right. We should go. Your uncle will be fine. I'm sure Nate just has a few more questions in order to rule Ralph out as a suspect."

Her friend could be right. But a niggling in her brain told her Liv wasn't right. It told her that her uncle could be in serious trouble.

"I have to call Summer and Frankie. They need to know what's going on and make sure Ralph gets a lawyer." Kelly reached down for her yoga bag, slung it over her shoulder, and then pulled out her phone from a zippered compartment.

"And you have to check on Breena. She was really distraught when she left," Liv said.

After taking Breena's statement, Nate had let her leave. He assigned an officer to drive her home. She had been crying and appeared to be in shock at finding Miranda dead. So much so that she even accused Ralph of killing Miranda. Yes, Kelly would blame the stress of the situation for Breena's unfounded allegation.

"You're right. I have to call and check on her." Kelly couldn't believe she'd stumbled upon another dead body. Was this the way it was always going to be for her? Stumbling upon murdered people? She gave herself a mental shake. A woman was dead. Now wasn't the time for a pity party. Now was the time to do something useful. Perhaps she kept finding dead bodies because she had some special knack for helping find justice for victims and their families.

Maybe, just maybe, this time, she was there to make sure an innocent man didn't get arrested for a murder he didn't commit.

Kelly said goodbye to Liv with a hug outside of Miranda & James and then headed to her boutique. Her steps were heavy and slow. The lightness she felt coming out of the Pilates class had been zapped by the ugliness of murder. She glanced over her shoulder and saw Liv had also lost the perkiness from the early morning fitness session.

She eventually made her way around her building and noticed the gray sedan parked in the space next to her Jeep. Good. Pepper had arrived for work early that day. Relieved, she entered through the back door. First, she'd tell Pepper what happened, and then she'd be comforted by some small action, like a cup of tea or a reassuring hug. She dropped her yoga bag on the floor after plucking out her phone. Her nose wriggled at the fragrance of freshly brewed coffee. Darn. She'd left her coffee from Doug's back at the shoe shop.

The door to the staff room swung open, and Pepper appeared.

"Good morning. I thought I'd get an early start today." She looked perkier than she had the other morning. Her hair had a gloss to it, and her face had a subtle glow Kelly suspected came from the radiance facial mask treatment Pepper had indulged in for her birthday. Based on the results, it was a worthwhile splurge. "I dropped off breakfast for Gabe, and since I was out, I figured I might as well come in."

"Oh...great." Kelly walked to the table and dropped into a chair.

"We already had a customer. Paul Sloan came in to consign some clothes."

Kelly's head tilted. "We don't sell menswear."

"It's his late wife's clothes. She died five months ago. He said he's finally ready to clear out her belongings." Pepper poured a cup of coffee and added cream to it. "I remember Dorie had a rough life before she met Paul. Her dad had been an abusive drunk. Her mom was so fragile and powerless against him. I believe that marrying Paul was the best thing that happened to the poor soul."

"Ah-ha." Kelly's thoughts were still back in the shoe shop. She turned over the events that led up to Miranda's life ending, from her two dead husbands to her arguments with too many people to count at the moment.

"What's wrong? You have a funny look on your face. Did something happen at the Pilates class?" Pepper dropped the spoon in the sink.

"No. Class was fine. It's what happened afterward."

Pepper moved quickly and joined Kelly at the table. "You're scaring me, dear. What happened?"

"It's Miranda Farrell." Kelly shook her head. She still couldn't believe it. Maybe saying it out loud would help make it real. "She's dead."

Pepper gasped, covering her mouth with her hand. After a moment, she asked, "Don't tell me you found the body?"

Kelly shrugged. "Sort of. Breena saw Miranda first."

"No! Oh my goodness. How is she doing? I can't imagine...."

"She was inconsolable, so Nate had an officer drive her home just to be safe."

"I don't believe this," Pepper said. Her forehead creased with concern as her eyes clouded with sadness. "Who? Why? Poor Breena. She must be so upset."

"It was awful. Truly awful." The image of Breena's face when she found Miranda haunted Kelly. All she wanted to do was pull her friend into a big, comforting hug. But she couldn't. She had to check on Miranda and make sure the scene remained undisturbed. Well, as much as was possible, considering four people had entered after the murderer.

"In her own shop? When was she…you know?" Pepper asked.

Kelly shook her head. "Do you want details?"

Pepper raised her palm before standing. She walked back to the kitchen counter where she'd left her coffee. "No. I don't need them."

Kelly understood Pepper's reluctance to hear the gory details like Miranda's lifeless eyes staring off into space.

"Do you know if Miranda had any family?" Kelly asked.

"I really don't know. It was twenty years ago, I think, when she lived here. I barely knew her then. We didn't travel in the same social circles."

"Well, Nate is going to notify Bud."

Pepper's head cocked sideways. "Why? Were they dating? Isn't he a little young for her?"

Kelly shrugged. "She wasn't that much older than him, right?"

"Guess so. Equal rights and everything." Pepper poured another cup of coffee and delivered it to Kelly before returning to her cup. "So, Nate is the detective on the case?"

Before Kelly could answer, the back door swung open, and her cousin Frankie barged in. Worry, anger, and confusion masked his typically boyish face.

"What the heck happened?" he demanded as he approached the table and propped his hands on his hips. "I've been trying to call my dad since you texted me, and he's not answering. So you really saw my father standing over Miranda's body?"

"I did. And so did Breena and Liv," Kelly said. "Why don't you pour a cup of coffee and try to calm down."

"Calm down? Are you serious right now? What on earth was he doing there? Did he say?" Frankie asked.

"No, all he said was that he found her like that," Kelly said. "He was probably trying to get her to break her lease again, since he hadn't had any luck the last couple of times they discussed it. But, you know, I sensed something else was going on between them. They have history, don't they?"

Frankie threw his hands up in the air. "I have no idea! I was a kid back then."

"Well, she accused him of leading a witch hunt against her twenty years ago," Kelly said.

"What are you doing, Kell? Helping the police find a motive for my father having killed Miranda?" Frankie dropped into a chair.

"I don't think she's doing that," Pepper said.

"Look, what I know is that my father didn't murder that woman." Frankie dragged his hand through his sandy blond hair. "Even if something happened between them back then, he's not a killer. You know that, Kelly."

"Frankie, please calm down. For all we know, your dad finished up with Nate and is in a meeting and can't take your calls." Kelly sipped her coffee, praying she was right.

"So, this is Nate's case? What does he think? Does he think my dad had something to do with Miranda's death?" Frankie leaned forward and waited expectantly for Kelly's answer.

Kelly thought back to Nate's questions about Ralph and Miranda's relationship. And how he detained Ralph longer at the scene. Why hadn't Nate asked more questions about the people Miranda clashed with at the luncheon? Maybe because he was going to speak to them directly. Yes, that must be it.

"Of course, I can't say for sure. What I can say for sure is that he's a good detective and professional." From the unconvinced look on her cousin's face, her words were falling hollow. "He'll keep an open mind and follow the evidence, which should lead away from your dad because he's innocent."

"He was found standing over a murdered woman he'd been arguing with…that's evidence." Frankie scrubbed his face with his hands. His surfing tan had started to fade thanks to cooler, shorter days. He spent as much time as he could on his surfboard when he wasn't working at his restaurant. He clasped his hands together and looked at Kelly. "Kell, I need you to do your *thing* and help find the person who killed Miranda."

Her *thing*?

"Hold on there," Pepper butted in. "I know what you're asking her to do. She's not going to do her *thing* because it has almost gotten her killed too many times to count. My son is a police officer, and I know that the LCPD consists of competent law enforcement officials who are trained to solve murder cases."

Frankie gave Pepper a pointed look. "No offense, Pepper, but this is a family matter, and you should stay out of it."

Pepper drew back as if she'd been slapped.

"Frankie! That was uncalled for. She's only trying to help." Kelly stood, swiping her mug up, and carried it to the kitchenette counter. There, she topped off her coffee, giving her time to cool off. Her cousin had just crossed a line, but because he was upset and stressed over the situation, she didn't want to overreact. But she set the coffee carafe down harder than she intended. Her plan wasn't working. "You know, Frankie, she is my family."

He squared his shoulders, and, in an instant, the worry and confusion of a son who had burst into the boutique moments ago had vanished and was replaced with a cold, calculated demeanor similar to his father's.

"Have you forgotten that *you* caused my dad's heart attack, and for that, you owe him?" Frankie asked.

Pepper whipped around, and she looked at Kelly. "What is he talking about? How did you cause Ralph's heart attack?"

Kelly pressed her lips together. Now Frankie had gone too far. She sprinted back to the table, and when she reached her cousin, she grabbed his arm. He tried to wiggle free, but she held on to him tightly as she guided him up onto his feet and dragged him toward the back door.

"Will someone tell me what's going on?" Pepper asked.

"I'm sorry...we need a minute in private. Do you mind?" Kelly asked, hoping that Pepper wouldn't be offended.

"No...of course not. I'll finish entering Paul's merchandise into consignment." Pepper's tone revealed she had been offended. She quickly discarded her mug in the sink and then left the room. After Pepper left and the door swung closed, Kelly looked at her cousin. Irritation swelled up inside her, and she was afraid she'd say something she'd regret, but there was no calming down. Not after Frankie had come perilously close to revealing his father's secret.

"What is wrong with you? How could you say that? And in front of Pepper?" Kelly asked.

Frankie remained quiet, which infuriated Kelly more.

"No one outside of our family...I'm talking you"—she pointed at him—"me, Summer, Caroline, and your dad know that Ariel is your sister. It's your dad's and Ariel's secret, and it's up to them when it becomes public. It's not up to you!" Kelly swung around and marched away from her cousin.

She had to calm down. But not until she got everything off her chest. She reeled back to face Frankie.

"And how dare you blame me for your dad's heart attack. He's the one who got all upset, pounding on his desk and yelling at me! I was only trying to help him. So don't you ever lay that guilt on me again. Am I clear?"

"Let me make it clear to you." Frankie's voice sharpened. It seemed he'd channeled his father's tone. They already shared the same narrow noses and squared chins. Now he was talking to Kelly the way Uncle Ralph did. "I need your help. You need to choose between your friends, which Pepper is, or your family, which includes my dad. When you make your decision, let me know." He turned and then stormed out of the staff room.

Kelly flinched when the door slammed shut. She'd never seen her cousin so angry. He'd always had a mild temperament. A creative soul, his mom used to say. Maybe that's why he hadn't succeeded in his dad's real estate business. He hadn't had the cutthroat mentality, the winner-take-all outlook, or the success-at-all-costs motivation like Ralph Blake had. No, Frankie was gentler, kinder, and that's why Kelly loved him so much. But, at the moment, she didn't like him very much.

Giving her an ultimatum.

Who did he think he was?

Maybe when he had time to cool his jets, he'd see that Pepper had only been trying to protect Kelly. She'd been right in pointing out that Kelly's *thing*, which seemed to be a natural gift for sleuthing, had put Kelly's life in danger a few times. Those times Kelly had stuck her neck out for people who weren't as close to her as Pepper, Frankie, or her uncle.

Gosh, Kelly hated it when Frankie was right. Ralph was her family, her blood. So she should at least try to help make sure he wasn't the only person the police looked at for Miranda's murder.

As she tidied the kitchen counter and sink, she let her mind churn over thoughts. Mindless tasks usually helped her clear her head. By the time she was done cleaning, she had the start of a plan. The first thing she needed to do was find out what happened after she left the shoe shop, aka crime scene. Pepper would understand. Right?

Chapter 6

Even her favorite long velvet duster in mustard yellow couldn't lift Kelly's mood the following morning. She'd added the duster for oomph, yes it was an official fashion term, over her V-neck white tee and dark wash jeans. To finish the look, she put on statement gold-tone jewelry in front of her mirror. Her reflection had radiated a comfortable, stylish look. Though, on the inside, she was a hot mess of emotions. Well, really, only one feeling—regret.

She hated how things ended with Frankie yesterday. He'd stormed out and hadn't returned any of her calls or texts. Then there was Pepper. She hadn't come out and asked directly, but she was curious about Frankie's statement that Kelly had caused Ralph's heart attack. She also seemed hurt by Frankie's comment that she wasn't family.

Insensitive jerk.

"I can't believe he almost came *this* close to blurting out Ralph's secret in front of her. What was he thinking?" she muttered to herself. The whole point of coming downstairs to the staff room early was to get some work done on the Shop Small project before the boutique opened. Now, she feared she'd have difficulty concentrating since she was already thinking about Frankie and the can of worms he almost opened yesterday.

Deep breaths. Deep breaths.

She focused her gaze on the large faux plant beside her desk. She'd bought it last week because she wanted to add a touch of green and Zen to the space. She'd considered a real plant, but she didn't have a green thumb like Pepper.

"Frankie knows Ariel doesn't want the whole world to know she's Ralph's daughter." She blew out a breath. The whole Zen thing wasn't happening.

She needed some good old-fashioned discipline. "Time to get to work." She scanned her desk for the computer mouse. "Shoot. Where is it?"

Last night, she'd left her laptop on the desk because she hadn't wanted to be tempted to work. All she wanted was a hot bath, a glass of wine, and to indulge in a marathon of *Project Runway*. She could have sworn the computer mouse had been right next to the laptop. Since she would be working on a spreadsheet, she preferred using the external device.

The back door swung open, catching Kelly by surprise. She looked up and was both happy and stunned to see Breena. Honestly, she hadn't expected Breena to come into work for another day or so. She'd had quite the shock the day before.

A velvet headband pulled Breena's auburn hair from her face, highlighting the silver hoops dangling from her ears. She layered a tartan overall dress over a long-sleeved white funnel neck sweater. She finished off her easy fall look with taupe booties. For someone who suffered a tremendous shock only twenty-four hours earlier, she looked good.

Kelly popped up from her seat and raced to Breena, pulling her into a hug. "I'm so sorry you had to be the one to first see Miranda."

Breena softened in the embrace and nodded. "Me too. I don't know how you do it. You were so calm and collected."

Experience, dear Breena, experience.

Kelly released her friend. "Are you sure you want to be here? You can take today and even tomorrow off. With pay."

"I appreciate the offer. Hopefully, staying busy will keep my mind off yesterday. All night, I kept seeing her body lying there with your uncle standing over her." Breena shuddered.

"About that." Kelly stepped back and then returned to her desk, where she continued to look for the computer mouse. "You accused him of murdering her."

Breena set her suede hobo bag on the table as she walked toward the coffee maker. Her head had tilted down slightly. Did she feel guilty for what she said?

"Well, it kinda looked bad for him." Her voice lacked the confidence it had the day before when she'd slung the allegation at Ralph. "He and Miranda have been arguing a lot the past week."

"That doesn't mean he killed her."

"Then what was he doing there standing over her?"

"I'm not sure why he was in the shop, but he was standing over her like we were because he'd also discovered her body." Yes, that made sense to

Kelly. And then a wave of sadness swept over her—Ralph had found the dead body first. That must have been horrible for him.

"What are you looking for?" Breena asked as she prepared a pot of coffee.

Kelly looked up. "The mouse for my laptop. It was right here last night." She jabbed her finger on the spot next to the computer where she last saw the device. Or, she thought she had.

Breena pressed the coffee maker's Start button and then moved to the table. She glanced at her watch. "I'll open in a few minutes. Is the cash register all set?"

Kelly shook her head. She hadn't had time to take the money bag out of the safe and fill the register.

"Okay. I'll do that." Breena crossed her legs and leaned back. "How's Frankie doing? Is he still upset?"

Kelly paused for a moment. Pepper must have spoken to Breena last night and filled her in on what happened when Frankie came by yesterday. When she called Breena yesterday, she didn't share that. Instead, she tried to keep the conversation away from the murder and the fallout afterward.

"I haven't spoken to him since he left here." Like Ariel, he was avoiding her. Why were relationships so hard? And where was the freakin' mouse? She bent over and pulled out her laptop bag. Maybe it had fallen inside there.

"So what are you going to do now?" Breena asked.

"I was going to work on Shop Small Saturday." Kelly frowned. The mouse wasn't in the bag. She dropped the bag back on the floor and considered where to search next.

"I mean about your uncle being like a number one suspect in Miranda's murder. He had motive, means, and opportunity," Breena said.

"What do you mean he had means?" The motive and opportunity were pretty much evident.

"It appeared Miranda had been strangled, and she hadn't been dead long before we found her. I heard one of the two officers say they had a fresh one." She made a face. "Ewww."

Kelly stopped her search and remembered when she touched Miranda's skin, it had still been warm. So she hadn't been dead for too long when they discovered her. But her uncle hadn't looked like he'd just strangled someone. For the exertion that would require, he would have been out of breath. He wasn't exactly in the best shape. He also looked pulled together in his suit, while the room had looked like there'd been a struggle. She retrieved a memory, an image. Uncle Ralph's diamond pattern dark gray silk tie hadn't looked askew. If he'd overpowered her after a struggle and strangled her, indeed, he would have been a little rumpled.

"Earth to Kelly," Breena said, snapping her fingers. "Did you hear me?"

"What?" Kelly snapped out of her thoughts.

"I asked you what are you planning to do? Are you going to help clear your uncle?"

"First, I have to find out if he's really under suspicion. I haven't heard from him or Nate." She'd left a voice mail for Nate before she called Breena last night but figured he was working late on the case. "There are some other people who seemed displeased that Miranda came back to town. Also, it could have been random. Maybe someone had broken in, and she surprised them when she showed up early."

Breena's head bobbed up and down. "Possibly. I hadn't thought to look for any signs of a break-in. Though, I think it's unlikely a random stranger killed her."

"Why do you say that?"

"For the same reason you think the police need to look beyond your uncle. I only worked for Miranda for a short time, but I also noticed she wasn't well received by a lot of people who have lived in town for a long time."

"Are you just talking about the other business owners on Main Street or customers?"

"Both."

"Interesting." Kelly rapped her fingers on her desk. "I'm curious. Who's James?"

"There isn't any James. Well, not anymore."

Another dead husband?

"What happened to him?"

"He died."

"How?"

"She said he died from cancer. It was a rough period. She'd had him for nearly fifteen years, and then one morning, she found him curled up on an old blanket, and he didn't look good. So she took him to the vet—"

"Vet?"

"Yeah. James was her cat. Who did you think I was talking about?"

"Another dead husband."

"Oh. No." Breena giggled. "He was definitely her cat. I saw his picture. She liked how the name Miranda & James sounded, so she decided to name her shop that."

Relieved there wasn't a third dead husband, Kelly returned to her inquiry about people who disliked Miranda. "Did anyone else come into the shop and argue with her?"

"No. Honestly, it was only your uncle." Breena stood and went to pour a cup of coffee and returned to the table.

Kelly resisted asking if Breena told Nate about those arguments. She really didn't want to put Breena in the middle of things. Though she kind of already was.

"Nobody else? Not Erica or Ricky or Ernie Baldwin?"

"Erica and Ricky came into the shop, but they didn't argue with Miranda, not like Ralph did. Sorry. Their tones were very unfriendly, but there were no scenes. It didn't take a rocket scientist to figure out they weren't happy with her."

"Miranda lived here twenty years ago. Though I don't remember her, and neither does Frankie. Pepper kind of does. She said she didn't run in the same social circles as Miranda had."

"Well, I have some info on that." Breena pushed her mug out of the way and leaned forward. "Miranda worked at the Lucky Cove Inn when she first came to town. There she met Daniel Parnell, an older widower. From what she said, it sounded like a whirlwind romance because, by Labor Day, they were married, and she was living in a big house and driving a fancy car." She expelled a wistful sigh.

Kelly suspected that to Breena, a struggling actress who returned from New York City to work odd jobs to raise her daughter, Miranda's life sounded like a fairy-tale romance. Kelly could almost hear Breena's thoughts—*some girls have all the luck*. But Breena would be wrong. Miranda had two dead husbands, one dead cat, and now she was dead. Not much of a fairy tale.

"What else did she say?" Kelly asked.

"A few of Daniel's friends had tried to warn him not to marry her."

"They thought she was a gold digger?"

Breena nodded. "But it turns out she wasn't after his money."

"Well, probably not at first." Kelly gave up on trying to find the computer mouse. Knowing, eventually, it would show up. "Did Miranda tell you that Daniel had been accused of embezzling from his clients?"

"So you know all about her first husband? The charges came by their first wedding anniversary, and a few days later, he died from a heart attack." Breena's eyebrows arched. "But what do you know about her second husband?"

"Only that he died." Kelly stood and went to the kitchenette. She pulled out a package of English muffins and prepared one for the toaster. "Tell me what you know."

"Six months after Daniel died, she married Nolen Briggs," Breena said.

"The name is familiar. Why?" Kelly pulled out a plate from a cupboard and a jar of jam from the refrigerator.

"Violet Briggs is one of our regular customers. He was her brother. Anyway, I've heard that some suspected Nolen of helping Miranda hide money—"

"Money that Daniel embezzled?"

Breena shrugged. "Possibly. Being a boat captain, he had access to a boat, and it's said that he and Miranda took several trips to the Cayman Islands."

"Oh my gosh. This all sounds like a soap opera." The English muffin popped up from the toaster, and Kelly quickly spread a heaping serving of jam on both slices. She returned to her desk with her breakfast and sat.

"I also heard Miranda has been seeing someone since coming back to town. And I think she was. I overheard her a few times on the phone talking all sweet," Breena said. "Though, she never talked about him."

Kelly took a bite of the English muffin and chewed. After she swallowed, she said, "She was seeing someone. Bud Cavanaugh. I'm positive."

"Poor Bud. He's so unlucky in love." Breena lifted her mug and then stood. "I'll open the boutique."

"Thanks." Kelly pulled open the desk's file drawer. Her list of things to do included reviewing invoices from the boutique's suppliers. "What the…" She reached in and pulled out the computer mouse.

"Hey, you found it!" Breena said.

"How the heck did it get in there? I didn't open this drawer last night."

"Are you sure?"

Kelly set the mouse on the desk's surface. "Yes. I'm sure." Wasn't she?

* * * *

By midmorning, there had been a handful of customers who'd left the boutique with stuffed shopping bags. All in all, it was turning out to be a good day, even though Kelly's thoughts kept drifting back to Miranda's murder and that her uncle was a likely suspect. She'd started forming a plan yesterday. But, since it wasn't thoroughly thought out, she decided not to act on impulse or let spontaneity propel her into something she'd regret. No, instead, she was going to think before leaping. Her therapist would be so proud of her. Well, if she hadn't fired her.

"I really only meant to browse," Minnie Clayborne said as Kelly folded the three blouses she'd just purchased and placed them into the customer's tote bag.

"Isn't that always the case?" Kelly ripped off the receipt from the cash register and handed it to Minnie, who looked thrilled that she'd scored not one, not two, but three Kate Spade blouses at such a ridiculously low price. A leopard print, a pink lace, and a floral bouquet. All three had just been put out on the sales floor. They'd come from Paul Sloan. His late wife had good taste, and Minnie had good timing. Kelly hadn't thought those blouses would last long when she first saw them.

Minnie thanked Kelly and then strutted out of the boutique with her head high and shoulders squared. She'd come, shopped, and conquered. Kelly giggled. She loved it when her customers left happy.

The bell over the door jingled, alerting Kelly to a new arrival.

In walked a woman Kelly didn't recognize. Tall, with a commanding presence, the woman was a stark contrast of dark and light. She wore black from head to toe—a longline cardigan, turtleneck, and knit pants. The strappy sandals she wore kept the look from being too heavy or somber. She paused, taking a long look around the boutique, when she spotted Kelly. A slow smile crept onto her bright red lips. The lip color and her smoky eye kept her fair skin from being washed out against the blackness of her outfit and her whitish gray hair that had an Elsa from *Frozen* vibe. She stepped forward toward the counter, and she extended her hand.

"You are Kelly Quinn." Her handshake was firm. "It's a pleasure to meet you. I'm Jocelyn Bancroft."

The name was familiar to Kelly, but she couldn't place it. "Nice to meet you. Welcome to my boutique. How can I help you today?"

Jocelyn took back her hand. "It's a lovely boutique. But I'm not here to shop."

Kelly's smile faltered a bit.

"And I'm not here to sell anything."

Kelly arched an eyebrow. Now she was intrigued by Jocelyn Bancroft.

"Then how can I help you?"

"Give me an hour or two of your time for an interview."

Kelly's smile slid back into place. She loved promoting the boutique, and media coverage always brought in new customers. Yes, she could do an interview. No matter how busy she was, there was always time to speak to a reporter or writer.

"I write true crime books." Jocelyn continued with her sales pitch.

Aha! That's where Kelly knew the name. Jocelyn wrote *Danger Next Door*, the book that was on the nightstand beside Courtney's mom's bed.

"I don't understand why you would want to interview me."

"Because my next book is about Diana Delacourte's murder." Jocelyn swept aside her fringe of bangs. "And the story wouldn't be complete without hearing from you."

Kelly swallowed. Diana Delacourte had been one of the wives on the reality show *Long Island Ladies*, and she had been murdered. A shudder rippled through Kelly's body at the memory of finding Diana in the snow and then her own near-death experience when she confronted the killer. That had been a treacherous, icy fight for her life. It definitely was a heck of a holiday season she'd never forget.

"You were instrumental in bringing Diana's killer to justice, and I'd like to talk to you about that. Of course, I'll be interviewing other people who worked with and knew Diana. Including your aunt, Summer Blake."

Technically, Summer hadn't worked with Diana. In fact, she barely knew the woman. Last December, Summer had been under consideration to replace Diana after she was fired from the show.

"To be honest, I'm not sure how I feel about your offer." Kelly couldn't help but think being featured in that sort of book wouldn't be the best publicity for her business. She wanted to be known for stylish resale fashion, not for solving murders. But maybe that ship had already sailed since her name was already connected with a handful of true crimes.

"Understandable." Jocelyn reached into her Christian Dior Bobby bag, a classic saddlebag Kelly lusted after, and pulled out a business card.

"Your participation in the book would really bring the story to life, so to speak. Local shop owner caught up in the dark side of reality television solved the murder of a real-life diva." She leaned forward. "I've also heard that Diana's murder isn't the only case you've been involved with."

"You've heard correctly." Kelly looked at the card and then at Jocelyn. "I need to think about this."

"Of course. I understand. Take some time to think about it." Jocelyn turned and left the boutique.

Kelly tapped the card against her fingers, thinking about the pros and cons of granting an interview to Jocelyn. On the one hand, good or bad, it would garner her some attention for the boutique. On the other, she'd be using a woman's murder for her own benefit.

Chapter 7

Midday, Kelly saw a window of opportunity to dash out of the boutique to make a bank deposit and do a little sleuthing. While she was writing up the deposit, she had an idea to visit the library for a quick search of old newspaper articles. Okay. Searching archived articles wasn't exactly a quick activity, but she had some spare time and her curiosity was getting the better of her.

With her banking done, Kelly headed to the library. Checking her watch, she had enough time to do that and make it back to cover lunch breaks. Her pace along Main Street was somewhere between gotta-get-there-ASAP and it's-a-beautiful-day. If she were still in New York City, she'd be moving at the speed of I'm-already-late. Instead, her movement slowed as she approached Turn the Page, Erica's bookshop. Peering in the window, she saw the shop was empty of customers, and Erica stood behind the counter reading a book.

Erica was about the same age as Kelly's mother, and she remembered they'd been friends before her parents moved down south. Erica always had her nose in a book, so it'd been surprising she had those explosive outbursts in the past. But you know what they say about the quiet ones.

After witnessing Erica's temper with Miranda and the death glare she gave Kelly the other night, Kelly hesitated before opening the door and entering the bookshop.

The shop had a calm, inviting, minimalist vibe with its white bookshelves and carefully placed books on display tables. It was very different from the original Turn the Page. Erica had purchased the shop from the previous owner after working there for a decade. Like Kelly, she'd made changes as soon as she took over. One of the changes made was the removal of the dark wood bookcases and creating an open space for author readings, complete with a beverage station.

The bookshop also had a bell over the door, and it jingled, announcing her arrival to Erica, who looked up from her book. Her expression remained neutral as she inserted a bookmark between the pages she'd been reading and then closed the book.

"Welcome, Kelly. Is there anything in particular I can help you find?" Erica's gaze drifted around the store. The walls were lined with floor-to-ceiling bookshelves, all neatly organized. At the same time, display tables ran from the front of the store to the back wall that separated the shop from the back office. Most of the tables displayed books, while others highlighted gifts perfect for the bookworm.

"Yes, yes, there is." Kelly stepped forward to the counter. Displayed in the long glass cabinet were rare first editions. Erica took quarterly antiquing trips and was always looking for a first edition.

"We have several new releases you might be interested in. Let me show you." Erica stepped out from behind the counter, revealing her midi-length green dress and wedge booties. She led Kelly to a table where five hardcover novels were stacked. "These are all murder mysteries."

"I do love a mystery."

"Everyone in Lucky Cove knows how much you love a mystery." Erica reached for one book and handed it to Kelly. "Perhaps this one might be of interest to you. The main character returns to her hometown and pokes around in what appears to be her neighbor's accidental death."

Kelly looked at the cover, then back up to Erica. "Guessing it wasn't an accident."

Erica stared, and Kelly got the message loud and clear.

"These all look great, but I didn't come in for a book. I came in to talk to you. Since there aren't any customers around, it looks like you have a few minutes to talk to me." Kelly set the book back on its stack.

Erica didn't look very enthusiastic about talking to Kelly. "If I say no, you'll just try again, won't you?"

Kelly nodded. The bright side about everyone knowing everyone else in a small town was that they knew the person's personality. It saved a lot of time.

"Fine." Erica walked past Kelly toward the beverage station. There she dropped a coffee pod into the single-serve coffee machine and placed a mug beneath the drip. She pressed a button, and the machine roared to life. "What about Miranda do you want to talk about?"

Surprised the bookshop owner was being so cooperative, Kelly followed and didn't waste any time in getting to the conversation.

"Let's start with the scene in the bathroom at the luncheon. What was that all about?" Kelly asked.

"It's really none of your business. But I sense you won't stop sticking your nose into my business, so I'll tell you."

"My uncle is under suspicion for her murder, so everything connected to Miranda and her death is my business."

"Your uncle has a temper and I wouldn't be one bit surprised if he snapped. Miranda had that way about her. Pushing people to their limits." When her coffee was finished brewing, Erica pulled out the mug and took a sip and then returned to the counter. "I wanted to make sure that Miranda knew I wasn't happy she decided to come back to town. We didn't need her kind back here."

"What do you mean by her kind?"

"Gold digger, cheater, liar. That pretty much summed up Miranda." Erica took another sip of her coffee. "I'd been the best friend of Daniel's first wife. We were as close as sisters, which meant I was very fond of Daniel. So when Ivy died, I did whatever I could to help Daniel. I cooked for him, got his dry cleaning, held his hand while he wept for his wife. It broke my heart."

"You were a good friend."

Erica scoffed. "Not good enough of a friend for Daniel to listen to me about Miranda."

"Did you know for certain she was a gold digger? That she only wanted Daniel's money?"

"What do you think? She was young, beautiful, and had absolutely no job skills other than bending over 'just so' to give Daniel a peek at her cleavage when she served him at the inn. Then she married him and became what my mother called a lady of leisure." Erica reached for her mug again. "She was quite good at it."

"What about the accusations made against Daniel about him stealing clients' money? Were they true?"

Erica's body tensed, and her eyes narrowed. "I was very disappointed when that was revealed. A lot of people, friends of Daniel's, lost money. But when he died, the money was never found. His estate was bankrupt, which meant there was no restitution for his victims. Mark my word, Miranda knew about all that money, and there's no doubt in my mind that she knew where Daniel had hidden it."

Kelly could see why Erica thought that. Married couples did share secrets. But would Daniel risk telling his new bride where the money he stole was stashed? By doing that, he risked her double-crossing him, or making her an accomplice to his crime. She inhaled a breath and gave a little more thought to what Erica had just told her.

"Did Daniel steal from you?"

Erica gazed at Kelly over the rim of her mug. "What difference does it make now?"

Kelly shrugged. "If you're correct about Miranda, she knew where the money was and probably has been living off it for years. Maybe you were trying to find out where the money was."

"I didn't ask her that question in the restroom at the inn. I just wanted her to leave town."

"Maybe not at the luncheon, but what about the morning of the murder? Where were you at that time?"

Erica slammed the mug down on the countertop, coffee sloshing. Her cheeks puffed out as her brows drew inward, and her narrowed eyes got smaller.

Not good, Kell.

"Are you asking me for an alibi? How dare you!" Erica came out from behind the counter with her finger jabbing the air and moving forward in one swift move, forcing Kelly to walk backward. "You come into my place of business asking me if I killed a woman? Who do you think you are?"

Oh, boy.

"I…I…I'm only trying to find the truth of what happened." Kelly continued moving precariously backward to the door. "If you were here with someone else…then there's no harm in asking, right?"

"No, you're wrong. There is harm. I have a reputation in town."

"Well, you have been known to lose your temper." Kelly bumped into a table, jostling the display of self-help books. She attempted to right them, but Erica intervened, setting the books down. But she didn't stop forcing Kelly to the door.

"Then you should have given more thought to coming here today and poking around my life." Erica sidestepped around Kelly, pulling open the door. "Get out! And never come back!"

"Please, Erica. I'm sorry I've offended you. Look, I'm sure you have an alibi for the murder. But, since you're a few stores from the shoe shop, did you see anything that morning that may help the police?"

Erica's transformation was instantaneous. Her face relaxed, as did her posture.

"Actually, I did see something that may help the police."

Yes! It looked like the visit to the bookshop owner, with anger issues paid off for Kelly.

"I saw your uncle sneak in through the back of the shop that morning. I had to take out some boxes I broke down for recycling. From what I saw, he acted like he didn't want anyone to see him. Thanks for reminding me. I'll have to call that handsome detective and tell him everything." She gave Kelly a shove out of the shop and closed the door.

* * * *

Kelly had finally put enough distance between herself and Turn the Page bookshop to feel a little calmer about being shoved out into the street. Right after the door closed in her face, she glanced at her hands, and they were shaking. Erica definitely could be scary. Now Kelly couldn't help but wonder if Erica could treat her like that, could she have snapped with Miranda and done something awful? Like murder?

She veered off Main Street and walked along the path toward the entry of the Lucky Cove Library. Set back from the sidewalk, the whimsical cottage was shaded by a canopy of scarlet-colored leaves from towering oak trees.

Passing a multipaned bay window, she caught a glimpse of Mrs. Glenn reading to a group of littles. They sat crisscross applesauce in a circle while Mrs. Glenn read from an illustrated book. The cheerful white-haired woman had been volunteering there for decades. When Kelly was a kid, she loved coming to the library with her sister and getting lost in stories. She'd pull a book from a shelf and find a cozy spot in the library to sit and read. Then she got her driver's license, and her leisure-time activities changed. She preferred browsing clothing stores to bookshelves. Life had been so simple back then.

She opened the door and entered the library. Built over a hundred years ago, the cottage had been added onto over the years to meet the community's needs. The new rooms were named in honor of Lucky Cove's prominent citizens. Even her uncle had a room named after him. The Blake Genealogy Room—ironic, wasn't it?—was to her left and past the lounge. Six deep leather chairs were arranged in a semicircle on top of a colorful rug. Thick tomes of literature donated over the years and a collection of local authors' novels filled the bookshelves. The quiet space had three patrons immersed in books and a newspaper.

Kelly snuck a peek into the toddlers' reading room. She couldn't resist. The room was a happy space, decorated in primary colors and books, lots of books. She smiled as she continued toward the circulation desk, where Lou Madison was working. The library assistant caught her eye, and she smiled warmly. She definitely wasn't your typical librarian. Her dark hair had a shock of bright pink, and each ear had multiple piercings. As Kelly got closer, she noticed a hint of a tattoo beneath Lou's three-quarter-length sleeve.

"What brings you by?" Lou pushed aside the stack of books in front of her and devoted all her attention to Kelly. She wore a bright orange shirt, and a chunky bead necklace filled in the neckline. She clasped her hands together and rested them on the counter.

"I need to do some research. I'd like to look at issues of the *Weekly* from twenty years ago."

The *Lucky Cove Weekly* had been a mainstay in the community for generations. If it happened in town, it was covered in the *Weekly*. Sometimes to Kelly's chagrin. There was that one article about the seance in her boutique, which didn't help business. No, it only encouraged those with inquiring minds about the afterlife to visit the boutique.

"Wow. That's pretty far back." A spark of curiosity flashed in Lou's eyes. "Does this have something to do with Miranda Farrell's death? I heard she lived here years ago."

Like Kelly, Lou was far too young to remember Miranda from that long ago. But since she worked with the public, she was privy to gossip.

"She lived here for a couple of years back then. Have you heard anyone talking about her?"

"Not really. The gossip grapevine isn't that active in here. Sorry." Lou tsk-tsked as she shook her head. "She came back only to get murdered." She made a sad face and then perked up as she stepped out from behind the counter. "Let me get you settled so you can do your research."

"I appreciate your help." Kelly walked along with Lou through the community reading room, took a right, and then a left to finally reach the technology room. Six tables were set up with computers, and two were already occupied.

Lou stopped at the third workstation and jiggled the computer mouse. When the screen brightened, she tapped on the keyboard and opened a file. Another click, and she was in the *Weekly*'s archive. Another couple of clicks brought her to the folder from twenty years ago.

Lou pulled back her hands from the keyboard and straightened up. "There you go. You're all ready to start. Good luck." She turned and walked away, quickly disappearing.

Kelly settled on the chair, dropping her tote to the floor and pulling out a notebook and pen. She opened the notebook to a blank page and then started clicking, looking for articles about Miranda, Daniel, and Nolen.

She dug into those stories.

There was a photograph of Miranda walking out of the church after Daniel's funeral service in one article. Beside her was a woman. Scanning the article, she found no mention of who that person was. Perhaps a family member? Maybe a friend? She had to have at least one, Kelly figured. She squinted, but it was hard to make out the details of the woman's face. She wasn't someone Kelly remembered.

Another article revealed that husband number two died from a head injury while on his boat. The official ruling was accidental.

Next, she found articles about Daniel's arrest and his alleged crimes. As she read, she jotted down notes.

As Kelly read article after article, she was disappointed to not have learned anything new that would lead her in the killer's direction. Then there was a quote that had her heart thumping against her chest.

"It's unbelievable to think she had no knowledge of her husband's crime. It's reprehensible that she's allowed to walk freely among us. She should be in jail."

Kelly stared at the name of the person attributed to the quote.

Pepper Donovan.

Kelly chewed on her lower lip and wondered why Pepper had acted like she'd barely known Miranda twenty years ago. Based on that quote, it was clear she had a lot of animosity toward Miranda. And for some reason, she hadn't shared that with Kelly.

"So, did you find anything interesting?" Lou asked as she approached the table, making Kelly jump. "Sorry. I didn't mean to startle you. Guess you found something."

Kelly turned her head slowly, still processing what Pepper had said twenty years ago.

"I think I did." The trouble with looking for the truth was that sometimes the truth could be inconvenient and disturbing.

* * * *

Kelly returned to the boutique without a plan of how to ask Pepper about the article she'd been quoted in. Straight and direct would be the simplest way…to earn her the infamous "Pepper glare" and get a lecture. On the other hand, hedging around the article could lead Pepper to reveal she'd been quoted and admit what she'd said.

She was seriously considering googling "how to ask a friend about harsh statements about a murdered person without coming off as accusatory" when the swinging door into the staff room opened.

"You look serious. Don't tell me you found another body." Pepper stopped after entering the room and set her hands on her hips, waiting for an answer.

"No, I didn't find another body." Kelly's belly quaked. She could google pretty fast, and Pepper wouldn't be any the wiser. She just had to stall her friend.

"Then what's the problem? Now you look as white as a ghost." The lightness in Pepper's features had darkened with worry. She hustled to the table and pulled out a chair. "Maybe you should sit down."

"Yes, we should sit." Settling at the table would buy Kelly a couple of extra minutes. As she sat, she dropped her tote on the table. "You know I love you, right?"

Pepper's brows drew together. "What have you done now?"

Spoken like a true, lifelong friend.

"I haven't done anything…well. I went to the library and looked at archived issues of the *Weekly*."

"Why? Never mind explaining. You were researching Miranda and her dead husbands." Pepper rested her forearms on the table and lowered her eyelids.

"I found several, and there was one in particular that had a quote I was surprised to find." Kelly dug into her tote and pulled the printout of the article from a folder. She set the paper on the table in front of Pepper.

Pepper pulled the document closer to her and instinctively reached for her reading glasses, which usually ended up on top of her head during her workday. But they weren't there. "I can't read this. It looks like a newspaper article."

Kelly took the paper back.

"It's from an article about Daniel's alleged crimes and Miranda's possible connection to them. A quote caught my attention." She didn't have to read from the article because Pepper's words had been seared into her brain.

"It's unbelievable to think she had no knowledge of her husband's crime, and it's reprehensible that she's allowed to walk freely among us. She should be in jail."

"Sounds about right." Pepper nodded. "Why are you telling me about this?"

"Because you're the one that said it to the reporter."

Pepper's mouth dropped open.

"When I mentioned to you that Courtney said Miranda lived here before, you seemed not to have known her. Then you vaguely remembered."

Pepper's mouth closed, her chin tipped down, and her gaze locked hard on Kelly, making her squirm. The infamous Pepper glare felt 100 percent more potent. Maybe broaching this subject wasn't a good idea.

"Tell me, what is going on in your pretty little head?" Pepper folded her arms just as the door swung open and Breena strolled in. "Are you thinking I'm a murderer?"

"Murderer? Who? You?" Breena blurted out, her voice shrilling in disbelief as she stared at Pepper.

"No, no, no!" Kelly raised her hands, signaling the conversation needed to stop. She needed a moment to collect her thoughts and straighten out the misunderstanding. "I'm not accusing Pepper of killing anyone. You would never do that in a million years."

"Of course she wouldn't," Breena chided Kelly as she joined them at the table. "Now, will one of you tell me what's going on?"

"Kelly dug up some old newspaper article that I'm quoted in saying that I believed Miranda was involved with Daniel's embezzlement and should have been in jail. It's not like I was the only person saying it," Pepper said.

"Then why did you act like you barely knew her?" Kelly asked.

"Because I didn't know her. It's not like we were friends." Pepper sighed. "Look, it was years ago, and up until now, I didn't remember speaking to the reporter. My memory is good, but it's not perfect."

"But you lost money because of Daniel, didn't you?" Kelly knew she was treading precariously close to crossing boundaries by talking about finances.

Pepper's gaze flickered away for a moment. When it returned to Kelly, any anger her expression held a moment ago had vanished.

"We did. It's not something we like to talk about. Clive and I trusted Daniel for our retirement planning. We lost a lot of money because of him. Why do you think I'm still working?"

"I thought you enjoyed working in the boutique," Kelly said.

Pepper reached for Kelly's hand and squeezed. "I love working here with you and Breena. Spending my days with you two young people keeps me young."

"And fashionable," Breena added.

"It certainly does. But the truth is, I should be able to retire by now. And so should Clive. Our savings took a big hit, and it's been hard to regain ground. First, there was Gabe's education to pay for, and then Clive had that heart thing a few years back and the bills piled up." She patted Kelly's hand before letting go. "Now, I don't want you two feeling sorry for me. I love working here. There's no other place I'd want to be clocking in." She winked.

Kelly set her hands on her lap and dropped her head. She wouldn't blame Pepper if she got up and walked out of her life.

"I don't know what to say. Other than I'm sorry," Kelly said.

"For what? Trying to make sure your uncle doesn't go to prison for a crime he didn't commit? We all know he's a bull in a china shop, but he's no killer," Pepper said.

Kelly's head lifted, and she gave a small smile. "He is, isn't he?"

"Maybe finding that old article has done some good," Pepper said.

"What are you talking about?" Breena asked.

"I'd forgotten all about this. When the news broke about Daniel's alleged embezzlement, I had lunch with a few girlfriends at the Gull Café. Two of my friends left before dessert, but Ronni and I wanted apple pie, so we stayed. Behind me, at a table, a woman was talking to a man. She was very angry with Daniel. She'd lost a lot of money, somewhere around a million dollars."

"Yikes!" Breena leaned forward. She must have figured the story was getting good.

"She believed Miranda had been involved too. Said it straight out, so you see, I wasn't the only one," Pepper said.

Breena looked deflated as she reclined back. Kelly felt the same way but did her best not to show it. Though she had an inkling there was more to Pepper's story.

"Do you know who the woman was?" Kelly asked.

Pepper nodded. "A nonfiction author."

Kelly's mouth gaped open.

"Back then, Jocelyn Bancroft was freelancing for magazines like *People*, and I think she was working on her first book. Isn't it interesting that all of a sudden she's popped into your life, Kelly?" Pepper crossed her arms.

Kelly couldn't deny that Pepper had a point. "It most certainly is."

Jocelyn knew about Kelly's involvement with Diana's murder case and her role in it. Since Jocelyn was a competent true crime writer, she must have researched Kelly and discovered the other investigations she had a hand in. Under the guise of wanting Kelly's help with her next book, Jocelyn could keep tabs on Kelly.

The bell over the front door jingled, and Breena sulked. "Darn. Just when this was getting good. Fill me in later." She stood and hurried out of the staff room.

"You think Jocelyn is trying to use me?" Kelly asked.

Pepper gave a half shrug. "I don't know. What I am certain of is that she has her own agenda, so you should watch your step around her."

"I'm sorry if it sounded like I thought you were a…"

"It didn't. Besides, if you hadn't asked me about what I said to the reporter, then I wouldn't have remembered Jocelyn also being a victim of Daniel's crimes." Pepper stood and walked around the table. She leaned in for a hug and patted Kelly on the back. "I love you like a daughter. That will never change. Even when you accuse me of being a murderer." She chuckled.

"Too bad Erica didn't feel that way when I talked to her." No, Kelly doubted there would be any forgiveness from Erica anytime soon.

"Oh dear. You know she holds grudges, right?"

Kelly nodded.

"Should make the chamber of commerce meetings interesting." Pepper released her hold on Kelly and left the staff room.

Kelly didn't want to think about those meetings. All she knew was that she'd stay out of the restroom when Erica was in there. She reached into her tote for her phone and searched for Jocelyn's card. When she had both out, she typed a message and sent it off to the writer.

I've thought about the interview. I have a few questions first. When are you free?

Chapter 8

Kelly waved goodbye to Breena from her desk at the end of the day. They'd closed up the boutique, and Breena was heading home to take her daughter out for pizza while Pepper had left an hour earlier to bring dinner to Gabe. With the boutique empty, Kelly settled down for a few more hours of work before calling it a day.

The boutique had been busy all afternoon. It was a good thing for her bottom line, but after eating her lunch, she worked the sales floor and couldn't get anything done for her committee. So now she was looking at a long work session and something reheated for dinner.

Before turning her attention to the computer, she checked her messages. Nothing so far from Jocelyn. Maybe the writer had changed her mind about including Kelly in her book. Maybe her intentions hadn't been fueled by wanting to keep tabs on Kelly. Maybe she was just busy and hadn't checked her messages.

Kelly set her phone down, placed her fingers on the keyboard, and started work.

The first document she opened was a catchall for ideas from the participating shops to drive customers to Lucky Cove on the Saturday after Thanksgiving. Emails had come into her inbox throughout the day. Her task was to go through each one and add the suggestions to the spreadsheet.

When she finally came up for a breath of air and a sip of lukewarm water from her reusable bottle, she stretched. Being hunched over her laptop was murder on her back. She then rolled her shoulders back and around a few times, and that was when she realized the time. It was getting close to dinner for her and Howard. There were a few leftovers in her fridge she could nuke in the microwave. Not much of a meal, but it would suffice.

She closed out of her spreadsheets and stood. Her plan was to go upstairs, but she looked over at the back door and had an idea for a change of plans. She'd been waiting all day for people to call or text. Ariel. Jocelyn. Frankie. Nate. Ralph. She was pretty fed up with waiting around. Her uncle didn't live that far away. She'd be back in time to make dinner and get another hour's worth of work done before crawling into bed. Then at least she could scratch one name off her waiting-on list.

Kelly grabbed her tote and then slipped on a cardigan before leaving the boutique out the back door. Behind the steering wheel in her Jeep, she navigated the vehicle out of the communal parking lot behind the shop and turned onto Main Street. Eventually, the quaint shopping village turned into a row of single-story motels booked to capacity in the summer. A turnoff of Main Street onto a residential side road led to several more turns, and she arrived at the Blake house a few minutes later.

She parked in front of the three-car garage, next to a dark Mercedes, and stepped out onto the fancy paver-block driveway. Every time she saw it, she shook her head at the cost. Of course her uncle and Summer couldn't have done a simple paved driveway like the rest of the world. Nope. Appearances were everything to them. As she walked across the patterned blocks, she had to admit it was stunning.

She glanced at the sleek sedan and wondered if Ralph's attorney was inside the house. If so, her visit was poor timing.

Kelly climbed the steps to the front door and pressed the doorbell. She tugged her cardigan around her body and waited for a moment before she heard footsteps approaching on the other side of the door.

She expected to see the housekeeper and was surprised to see Summer standing there with one hand on the doorknob and Juniper, her one-year-old, hitched on her hip. She looked relaxed with her hair pulled into a high ponytail and diamond studs sparkling in her ears. Summer wore jogger pants and a pullover sweater with leather slip-on sneakers. Kelly knew where her aunt liked to shop, and there was no doubt Summer was lounging in designer style. And so was little Juniper. She was dressed in a pink sweater onesie with ruffle details at the shoulders and owl intarsia on the front that probably cost more than Kelly's seasonal wardrobe budget.

Juniper smiled and opened and closed her tiny little hand at Kelly.

"Hey, sweet girl." Kelly leaned forward and tickled Juniper's belly, prompting the baby to giggle as she waved her hands excitedly.

"I was just about to get her ready for bed. Come on in." Summer pulled the door open wider and stepped aside for Kelly to enter. Before she closed the door, she handed her baby to Kelly.

Kelly started bouncing, and Juniper's laugh intensified. "This is the best part of my day." And it was. She loved her little cousin and never missed an opportunity to babysit.

"I guess you're here to see your uncle," Summer said.

"Yeah. But if he's with his lawyer, then..."

"Jared isn't here."

"Well, then whose car is parked in the driveway?"

"Jocelyn Bancroft's. She got here a few minutes ago. I couldn't believe she called and asked to come over. She wants to include me in her next book!" Summer hadn't gotten the part on *Long Island Ladies*, so being in the book could be seen as a consolation prize. She'd get some notoriety out of it.

Summer walked past Kelly toward the family room.

"She's here?" Kelly turned and followed.

When they arrived in the room, Summer headed for the sofa near the play mat and sat, crossing her long legs. The former model had legs that seemed to go on forever. However, Kelly stood rooted in the doorway, staring at Jocelyn, who looked at ease seated on the sofa.

"Are you coming in?" Summer gestured for her niece to enter the room. Despite the high ceilings, expensive furnishings, and high-priced artwork, the room had a warmth to it. Perhaps it came from the working fireplace that crackled and emitted a fiery glow, or the cozy throws draped over the upholstered furniture, or the play area that had been set up for Juniper. Whatever it was, that was the only room Kelly truly felt comfortable in when she was at the Blake house. There were no pretenses in there.

"Jocelyn, I'd like to introduce you to our niece, Kelly Quinn." Summer gestured again for Kelly to enter the family room.

"Ah, we've already met." Kelly entered and carried Juniper to the play area. She then got down on the floor with her. Mindful that it was bedtime, she did her best not to overstimulate the baby. "I hope I'm not intruding." She knew it was wrong to fib. She was thrilled to have run into Jocelyn.

"You have?" Summer asked.

"I popped into her boutique and introduced myself and requested an interview," Jocelyn said. She wore a houndstooth patterned top and black side-vent ankle pants paired with stiletto booties for her evening visit. Next to her on the cushion was a floral quilted jacket. "Like you, Summer, she's a big part of Diana Delacourte's case." Jocelyn's gaze shifted to Kelly.

"Of course she is. She's the one who found Diana's body and proceeded to insert herself into the police investigation." Sharing the spotlight wasn't something Summer liked doing. “And it was a good thing she did, or I believe Diana’s killer would have gotten away.”

Kelly did a double take at Summer. Had she heard what she thought she heard? It almost sounded like a compliment.

Jocelyn cleared her throat. “I’m pleased that you’ll be a part of this project, Kelly. You said you had a few questions for me. Since we’re both here now, why don’t we discuss them?”

“Yes, let’s discuss them.” Though she didn’t want to have the discussion in front of Summer. If only she could get a few minutes in private with the writer. Kelly jiggled a stuffed bear in front of Juniper. The baby’s sleepy eyes danced with delight, but Kelly could tell her cousin’s energy was waning. Within seconds, Juniper started fussing, and Summer stood. “Are you going to take her upstairs to bed?”

Summer bent over and scooped her daughter up. “It’ll only take me a few minutes.”

“No need to rush.” Kelly untangled her legs and stood, moving to the spot on the sofa Summer had just vacated.

“She is an adorable baby,” Jocelyn said as mother and daughter left the room. “Now, what questions do you have? Truthfully, the process is pretty cut and dry. First, though, there is a release form you have to sign. My publisher insists on it.”

That seemed reasonable to Kelly. But she wasn’t sure if she would participate in the book. Though, she was sure that she had questions for Jocelyn about Daniel and Miranda.

“My concern is that the publicity around the book could overshadow my business. I’m working hard to establish the Lucky Cove Resale Boutique as a fashion-forward consignment shop. You know, as a viable option to all the other boutiques in the area.”

“Well, I don’t think you need to worry about that. I think the opposite would happen. People will flock to your shop once they read about your efforts to track down a killer.”

“Hopefully, once they’re in the boutique, they’ll buy something.” Kelly gave a light laugh. She was about to transition to asking questions Jocelyn had no idea were coming, so she was a little nervous. Turning the tables on a person who made her living asking the questions was no easy feat. “You know, I’m kind of involved in the latest murder here in town.”

“I have heard that you found her body. That must have been awful for you,” Jocelyn said.

“What actually happened was that my friend, Breena Collins, first discovered Miranda’s body, and then I rushed into the room when I heard her scream. It was awful. I got the sense the day before that there were people in town who disliked her because of something that happened twenty years ago. Are you familiar with her late husband's alleged crimes?"

"It was quite a famous case in its day. I don't see how anyone who lived in this area didn't know about it." Jocelyn swept her bangs to the side, and she adjusted her seat.

"From what I've learned so far, none of the money he stole has been found. Which I guess is why a lot of people thought Miranda knew where the money was and had it. In fact, didn't you lose about a million dollars because of Daniel's embezzlement?"

"I don't know where you've gotten your information from, but I can assure you that you're wrong."

"I don't think so. My sources are pretty solid." Though Pepper's memory of a conversation she eavesdropped on two decades ago was pretty far from solid. "You didn't lose money because of Daniel Parnell?"

"It was so long ago, and I've made peace with never getting the money back. What happened just forced me to work harder. As far as my finances are concerned, I'm doing okay."

"Then you didn't hold Miranda responsible?"

"And what, kill her? Are you seriously asking me if I killed Miranda Farrell?" Jocelyn jumped up from the sofa.

"Kelly! What are you doing?" Summer burst into the room, and if she hadn't had a face full of injectables, she'd be giving Kelly a look that beat Pepper's glare. "Are you accusing her of murder?"

Kelly shrugged. "We were talking about Daniel and Miranda."

"Let me tell you something to help with your investigation." Jocelyn stepped forward and glared down at Kelly. "Maybe the question you should be asking is not who lost money because of Daniel, but who had helped him embezzle the money and wanted their share."

"What are you talking about?" Summer walked farther into the room and stood behind Kelly. "You think someone besides Miranda helped him?"

"Who was his best friend? Who has had constant arguments with Miranda since she returned to town? Who was standing over her body?" Jocelyn asked.

"Now, wait just a minute. How dare you insinuate that my husband was a part of Daniel's scheme?" Summer bolted from around the back of the sofa, heading straight for Jocelyn. Kelly sprang up, grabbing her aunt's arm. Summer stopped in her tracks and took a deep breath. "I think you should leave now."

Jocelyn gave a curt nod and then picked up her jacket and left the house with less drama than Kelly had expected.

"Can you believe the nerve of that woman? Saying something like that could damage his reputation." Summer dropped onto the sofa and crossed her legs. "Why are people trying to hurt my Ralphie? He's not a bad man. He'd never steal or kill anyone. You know that, right? Can you tell your boyfriend detective Ralph is innocent?"

"Nate isn't exactly my boyfriend. We haven't had that conversation yet."

"Whatever he is to you, I'm worried he won't look any further than Ralph to solve his case." Because of Summer's faithful visits to her dermatologist, her face belied the grave concern of her voice. There wasn't an ounce of worry on her smooth, unwrinkled face.

"Nate is a good detective, and I can't see him ignoring other leads and suspects. I'd like to know why Uncle Ralph was at Miranda's shop that morning. Why was he trying to get her out of the lease? Why couldn't he wait until the lease was up? It's only a year."

"You know, he rarely talks to me about his dealings. However, I do know that Bitsy London wants to rent the whole building. The company wants to create one large shop from the two smaller ones, and they want the upstairs for offices."

"Bitsy London wants to open a store here?" Bitsy London, or BL as they were more commonly referred to, was a cross between Lilly Pulitzer and Kate Spade with the enterprising spirit of Tory Burch. From a tiny booth at the Queens Mall forty years ago, Bitsy built an empire that included a flagship store on Madison Avenue. "They have a shop in Southampton." Kelly had only window-shopped there because the prices were way out of her budget. Especially for a sundress.

"Not after next summer. Bitsy's daughter is now the CEO, and she is over the Hamptons." Summer rolled her eyes. She clearly couldn't fathom anyone ever being over the social mecca of the resort community for those who wanted to be seen. Even though Summer lived in a beach town on Long Island, she spent at least two weeks in July at a rental house in East Hampton.

"Now I understand the urgency in getting Miranda to move out of the location." Yes, it was all coming together for Kelly. Her uncle couldn't pass up the chance to land a hugely successful deal with a popular brand-name shop.

"I'm also sure you can understand my concern for Ralphie. He had a heart attack a couple months ago, and he hasn't been following the diet or exercise plan that was created for him." Summer uncrossed her legs and slapped her hands on her lap. "He truly is maddening. All I want is for him to be healthy, and all he wants is to work himself into the ground. Now this…this stress from being suspected of murdering someone."

"Miranda wasn't just someone; she was a person from his past that he didn't like back then, and she was now blocking him from what sounds like a big deal happening," Kelly said. "I'm also concerned that Jocelyn might not be the only person who thinks Ralph was involved with Daniel's embezzlement. So I'd like to talk to him."

Summer shook her head. "I don't think it's a good idea. Not in the mood he's in. Right after dinner, he secluded himself in his study…with the door closed." She scooted closer to Kelly and placed her hand on Kelly's knee.

Kelly looked at Summer's hand, slender fingers adorned with diamond rings, and tried to figure out what was happening.

"This isn't easy for me to say." Summer's lips quivered. "I want to thank you for helping my family."

"Thank me? For what?"

"Your sleuthing or whatever you call it. I know Juniper and I can rely on you to find the person who killed Miranda Farrell. You've done it before for other people. When I heard you grilling Jocelyn, I knew you were already at work. I thank you. And so does Juniper. She needs her daddy." Summer got teary eyed and reached for a tissue.

"Wait…what?" Kelly's confusion was warranted. Summer had made it clear in the past that she hadn't appreciated Kelly's sleuthing. It was right up there with owning a secondhand shop. Unseemly for the Blake family. Now she was thanking Kelly.

"What are your next steps?" Summer sniffled and then dabbed her eyes, taking obvious care not to smudge her concealer or foundation. "Who are you going to question next? We don't have much time for this to drag on. The longer it takes to clear Ralph's name, the more damage will be done to his reputation. And you know reputation is everything."

"You want me to investigate Miranda's murder?"

"Well, you're doing it already because you can't help but stick your nose into police matters," Summer said.

Not exactly the right way to ask for a favor.

Kelly was still unsure of what she was hearing. "Wait…what?"

Summer heaved a sigh. "Really, Kelly, sometimes you can be so difficult. I'm not sure what you're not understanding." She stood and propped her hands on her hips. "I want you to find the person who killed Miranda Farrell so my husband will be in the clear. I'd appreciate it if you could do this as quickly as possible. Can you do that?"

Okay, that sounded more like the Summer she knew. Now she was certain she wasn't dreaming.

Kelly nodded. "I can. I can do that."

"Good. Now I have to get to bed because I have an early morning class. And you have to get home and rest up. You have a killer to find." Summer stood and gestured to Kelly as she walked out of the room.

Kelly followed and said good night at the door. She dashed to her car and slid into the driver's seat. She'd just reached the top of the driveway when she got a text from Gabe that had her slamming on the brakes.

Are you crazy accusing my mom of killing Miranda?

Chapter 9

Kelly's whole body tensed as she read the text from Gabe. *This is bad.* Even though Pepper had said she accepted Kelly's apology and they'd made up, it appeared she was still upset. Otherwise, why would she have told Gabe?

She shifted the car into Park and then tapped on her phone, calling Gabe.

"Pick up, come on, pick up."

She waited impatiently for him to answer.

"I didn't accuse your mom of murder. I swear!" Kelly banged her head against the car seat. "I only asked about a quote in an old newspaper article."

"Does Detective Barber know you're interfering in his case?" Gabe asked, sounding more like a police officer than Kelly's lifelong friend.

"I'd be surprised if he didn't. It's not like I'm sneaking around behind his back. Besides, I was only looking for information, and there's no law against that."

"You may be dating him, but he's a police detective, and he won't tolerate your interference. And stop accusing my mother of murder. I could hear in her voice that she was upset."

"She accepted my apology and I thought we were okay. I am sorry. Though, I don't think she's upset with me. I think it's the situation."

"What do you mean?"

"I'm guessing it was a big chunk of money your parents lost because of Daniel, and it hasn't been easy for them to get back on their feet financially. My questions probably brought up a lot of bad memories. I promise I won't mention it again. Do you forgive me?"

There was silence on the other end of the call. It stretched out to eternity before she heard Gabe chuckle.

"Yeah, I do. There's never a dull moment with you, Kell."

Kelly smiled as her body relaxed. "You wouldn't want it any other way. But, hey, when do you go back to work?"

"Tomorrow. I better get going. I need my beauty sleep." He ended the call, and Kelly shifted her car into Drive, continuing out of the driveway.

He wasn't the only one who needed beauty sleep. Exhaustion was sweeping through Kelly, and she couldn't wait to get home and crawl into her bed for a good night's sleep. She said a little prayer that Howard wouldn't wake for his middle-of-the-night crazies episode where he raced through the apartment and eventually ended up back in bed, pouncing on Kelly just to let her know he was back.

A girl could wish.

* * * *

Kelly finally made it back home, and a yawn escaped as she parked her Jeep in her spot, which was only a few steps from the boutique's back door. Once she put out that fire with Gabe, her mind had gone back to churning over Summer's unexpected gratitude and encouragement to continue investigating the murder.

Surely, pigs were flying somewhere, and double denim outfits were making a big comeback. She climbed out of the vehicle and headed to the door. The automatic light above the entry flicked on as she got closer. Her key was out, ready to unlock the door and get out of the nippy night air. Her cardigan wasn't warm enough for the dipping temperature.

She halted when she noticed the door slightly open.

"Did I forget to lock it when I left?" Her mind replayed her departure earlier, combing through each clip as if it were a video. She remembered slipping on her cardigan, grabbing her tote, opening and closing the door, then jiggling it to make sure it was secure.

"I did lock it." She was certain. "I think I locked it?"

Now, standing there in the blackness of the chilly night with a murderer on the loose, she wasn't so sure. Her spidey senses kicked into overdrive. Something wasn't right. She felt it in her bones. She glanced through the glass pane but didn't see anyone. The staff room was dark because she'd flipped off the light when she left. Kelly took a few steps back and looked up to her apartment windows. Also dark. No shadowy figure moving about up there.

She chewed on her lower lip, not sure of what to do.

Go inside and possibly stumble in on a burglary?

Stay outside and do what?

Go back to her uncle's house? Stay there for the night? And spend tomorrow wondering if someone had broken in?

Call the police and settle the matter?

Right, I'm calling the police.

She dialed 9-1-1 and reported a possible break-in. The dispatcher told her to remain outside, and she agreed with that instruction. In fact, she went one step further and locked herself inside her Jeep. From there, she kept a lookout for an intruder to burst out of the boutique and for a police cruiser to arrive.

No escaping intruder, though a police vehicle finally drove into the parking lot. When the car pulled up alongside the Jeep, Kelly felt safe enough to get out.

"Good evening, ma'am. You reported a break-in?" The clean-shaven officer, barely out of high school, took a solid stance and looked expectantly at Kelly. She let the ma'am comment slide. After all, she was under thirty and had every right to be offended.

"A possible break-in. I'm certain I locked the door when I left to visit my uncle and his wife, but now I'm unsure. The door is open. See." She pointed and took a step forward.

The officer held out his hand to keep her back. "You stay here while I go in and check it out. Okay?"

"Sure. No problem. I'll stay right here." Kelly remained planted in place while Officer Barely Out of Puberty turned and walked toward the door with his flashlight drawn and his other hand resting on his holstered weapon. He pushed opened the door and entered, disappearing into the darkness.

She saw a stream of light from his flashlight as the officer methodically searched the space. Then, the beam of light faded, and she wondered what had happened. Had he been overpowered by an intruder? Did she need to call for backup? The seconds she fretted seemed like hours until the interior lights went on and the officer emerged from the building.

"All clear, Miss Quinn. It looks like you did forget to secure the door when you left earlier." The officer jammed his flashlight back onto his utility belt.

Kelly let out a breath of relief, and then she felt her cheeks warm. How embarrassing. She'd made a big fuss over nothing.

"I'm so sorry for wasting your time. I don't know what I was thinking." She'd been thinking for once she'd listen to her internal alarm system and not ignore it until it was too late.

"There's no need to apologize. You did the right thing. It's better to be safe than sorry." He grinned. She guessed he was used to responding to calls that turned out to be nothing.

"I appreciate your help this evening."

"Have a good night." The officer walked back to his vehicle and, within a few moments, drove out of the parking lot.

Kelly slogged to the back door and entered the staff room. "How could I have not locked the door?" she muttered as she closed the door and double-checked that it was locked before going upstairs to her apartment. "Maybe I do need a vacation."

* * * *

The following morning, Kelly pressed the Snooze button three times before finally opening her eyes. Then she dragged herself out of bed, and, with the energy of a sloth, she dressed in her running clothes. At the apartment door, she tucked her key holder and cell phone into her hip pack and tied her laces. She was about as ready as she could be for a shortish run.

The morning air was cool, which was perfect for her run. It snapped her out of her sleepiness and also gave her an excuse to don her favorite puffer vest. It had been pricey, but thanks to her then employee discount at Bishop's department store, she'd been able to afford it. Those were the days. She missed her discount.

Right out of college, she landed a coveted job at the iconic retailer on Manhattan's Fifth Avenue. She worked her way up to assistant buyer and was on the path to becoming the VP of fashion merchandising one day. Or, so she believed. Until a series of disasters put her in the crosshairs of Serena Dawson, aka the Dragonista of Seventh Avenue.

It had been humiliating. She'd barely kept her composure as she carried out a small cardboard box that contained all her personal items from her desk. But she'd had no intention of giving Serena the satisfaction of knowing how sad and hurt Kelly was. Then last spring, Serena blew into Kelly's life asking for a favor.

Kelly shook her head. Now wasn't the time to think about the Dragonista. No, it was better to focus on the positive things from her time at Bishop's. Like the puffer vest that kept her warm during the run.

With the three-mile run done, she stopped into Doug's for a coffee. The run wasn't as shortish as she'd planned when she left her apartment. Once she got into the zone, she just kept going. Stepping out of the store with her coffee in hand, she took a few steps before stopping and taking a sip.

Delicious. It hit the spot. Instead of a flavored coffee, she ordered a plain one since the primary goal was to get a caffeine infusion.

Last night she barely slept a wink because she tossed and turned over the unlocked back door. The more she thought about it and replayed her movements before leaving the boutique, she was certain she'd locked the door.

So she had no explanation of why the door had been open when she returned.

She swallowed another drink and almost choked on it when she saw Ariel heading in her direction. She pulled the cup from her lips and coughed.

She'd been waiting weeks to "bump" into Ariel while out and about.

Her stomach fluttered with worry, apprehension, and happiness. She'd missed her friend so much. To help stack the deck in her favor that she'd get to talk to Ariel, she began walking to meet her friend halfway.

Ariel, whose bad bangs experiment had grown out to soft layers framing her face, kept a neutral expression as they got closer. Kelly took that as a good sign.

"Good morning," Kelly said in her most hopeful voice. "It's good to see you."

Ariel halted her wheelchair. Her neutral expression gave way to annoyance with the narrowing of her brows and the subtle twist of her lips.

Kelly struggled for grace. She often thought of what it would feel like if she were in Ariel's position, so she understood Ariel's anger. What she couldn't understand was why her friend was so angry with her. Or why Ariel couldn't muster up a simple "good morning."

"You can't avoid me forever. Lucky Cove isn't Manhattan," Kelly said.

Ariel glowered and then spun her wheelchair around and hurried off.

Kelly let out an exasperated sigh as she stomped her foot. Ariel could be so infuriating.

"Hey, Kelly, is everything okay?" Courtney came up beside Kelly. She wore a dark gray parka, and a red knit hat was pulled down over her hair.

"Huh?" Kelly figured Courtney had seen Ariel whip her wheelchair around and speed off. Of course she'd be curious since Ariel didn't usually do that. So much for keeping their estrangement private. "Yeah, everything is okay," Kelly lied before she sipped her coffee. "How are you doing? How's the clean-out of your mom's house coming along?"

"Slowly. There's so much stuff, but the good news is that Walt is taking a lot of the furniture. I had no idea my mom had such a keen eye for antiques." Courtney sounded pleased by the turn of events. The more furnishings Walter took, the less she had to worry about moving out of the house. "What has me feeling uneasy is Miranda's murder. I can't believe she was killed right there in her own shop. It's scary that could happen. Happen to any one of us."

Kelly couldn't disagree. Like everyone else in town, she liked to believe they were immune from such violence. Still, the reality was that nowhere was truly safe.

"I have to ask you about the other morning at your house. You got weird when I mentioned inviting Miranda to the luncheon. What was that all about?" Kelly asked.

"Come on, let's walk. I have to put out inventory before the shop opens. I got a new shipment of candles yesterday. You're going to love them." Courtney started walking. "My parents had trusted Daniel with their savings. They ended up losing a lot of money. They had to sell their home, and their retirements were pushed back for years. My dad died before he could enjoy his golden years. All because of Daniel's greed."

"Did your parents think that Miranda was involved with the embezzling?"

"Of course they did. She was his wife, and she was a great deal younger than Daniel. Miranda was only after one thing—money."

"She wasn't charged with any crime."

Courtney stopped walking. "I don't think the police looked very hard. Daniel was dead, and the money seemed to have vanished. I think she knew about his crimes, and I think she used Nolen to help hide the money and then killed him when she no longer needed him."

"In that scenario, she sounds like a cold, calculating murderer."

Courtney shrugged. "If the shoe fits. Look, I'm sorry she's dead, but I'm not going to grieve for that woman. And neither should you." She broke away and continued toward her shop.

Kelly stood, frozen in place. She'd never heard Courtney sound so cold and bitter. *Cold and bitter enough to kill?* She shook off the thought as quickly as it came. Courtney wasn't a murderer. Then again, Kelly had the same opinion about other people who turned out to be killers.

As much as she didn't want to think about it, a brief whisper of doubt about Courtney niggled in her brain. If she was going to find Miranda's killer, she needed to keep an open mind about everyone. She felt a clutch in her chest. *Including friends.* Her lips formed a frown, but luckily that didn't last too long. As she approached her boutique, Nate came into view.

He stood solid and extraordinarily handsome by the curb, talking on his cell phone. He wore a leather jacket over his dark pants and white shirt that morning. In midsentence, he noticed Kelly and seemed to wrap up the call quickly. By the time she reached him, he had said goodbye and clicked off his phone.

"Hey there. This is a surprise." She got close and kissed him. Her nose wriggled at the spiced scent of his aftershave.

"Good morning." He pulled her closer to him. "I thought I'd stop by and see how you're doing. I heard about the break-in last night. Why didn't you call me?"

"It was late, and it wasn't a break-in. I guess I forgot to lock the back door when I left to visit my uncle. It was truly embarrassing."

"You shouldn't feel embarrassed. That's why we have a police department, to ensure our citizens are safe. I'm glad you called before going inside."

"You know, I was just talking to Courtney, and she's also on edge about Miranda being killed in her shop. So maybe that's why I overreacted and called for help last night. I don't know."

"You're safe. And there was no harm in making the call." He let her go. "How about dinner?"

"Yes!" She made a face when she realized how quickly she answered the question and then laughed. "Sorry. I've missed you. But I know you've been working hard on Miranda's case."

A tiny smile twitched on his lips. "Speaking of which…dinner comes with a condition."

She had an inkling of what he would say. "Really? What's the condition?"

"No talk about Miranda or her murder. It's my job, and I don't want to discuss work over dinner. Deal?"

"You mean you don't want to talk about my uncle being a suspect over dinner."

"That is a part of my job, so yes, I don't want to talk about your uncle."

Kelly didn't like conditions on what she could or couldn't say. It felt like Mark Lambert all over again. But she quickly reminded herself that Nate wasn't Mark. And his request wasn't entirely unreasonable.

"Fine. I agree. No talk of your case while we're at dinner."

"That was easy," he said suspiciously.

"I'm full of surprises. Haven't you learned that yet?" She couldn't help but flutter her lashes. "Come on, walk me around back."

"What other surprises do you have for me?" he whispered in her ear as he wrapped an arm around her waist. Together they walked along the side of the building.

"Since you asked, I do have something to tell you. Not really a surprise, but I think you'd be interested. When I was talking to Courtney, I found out her parents lost money because they'd invested with Daniel Parnell."

"Kelly." He loosened his hold on her.

"She said that her parents believed Miranda was involved. The money hadn't been recovered because Miranda hid it with the help of her second husband, Nolen. And Courtney said she wasn't about to grieve for Miranda. She sounded so angry and cold.... I don't want to think she could be capable of murder. But if she confronted Miranda about what happened twenty years ago...who knows what could have happened?"

Nate stopped. "What did we just agree to?"

"We wouldn't talk shop over dinner. But this isn't dinner."

"You know I don't like you snooping around an active investigation."

"All I asked is why she got weird the other morning when I said I wanted to invite Miranda to the chamber luncheon. She just kept talking about her parents, and I listened, and now I'm passing the information onto you. You're welcome."

"For what?"

"For giving you a lead. A possible suspect. A possible motive. I'm happy to help."

"Your helping can get you into trouble."

"I know. Text me later with the time and place. I have to take a shower and change for work." She kissed him on the cheek and hurried inside. After closing the door, she glanced out the window and watched Nate walk back to Main Street. She might have agreed not to discuss the murder case over dinner, but she didn't agree not to investigate.

Chapter 10

Once the closed sign was flipped over and the front door unlocked, customers streamed in at a steady pace for buying and consigning. Kelly had been going nonstop since she got back from her run. After a quick shower, she dressed in one of her most effortless looks—a thermal waffled knit dress and booties—and then dashed downstairs to open for the day. She buzzed through the first half of the day, ticking off things on her to-do list. But boy, it felt like she'd run a marathon, and it wasn't even eleven o'clock yet. She and Pepper were pleased with the brisk business and hoped it was an early indicator of Black Friday. While it was weeks away, she knew how fast the holidays would arrive. In a blink of an eye, her granny used to say.

She took a sip of her water and glanced at the rack of newly consigned garments. Beneath the clothes were stacks of shoeboxes. She'd have to find time later in the day to get them all into inventory and out on the sales floor. Which meant she also needed to look at the merchandise that hadn't sold and mark it down.

"Something must be in the air today." Pepper bagged Mrs. Tillman's purchase—three blouses, two scarves, and a pair of brand-new loafers.

Kelly nodded in agreement. She set her water bottle down and stepped forward to take the next customer, who dropped a pile of sweaters on the counter and then browsed the bracelet display.

While Kelly and Pepper were ringing up sales, Breena was busy at the changing rooms. She was helping two customers find sizes. Being a consignment shop meant they didn't have an assortment of sizes in all clothing styles. Breena worked hard to find something similar to what the customers were trying on in a different size.

The bell over the door jingled; when Kelly looked up to see who had just entered, her breath caught, and a tremor of trepidation shot through her body.

Aurora Cavendish.

The seventy-year-old was a prickly woman with a drama queen reputation. As she entered, a few heads turned followed by some whispers, which Aurora seemed unaware of. She'd only once before been in the boutique, and that was when Kelly had first inherited the business. Kelly considered herself lucky not to have the woman as a regular customer because there were some horror stories about her up and down Main Street.

"Oh, boy," Kelly muttered. When Pepper looked at her, Kelly nodded toward the door. "What's she doing here?" Suddenly she had an urge to drop down and hide behind the counter.

Pepper took in a deep breath and then shrugged. "Maybe she's only going to browse," she said before handing the shopping tote to Mrs. Tillman. "Thank you for shopping with us. Have a great day."

"Good luck with her," Mrs. Tillman whispered and then exited the boutique.

Kelly discreetly watched Aurora, who was dressed in a simple sheath dress with a cardigan over her shoulders, stop between garment racks. She perused the clothing, but nothing seemed to catch her attention. Then, passing by the sales counter, she looked at them, her mouth set in an ever-present downward slant.

Aurora disappeared into the back room that once housed home accents and furnishings. Kelly's granny had added the square room to the house in hopes of bringing in more income. According to Pepper, it had for a while, but sales slowly declined. When Kelly inherited the boutique, the square footage wasn't pulling its weight in the sales department. So she completely redesigned the space, selling what she could and donating what was left. Days of painting and DIY projects resulted in an area that sold accessories—hats, shoes, purses, and more. Now the accessories department was contributing positively to the boutique's bottom line.

"Why do I have a bad feeling?" Kelly asked.

"Because where there's Aurora Cavendish, there's a scene."

"What's her deal?"

"Spinster. Know-it-all. Demanding. High maintenance."

"Is that all?" Kelly laughed, and Pepper joined in. The moment of levity felt good, but unfortunately, it didn't last very long. A piercing scream from the accessories department cut through the air.

"What the..." Kelly's eyes bugged out at the bloodcurdling scream, and she darted out from behind the counter. Pepper was by her side, and they raced through the boutique. By the time they reached the accessories department, Breena was behind them. They paused in the doorway and exchanged confused looks.

Aurora was standing in the middle of the room as the other customers exchanged bewildered glances.

"Who screamed? What's going on?" Breena asked.

Pepper shrugged. "No idea."

"Is everything okay, Aurora?" Kelly asked hesitantly.

Aurora's body jerked when she sneezed. And then she sneezed again. Kelly noticed the woman's red eyes and that she was about to scream again, but another sneeze cut off the shriek.

"God bless you," Breena said.

Kelly's gaze drifted downward, and that was when she noticed Howard slinking around the woman's legs.

"No, no, no!" Kelly lunged forward and scooped her cat up. He let out an annoyed meow while Aurora pierced Kelly with a scowl she felt to her core. "I'm so sorry. He shouldn't be here."

"I should think not!" Aurora sneezed again and then reached into her purse for a tissue.

"Are you allergic to cats?" another customer asked.

"Highly. What on earth is that *thing* doing here?" Aurora asked before blowing her nose.

"Yes, Kelly, why is Howard downstairs?" Pepper leaned over Kelly's shoulder. "How did he get out of your apartment?"

"I...I..." Kelly stammered as she replayed her movements after coming back from her run. "I don't know. I closed the door behind me when I came downstairs." Kelly looked at her cat. Of all the times to become an escape artist. And he had to zero in on the one person who was highly allergic and a drama queen to boot. "I'm so sorry, Aurora."

Aurora sneezed again. Her eyes were redder, and she started coughing. "I should think you would be. Get that thing away from me." She pointed to Howard and dismissed him with a wave.

Kelly opened her mouth to protest her beloved cat being called a thing, but Breena intervened and took him from Kelly's arms.

"I'll take him to the staff room for now." Breena carried Howard out of the accessories department.

"Is there anything we can get you, Aurora? Maybe an antihistamine?" Pepper asked. "We have some in the staff room."

Aurora shook her head sharply. "No. Absolutely not. I'm going to have to go to my doctor immediately. Let me assure you that you can expect my medical bill. Letting an animal loose in a place of business is unprofessional. You can be certain I won't be shopping in this store ever again."

"He never comes downstairs. I assure you this was an accident," Pepper said. Kelly knew she was using her most apologetic voice to try to appease Aurora. Unfortunately, though, the customer looked unimpressed by the assurance.

Aurora sneezed again, and she muttered something under her breath Kelly couldn't make out. She blew her nose again and then stormed out of the accessories department.

A moment later, the boutique's front door slammed shut, and Kelly jumped at the sound. Talk about a dramatic exit. The only good thing to come out of the situation had been Aurora's promise not to come back to the boutique. She looked around at the other customers, still gawking at her and Pepper. Gosh, she wished the floor would open up and swallow her whole.

No such luck.

"I apologize for the commotion." Kelly's cheeks burned with embarrassment. How had Howard gotten out of the apartment? "Please continue with your shopping."

Another customer sneezed. "I'm sorry, I'm allergic to cats too." She darted out of the boutique.

"I have asthma, and being around cats isn't good for me," another customer said before she hurried out the door.

Kelly turned and faced Pepper, who hadn't looked one bit thrilled. "Please, no lectures."

"Who, me? Why on earth would I lecture you?" Pepper followed Kelly out of the room and to the staircase. Its door was partly opened, leaving just enough space for Howard to get out.

"I know I closed this door. I do every day when I come downstairs." She ran her fingers through her hair. "You're looking at me like I'm…I don't know…crazy."

"Kelly, you have been forgetting things. For example, last night, you forgot to lock the back door when you went out."

"How do you know about that?"

"My son is a police officer. He knows things. I'd like to know why you didn't tell me."

Kelly pulled open the door and climbed the staircase with Pepper following. "It didn't seem important." Her pace up the stairs was faster than Pepper's, and she reached the small landing. At the sight of her apartment door open, she sighed. "I swear, I closed this door when I came downstairs to work."

"What about the missing computer mouse?"

So Breena ratted on her too. "I simply misplaced it."

Pepper finally reached the landing. She looked at the door and then at Kelly. She didn't have to say a word. Worry was written all over her face. She took Kelly's hand in hers. "I'm concerned about you. Maybe you should go back to the therapist."

"What? No. I'm not crazy."

"No one is saying that. You didn't start seeing the therapist because you were crazy. You went to her because you were dealing with Becky's death. Now you're burying yourself in work, and you're poking into Miranda's murder investigation."

"My family needs my help," Kelly said.

"And it's admirable you want to help them, but you need to take care of yourself. You're avoiding dealing with Becky's death. And it's starting to manifest in unhealthy ways. Just promise me you'll think about going back to therapy."

"I'll think about it. I promise."

"Good." Pepper touched Kelly's cheek and smiled. "In the meantime, you probably should consider taking a couple days off. Some R&R. Don't say anything. Just think about that too. I'll go get Howard and bring him up. Just make sure this time you keep him in the apartment." She turned and descended the stairs.

Kelly stepped into her apartment and continued into the living room. She stared out the window, which looked out onto Main Street. Had she forgotten to close both doors? She blew out a breath. It seemed she had. Okay. Maybe she was working too hard. Perhaps a day off and more sleep would help.

* * * *

There was a lull midday in the boutique, which allowed Kelly to step out and pay a visit to her uncle. She had Pepper call her sister-in-law, Camille Donovan, who worked as Ralph's secretary, to confirm that he was indeed in his office. Camille had promised to keep him there until Kelly arrived.

When Kelly reached his office, she hesitated before entering. The last time she visited him there, he had a heart attack after their intense conversation about his relationship with Ariel. She made a promise to herself that she wouldn't upset him today. Yes, she'd tread lightly, walk on eggshells, whatever it took not to stress him. And that way, Frankie wouldn't have another thing to hang over her head.

Entering the office, Kelly admitted that keeping the promise would be more than a little challenging.

"Good afternoon, Kelly." Camille looked up from her desk. During the summer, she'd asked Kelly to consign her enormous wardrobe. Having lost over seventy pounds, she'd gone down several sizes and had been addicted to subscription-style boxes. Now, with the help of Kelly, Camille had ended all those subscriptions and had a new minimal wardrobe that she looked and felt amazing in.

"Hi, Camille. Thanks for your help." Kelly noticed the heather-gray surplice wrap dress Camille wore. It complemented her silver hair and the sterling silver jewelry she wore.

"Go right on in." Camille hitched her thumb in the direction of Ralph's office. "I'll hold his calls." She winked.

Kelly pushed off, and as she walked along the carpeted hall, she repeated, *I won't upset him, I won't upset him.*

She arrived at his office and rapped her knuckles on the open door.

He looked up from the spreadsheets on his desk and scowled.

I won't upset him. I won't upset him.

Not waiting for an invitation, she entered the impressive office and closed the door behind her. "We need to talk about Miranda."

"Not much to talk about." He removed his reading glasses, set them on the desk, and then leaned back in his supple leather chair. He'd spared no expense in furnishing his office, from the dark wood desk expertly crafted to the plush seating area for informal discussions to the unique artwork hung on the walls. This space showed just how far Ralph Blake had come since getting his real estate license after graduating from college.

"I don't agree." Kelly sat on one of the chairs in front of the desk. "You were found standing over her body. The two of you had been at odds over her lease. And there's some history between the two of you."

He scoffed.

She sighed. "I only want to help."

"Like you did with Ariel?"

I won't upset him. I won't upset him.

"Because I kept your secret, which I had no desire to know in the first place, I've probably lost a friend for good."

Ralph rubbed the bridge of his nose. "I'm sorry she's taking it out on you. I'm the one she should be angry with, not you."

Kelly glanced upward to see if pigs were flying because she could have sworn her uncle just apologized. What was going on with him and Summer? Were the dynamics of her relationship with them shifting?

"Thank you for saying that. I probably shouldn't be so doom and gloom about it. I guess there's always hope, right? Anyway, let's get back to Miranda. What was going on between the two of you? It had to be more than just the lease."

Ralph stood and walked to the bookshelf opposite his desk. A handful of books were displayed, but mostly the shelves were filled with memorabilia and photographs. He took a framed photo off a shelf and showed it to Kelly. It was a photo of three men on the beach.

"That's us. Best friends for years." He tapped the photo. "Ricky van Johnson and Daniel Parnell."

Kelly took the photo. She saw the resemblance between her uncle and Frankie. They shared the same smile. Though she rarely saw her uncle ever smile. But in that photo, he was beaming. So were Daniel and Ricky.

"When was this taken? The three of you looked happy."

"We were. It was the end of the summer, about thirty years ago, and it had been a hell of a year for all of us. I'd just landed a deal to convert an old mill into a condo development. Ricky just bought Gregorio's, and Daniel had started his own financial firm. At that moment, we were on top of the world. There wasn't anything we couldn't do."

Reminiscing, Ralph sounded wistful. And for the moment, Kelly felt close to her uncle. And it was nice.

She handed the photo back to her uncle and leaned into the chair. "Daniel was married to his first wife at that time, right?"

"Ivy." Ralph returned the photo to its spot on the shelf. "The woman was a saint, so when we got the news she had cancer, we were all devastated. Daniel took it hard."

"How long after Ivy's death did he remarry?"

"One year. He met Miranda when she was working at the inn. He fell hard for her. And she didn't waste any time."

"Erica told me she believed Miranda was only interested in Daniel's money."

"She was Ivy's best friend. And I agreed with her. But there was no talking to Daniel. He was head over heels in love and happy. Then we learned about his embezzling scheme."

"Did you lose any money?"

"Some. But I was in a position where I was able to weather it. But most of his clients couldn't. So, to be honest, I started to think Daniel got what he deserved when he married the gold digger turned black widow."

Kelly's core chilled at the deadly label. "You think she murdered him?"

"I think his heart attack was convenient, given the timing. But, you know, some drugs and poisons can mimic a heart attack."

Kelly wasn't sure which substances could do that, but she knew what her uncle said was true based on what she'd read online. Could Miranda have murdered Daniel, disguising it as a heart attack, and then kept all the money for herself? Would Daniel have confided in his new bride about his stealing?

"Was he embezzling from his clients before he met Miranda?" she asked.

"Yes. If I recall correctly, for several years. Why?"

She shook her head. "Just curious." Could Miranda have already known he'd been stealing from clients before she married him? Now, with her dead, she'd never know the answer.

"Then Miranda wasted no time in remarrying. A boat captain, no less. Guess it made it very convenient to access the money that Daniel probably stashed offshore."

"Erica said the same thing," Kelly said.

Ralph returned to his chair. "She has good instincts. Always has."

"Why do you think Miranda came back after all this time? To a place where she knew she wouldn't be welcomed?"

"I have no idea. Miranda had a pretty good life in New Jersey, from what I could piece together. She had several businesses. My guess is they were funded by the money Daniel had stolen."

"Wouldn't she have lived a more luxurious life if she had all that money? I know I would have." Kelly shifted in her seat. "Do you remember if the police investigated the deaths of Daniel and Nolen?"

"Sure they did. Paul Sloan was the detective for both cases and ruled out any foul play."

There was a knock on the door, and then it opened slowly. Camille popped her head in and flashed an apologetic smile. "Ralph, you have to get going to make your meeting with Bradford."

Ralph glanced at his Rolex and nodded. "Thank you."

Camille drew back and closed the door.

"I should get going." Kelly had gotten more information out of her uncle than she'd expected. "One more thing, and I don't want it to upset you, but you probably should know what was said. Jocelyn Bancroft, she's a true crime writer, insinuated that you were involved in the embezzling, and that's why you killed Miranda."

Ralph's cheeks puffed out as his eyes widened in anger. "I know who she is." He slammed his fist on his desk. "That woman stirs up nothing but trouble. Is that the reason why she wanted to talk to Summer about Diana Delacourte's murder?"

Kelly nodded. "And Summer defended you. I don't think she'll be talking to Jocelyn again."

Ralph seemed to soften. His rage passed swiftly. Maybe he was heeding the advice from his wife and doctors.

"I have one more question," Kelly said as she stood. "Did Miranda have any close friends when she lived here? Maybe a girlfriend?"

"Yeah, yeah..." He snapped his fingers as he tried to recall a name. One of the most significant assets in his business was his ability never to forget a name. "Eve...Eve Marlow. Don't know if she still lives in Lucky Cove."

"I'm sorry, but I have to ask." She realized she might be pushing it, but she was dying to know. "Why did you go to Miranda's shop that morning?"

"To find out why she refused my plumber entry to the basement. He went there the day before, and she sent him away. She may have been leasing the store, but she couldn't prevent me from maintaining my building." Ralph stood. "Now, can I go?"

"You think she blocked him from going to the basement just to be difficult?"

"Why else would she? Look, I have to go, which means you have to go."

Her uncle had never been subtle. Kelly nodded as she spun around and headed for the door. As she made her way out of his office, she wondered if Miranda's reason for turning away the plumber had been so simple. Or was there a reason why she didn't want anyone in the basement?

Chapter 11

Leaving Ralph's office, she waved goodbye to Camille and stepped out onto Main Street, which was quiet. Only weeks earlier, before summer had faded and the temperatures dipped, tourists had filled the hub of Lucky Cove. They browsed, shopped, and dined. Once the season changed, the number of tourists dipped significantly. That was why she and her fellow Main Street business owners needed to come up with ideas to draw tourists back to Lucky Cove for the holiday season. She knew she told Pepper she'd take a day or two off, but there was too much work to do. She had to come up with a hook for the Shop Small event. Something big. Something that shoppers couldn't resist. Her cell phone rang, interrupting her thoughts, but the caller ID had her smiling.

Marvin Childers.

"Good afternoon, Marvin." She'd known the illustrator for almost a year. He'd been a close friend of her granny's. So close, they eloped while in Las Vegas years ago on a trip with the senior center. When Kelly first found out about the Vegas ceremony, she was worried that he'd take away her inheritance. But when she discovered the marriage hadn't been valid, she was disappointed. Marvin turned out to be a kind, sweet man who wouldn't have taken away the boutique or Howard. In fact, he would have been a wonderful step-grandpa.

"How's my favorite girl doing?"

Kelly got all warm and fuzzy inside. She loved being Marvin's favorite girl.

"Okay. We had a bit of drama at the boutique today." Crossing the street, she filled him in on what happened to Aurora Cavendish.

"Oh, dear. It sounds like you've had an eventful morning. How about dinner tonight? My treat."

Kelly balled her hand into a fist and punched it into the air. Shoot.

"I'd love to, but I'm having dinner with Nate. I'm sorry." She hated disappointing Marvin. He was finally back living full-time in Lucky Cove after a summer out on Montauk to work on new paintings. He'd hoped to become inspired, and from what he'd told her about the work he accomplished, there seemed to have been inspiration overload.

"Don't be, dear. I'm happy to hear that you're having dinner with your beau."

Beau. Kelly giggled.

"How about breakfast tomorrow? It'll be my treat," she offered.

"Breakfast sounds good. But I'm not going to let you pay. Meet me at the Lucky Cove Inn tomorrow before the boutique opens. Okay?"

"Great. See you then." Kelly ended the call and continued walking toward the boutique. She'd glanced at the time and realized she needed to get back. Even though it was slow when she left, she hadn't liked leaving Pepper and Breena. She was the boss, after all.

"Hey, Kelly!" Walt Hanover called out from across the street. "Wait up!" He jogged across the two-lane road when there was a break in traffic.

"Hi, Walt. What's up?"

"Are you finished at Courtney's mom's house?" he asked.

Kelly groaned. "No. Darn it. Things have been so crazy that I haven't gotten a chance to get back over there." And after their last conversation, she wasn't sure if Courtney still wanted her to continue with the job. Maybe she'd just carry on like nothing had happened. But at some point, they'd have to hash out what they said to each other.

"Well, if you can get over to the house today, one of us will be there. Bud was supposed to be there by now, but he called to let me know he'd be late. Miranda's death has hit him hard," Walt said.

"Understandable. Do you know when they met?"

"Not sure. I think it was last year when Bud left town for a few months to help his parents sell their tree farm in New Jersey. He came back in a better mood than he'd been in. And then Miranda showed up."

"Walt, do you know Eve Marlow?"

"Wow. That's a name I haven't heard in years. She used to manage the waitstaff at the Lucky Cove Inn. She left town about five years ago after she retired."

"Do you know where she went?"

“Florida? Not sure. But probably someone at the inn would know. Look, I have to get back to the shop. Hopefully, we’ll see you at the house later.” He took off, walking in the direction of his antiques shop.

“Sure,” Kelly mumbled. She wondered how hard it would be to track down Eve Marlow. Maybe Renata would have some information about the woman. All in due time. Now she had to get back to the boutique and put in an honest day’s work.

* * * *

After Kelly returned to the boutique and rang up three sales, Pepper slipped into the staff room for a cup of tea while Breena steamed a rack of clothing that had been recently consigned. Kelly remained at the sales counter on her phone, reading through emails from the other shop owners about Shop Small Saturday. The bell over the door jingled, and she looked up.

Paul Sloan entered carrying a shopping bag. In his midsixties, he was tanned and fit. His salt-and-pepper hair was buzzed, and his steel gray eyes looked like they could decipher a lie from a truth in a nanosecond.

“Hi, Paul.” She tapped off her email inbox and set her phone aside. She was happy she didn’t need to track him down to ask about Daniel’s and Nolen’s deaths.

“Good afternoon, Kelly.” He lifted the shopping bag onto the counter. “I’ve brought more clothes to consign. I hadn’t realized how cathartic going through Dorie’s things would be.”

It wasn’t the first time Kelly had heard the sentiment. She knew the first few times surviving family members attempted to sort through their loved ones’ clothing was fraught with overwhelming emotion. But once they were able to go through the process once, even if they only cleared out one or two items, the subsequent attempts were easier and helped with their grieving.

“I’m sorry for your loss. And I’m happy to help you with this.” Kelly reached into the bag and pulled out a bundle of clothing. “I saw the other things you brought in. Your wife had great taste.”

“Thank you. Dorie always looked beautiful. She always liked what I picked out.” He took the empty shopping bag and folded it. “I hope you will too.”

Kelly sorted through the garments, which were all three-quarter zip fleece tops. It appeared that Dorie liked to be cozy and warm. She inspected each top and then folded them, creating a pile off to the side.

“You know, your name came up just a little while ago while I was talking to my uncle.”

"It did? How did that happen?" he asked with a chuckle.

"We were talking about Miranda's murder. My uncle had been good friends with her first husband, Daniel. It's so hard to believe he could have stolen from his friends. And then he died before justice could be served."

"You know, there are some cases that keep cops up late at night. I have a few." He waited for a beat before continuing. "Daniel's case isn't one of them. He had a heart attack, and it killed him. And I share your sentiment about justice not being served."

"Her second husband, Nolen Briggs, then died in a boating accident?"

"It wasn't exactly a boating accident."

"No?"

"He was on his boat at the time of his death. However, the investigation determined he slipped and fell, hitting his head."

"Wasn't it suspicious that she had two husbands die within, what, a year?"

"In real life, not every death is a murder. What I concluded was that Miranda had been unlucky in love."

"That seems to be an understatement," Kelly said as she reached for the folder of blank contracts from beneath the counter. She pulled one out and set the folder aside. After filling out the form, she slid it to Paul for his signature.

"Looks like we're all set now," he said as he set down the pen.

"We've already sold several of the clothes you brought in earlier. I'll have a payment ready for you next week."

"It's a pleasure doing business with you." Paul stepped back from the counter and slid his hands into his jacket pockets. "There's not much more to tell about the deaths of those two men, but if you have any more questions, don't hesitate to call me."

"Thank you. I'll keep your generous offer in mind."

Paul nodded and then turned and walked out of the shop.

Even though Paul had been a skilled investigator, she wasn't comfortable with his findings of Miranda having been unlucky in love. No, she didn't believe it had been that simple.

* * * *

Kelly clicked on the report for her weekly newsletter. After processing Paul's consignments, she ducked into the staff room to get some administrative work done. Top on that list was her newsletter. She reviewed the first segment that had been sent the email. They were the subscribers who always opened and clicked on the newsletter's content. She scanned the percentages of clicks, unsubscribes, and bounces. Then, she transferred the data to her spreadsheet. The sheet was her bible. The data recorded there allowed her to improve her newsletter each week. She believed an engaged customer was a customer who spent money in the boutique.

Her ringing cell phone dragged her from her beloved spreadsheet. She glanced at the screen—Frankie. She hesitated a moment before tapping on the screen to accept the call.

"Hey, what's up?" What was she saying? *What's up?* It should have been more like, what the heck was his problem? Not returning her texts or calls? But she opted to remain calm. Since he must have been calling to apologize for his behavior, she didn't want to throw up any obstacles.

"How's it going? What have you found out?" he asked.

Not exactly what she expected to hear. She replayed his words in her mind, and she was pretty confident it wasn't an apology.

"I don't work for you." Kelly drew in a breath and reminded herself that her cousin, even if he wouldn't admit it, was scared and felt helpless. Acknowledging those feelings helped her return to a place of calm and allowed her to speak to him in a quiet, steady voice.

She briefed him on Miranda's relationship with Bud, that Courtney's parents lost money through Daniel, Erica believed Miranda was a gold digger, and Jocelyn was throwing some shade Ralph's way.

"That's all?"

Kelly rolled her eyes. Sometimes her cousin could be so clueless. While he knew how to make delicious creamy crab bisque, he hadn't an inkling of how to investigate a murder.

"Did you expect the killer to walk into the boutique and confess?" Now that would save her a lot of time and effort.

"I don't know. Honestly, I have no idea of what to do or how to help my dad."

"We need to focus on the bright side."

"What would that be?"

"Your father hasn't been arrested." Every day that didn't happen meant the police didn't have evidence. And they wouldn't because her uncle wasn't a murderer. "Have you talked to Ariel?"

"Ah…hmmm…kind of." Frankie went silent for a moment. "All right, we had dinner last night."

Kelly stared at her spreadsheet. It felt like a knife had been stuck in her heart. And it saddened her because she should be happy for Frankie and Ariel. They were siblings and should be getting together and bonding. She just wished she could have a meal with her friend again. She sighed. And then she decided to look on the bright side. If Ariel talked to Frankie, maybe she'd start talking to Kelly again. At least she hoped so.

"I'm happy to hear that. You both should be getting together and start forming that brother-sister bond." Kelly tapped the speakerphone button on her phone and then set it down so she could save her spreadsheet file. She resisted the urge to ask if Ariel mentioned her over dinner. It wouldn't be fair to put her cousin in the middle of her fractured relationship with his sister.

"Thanks, Kell. Look, I'm sorry about almost spilling the beans in front of Pepper about Ariel. I understand her need for privacy in the matter. So much of her life has been public since the accident, and not wanting people to know that she's Ralph Blake's biological daughter is understandable. We both know how the gossip mill works in town."

"Good to hear. I need to get back to work. Don't worry, I'll keep you updated." She ended the call. With her newsletter stats done, she turned her attention to her presentation for the chamber of commerce. Tomorrow she was scheduled to present it, and she wanted it to be perfect.

'Tis the Season to Shop Small in Lucky Cove.

That's the slogan she came up with. She thought it sounded catchy and could be used again next year.

She tapped on her computer's keyboard, and when the file opened, she went through each slide. A few ideas seemed a bit extravagant, but Lucky Cove needed something bold and unique to stand out.

The slides presented ideas for events during the long weekend, social media posts, and signage.

"If I say so myself, this presentation is looking pretty good." She leaned back and smiled. "We're going to have a great holiday season."

Her phone rang again, and the caller ID alerted her that Walt Hanover was on the other end. She tapped on the screen.

"Hi, Walt. Are you at the Travis house?" she asked, shifting in her seat.

"No. I'm stuck at the shop with a customer, but Bud is at the house, and he'll let you in."

"He's there by himself?" Without Walt at the house, she'd be able to talk to Bud about Miranda. "Okay. I'll head out now. Thanks for letting me know." She ended the call and then closed her presentation file. Popping up from her chair, Kelly moved quickly. She told Pepper where she was going and that she'd be back as soon as possible.

* * * *

Kelly arrived at the Travis house and parked behind Walt's box truck. Not needing her purse, she plucked her cell phone out and opened the Jeep's door. She expected she'd only be making one trip out of the house with clothing. Maybe two, depending on how bulky the coats were. When she reached the front door, she found it open. Bud must have been moving a lot of stuff out.

She stepped into the foyer and looked in the living room. It looked sparse compared to the other day she was there. She wondered how much Walt took and how much Courtney donated.

"Bud! It's Kelly." She looked in the dining room, which was opposite the living room. The dark walnut table remained, but the glass-front cabinet had been emptied of its collection of plates and glasses. "Bud!"

On the drive over, she thought about how she'd approach him with her questions. She'd have to be delicate and tactful. After all, his girlfriend was murdered. But she had so many questions. Probably the best way to approach him was to prioritize her questions. Like, how had they met in New Jersey? It seemed like a coincidence that two people from Lucky Cove would meet and fall in love there.

New Jersey.

She remembered something her uncle had said earlier. He mentioned that Miranda had started a few businesses in the Garden State. How had he known that? He knew because he kept tabs on everything and everyone. He'd admitted he'd lost money because of Daniel, and if he thought Miranda had access to the stolen funds, he'd keep an eye on her or hire someone to do it for him. That wouldn't look good for him if the police found out.

She pulled back from the dining room and looked around. Where was Bud? Maybe in the kitchen?

She walked through the dining room to get to the kitchen. She pushed the swinging door, and before she could call out Bud's name, her body jerked to a stop, and a scream made its way out of her throat.

Bud lay facedown on the tile floor. The back of his head was cracked and bloody.

"Bud!" When the shock wore off, Kelly rushed to his body and checked for a pulse. There was none. "No, no, no. Bud." She rocked back as the gruesome discovery settled over her. Then she realized she had to call for help. She pulled out her phone and dialed 9-1-1. She relayed all the pertinent information to the emergency dispatcher and then retraced her steps through the house and exited, careful not to touch anything.

The Travis house was now a crime scene.

Chapter 12

Outside, she waited for what seemed an eternity for the first police officer to arrive. A nip in the air settled around her, and she tugged her cardigan closer to her body. Though, the coldness that had seeped inside her wouldn't be warmed away by a layer of clothing. When she heard a car's engine, she pushed off the side of the Jeep and turned around in time to see a police vehicle pull into the driveway. She caught a glimpse of the driver and gulped. Gabe was back at work. So, of course, he'd be the responding officer to her call for help. He parked behind her vehicle and got out. His eyes narrowed on her as he propped his hands on his utility belt and shook his head.

"I know what you're thinking," Kelly said.

"Do you?" Gabe's stride forward was purposeful, and he passed right by her, headed to the front door. "Stay here."

"He's in the kitchen!" she called out as Gabe disappeared inside the house. She crossed her arms and then leaned back against her vehicle. She tapped her foot on the spot where she suddenly seemed rooted.

Various scenarios raced through her mind. With each one, the gruesome discovery she made minutes ago settled over her. And the fact that Bud had been murdered became more real. As did the way he'd been murdered. The bash on his head was no accident.

She couldn't help but wonder if the attack had been a surprise. Had Bud known the attacker was in the house behind him? Had he known his murderer? Had he let the person in the house? Or had the attacker snuck in?

She rubbed her temples to ease the pain of the headache forming. She was supposed to be sorting through outerwear, not sorting out Bud's murder.

The sound of another vehicle pulling into the driveway had Kelly looking over her shoulder. She immediately recognized Nate's sedan. She let out a huge breath. Then, eagerly, she waited for him to exit his vehicle. All she wanted was to fall into his embrace and forget about Bud lying dead in the kitchen.

Nate rushed toward her and quickly pulled her into a hug. One hand cradled her head while another kept her body pressed against his. "Are you okay?"

She nodded, not trusting herself to speak. It was taking every ounce of self-control not to break down into a blubbering mess.

Nate pulled back and then tilted her chin up with his forefinger. "Can you tell me what happened?"

She nodded again and then swallowed, willing herself to speak. "Walt told me Bud was here. I arrived, and the front door was open." She pointed to the home's entry. "I didn't think anything of it because I knew Bud was moving furniture out of the house. When I went inside, I called out for him. He didn't answer. Then I called for him again. Still no answer. I looked in the living and dining rooms. No Bud. The next room I checked was the kitchen." Her face scrunched, and she had to fight hard not to cry. "I checked his pulse. He's dead, Nate. He's dead."

Nate caressed her cheek. "I'm sorry you had to find him."

Kelly let out a steadying breath and managed to compose herself. Being an emotional wreck wouldn't help Bud now. Instead, she had to pull herself together to help get justice for him.

"You know, he was dating Miranda." Clarity started to return to her thinking. "Maybe their murders are connected." Her mouth formed an O, and she pointed at Nate. "Maybe he knew the murderer."

Nate's gaze leveled on her, and it wasn't very sympathetic. She knew what was coming next.

"Kelly, right now, there's no evidence of that."

"Well, of course not. Evidence is being collected as we speak. Surely you have to consider the fact that two people who were dating and then were murdered isn't a coincidence."

"You know I don't believe in coincidences."

"Exactly. I'm telling you, whoever murdered Miranda killed Bud. Why else would someone kill him? Everyone liked Bud." Except for his last girlfriend. Then again, Cara was the one who dumped Bud like every other boyfriend she'd had.

A flash of exasperation crossed Nate's chiseled features. It happened so fast, Kelly almost missed it. "I assure you, we will look at every possibility. Do you happen to know where your uncle was earlier?"

Kelly gaped and pulled back from him. "Seriously? You still consider my uncle to be a murder suspect? What on earth do you think he had against Bud?"

"You said Bud may have known Miranda's killer. Let's suppose your theory is correct. There was a confrontation and Bud was murdered—"

"By my uncle?" Kelly stepped back, putting more space between them. "Wow. I can't believe you think my uncle Ralph is a murderer. He's a lot of things, but he wouldn't kill two people. He's not a monster."

"I'm sorry." Nate raised his palms in surrender. "I shouldn't be speculating at this point, especially with a civilian." His tone had shifted from concerned boyfriend to professional detective.

"Will you or Gabe be taking my statement? I'd like to leave as soon as possible. I'm sure you can understand why." She realized her voice had an icy tone, and she didn't care.

"Kell, don't be like this. It's my job to look at every possible—"

"Suspect," she finished his sentence for him, and it left a bitter taste in her mouth. "I know. I get it. What about my statement? I'd like to give it now so I can leave. I don't want to stay here any longer than I have to." Her lower lip quivered. "Bud was a friend."

Nate's expression softened. "I understand." Another police cruiser pulled into the driveway. "I'll have Officer Devlin take your statement, and then you can leave. I'll follow up with questions if I have any."

She nodded. "What about Walt? Who will tell him?"

Nate gestured to the other officer to come forward after she exited her vehicle. When she approached, he instructed her to take Kelly's statement. "I'll take care of notifying him. And also Courtney."

In other words, *stay out of it, Kelly.*

The message was loud and clear. While Officer Devlin joined Kelly by the Jeep to take the statement, Nate entered the crime scene to do his job.

Kelly recounted her steps from when she pulled into the driveway to entering the kitchen for Officer Devlin. When the statement was finished, the officer dismissed Kelly with a compassionate smile. She too had known Bud.

So much loss in only a few days. As Kelly navigated out of the driveway, she thought she should be used to this feeling—a mix of hollowness, sadness, and anger—coursing through her body. How could someone take another person's life? Did the person who killed Miranda and Bud believe they would get away with it? That they could avoid punishment? The person who killed Diana Delacourte last Christmas had thought that and had been shocked when Kelly had figured it out. Maybe she should grant Jocelyn Bancroft the interview request even though she had made a baseless allegation against her uncle. The more voices speaking out against senseless murders and speaking out for justice for all victims would put those heartless, soulless people on notice.

But first, she needed to get back to the boutique. She flicked on the blinker and waited before making the turn onto Main Street. She had to break the news to Pepper and Breena. For that, she should bring something sweet and tasty to help ease the blow. Luckily, there was a space in front of Liv's bakery.

Kelly opened the bakery's door and stepped inside. The aroma of vanilla, sugar, and freshly baked bread enveloped her like a hug from her granny. Gosh, how she missed those hugs. And how much she needed one right now.

The third-generation bakery had no expensive coffee machines, fancy pastries, or Wi-Fi access. Instead, what Sweets on Main offered was yummy cookies, delicate pastries, and loaves of bread baked by Moretti women.

Behind the counter, Kelly spotted Liv filling a basket of rustic focaccia. Her aunt, Mia, talked on the phone while scribbling on a pad of paper.

Liv placed the last loaf of bread into the basket and turned to greet Kelly. "What's up?"

When Kelly sighed, Liv's smile faded. "Oh, no. What happened?" Liv searched Kelly's face for answers, and she pointed a finger. "I know that look! Don't tell me you found another…"

Kelly nodded.

"Who?"

"Bud Cavanaugh."

Liv's hand flew up and covered her mouth. Her eyes instantly darkened with sadness.

"I found him at the Travis house. In the kitchen." Kelly drifted to one of the café tables and dropped onto a chair.

"How awful." Liv rushed out from behind the counter and joined Kelly at the table. "What happened?"

"Walt called me to let me know Bud was at the house." Kelly propped her elbow up on the table. "I needed to get the rest of the clothes for consignment. When I got there, he was dead. Murdered."

"Oh my goodness. Kelly! You could have encountered the killer." Alarm sounded in Liv's voice and on her face. She grabbed Kelly's hand and squeezed tightly. "Why do you keep finding dead bodies?"

"What's going on? Come on, tell me." Mia approached the table. Like her niece, she was slender with dark hair. She wore jeans and a black shirt with an apron that featured the bakery's logo—a cupcake topped with blue icing.

"Bud Cavanaugh is dead," Liv said. "Kelly just found him at the Travis house."

"Oh dear." Mia slumped onto a chair. The glow her porcelain skin had radiated now faded. "How tragic. He was such a nice man. Though, very unlucky when it came to women. He came in every Friday afternoon for two cupcakes and every Sunday for a loaf of bread."

"First Miranda and now Bud. Do you think their murders are connected?" Liv asked Kelly.

"I do. And can you believe Nate asked if I knew where my uncle was earlier today?" Kelly said.

"No, he can't think Ralph killed those two people." Mia stood and walked back to the bakery case. She grabbed a plate and then plucked three cupcakes out of the case. "Ralph shouldn't be the only person the police look at. Unfortunately, Miranda was disliked by many people."

"So I'm learning." Kelly's mood lifted a little when Mia came back to the table with the plate of cupcakes and set it down. "And it's all because of her first husband's financial crime."

Mia picked up a chocolate cupcake and pulled back its wrapper. "That succinct recap sounds so impersonal, but trust me, when it happened, it was very personal for many people. Like, Courtney's parents."

Kelly lifted a cupcake from the plate and took a bite. After she swallowed, she said, "I've heard they lost a lot of money."

Mia swallowed her bite of cupcake. "Sadly, yes. They believed that Miranda killed Daniel to get her hands on the money. I think…" Her gaze drifted off as if she was trying to recall a memory. "If I remember correctly, they hired a private investigator."

"Are you sure?" Kelly asked just as she was about to take another mouthful of the cupcake. It was so moist and tender. She could easily devour a dozen of them, though she was sure she wouldn't be able to fit into her jeans if she indulged.

"It was twenty years ago, but I'm pretty sure Courtney's mom mentioned it," Mia said.

"Many people were devastated because of Daniel's crime, and as sad as it is, I'm not surprised that someone has sought the ultimate revenge."

"It seems like whoever gets tangled up in Miranda's life ends up dead," Liv said ominously.

Kelly paused midbite and let Liv's words settle over her as she finished chewing. The observation seemed spot-on. But she was more interested in the private investigator and what he might have found out about Miranda back then.

Kelly left the bakery with a box of Italian cookies. She hoped the baked goods would soothe the news she was about to deliver to Pepper and Breena. On her drive along Main Street back to the boutique, she caught a glimpse of Courtney's Treasure's front door. The closed sign was visible, but the inside lights were on. Kelly suspected that Courtney had been notified about the murder. When she drove to the lot behind her boutique and parked, Kelly made a quick detour to Courtney's shop before heading inside the boutique with the cookies and bad news.

* * * *

At the shop, Kelly looked in through the front window. She spotted Courtney behind the counter, closing the register. She knocked on the door and hoped she'd be let in. To Kelly's relief, Courtney motioned she'd be there in a minute and returned to her task at hand. Once the register was closed, and the money bag zipped and locked, she came out from behind the counter and opened the door.

"Closing early today?" Kelly asked.

"Yeah…I just heard about Bud. Detective Barber said you found his body." Courtney stepped aside for Kelly to enter. "Are you okay?"

Kelly shrugged. "It was a shock."

"What the heck is going on?"

"I have no idea. I'm trying to make sense out of it."

Courtney closed the door. "Well, I think that should be left up to the police. Detective Barber seems competent, don't you think?"

"Absolutely. Nate is a good detective," she agreed, despite the fact he seemed intent on pinning the murders on her uncle.

"This is so awful. It doesn't feel real." Courtney returned behind the counter and tidied the space. "I have to call my real estate agent. The new owners need to be notified that there was a murder in their new home. What happens if they back out? Nobody will want to buy the house." Her reaction struck Kelly as a little callous, but she tried to understand Courtney's position. She had a lot to lose. But the truth was, Bud had lost his life.

"Maybe it's best to take it one step at a time, like making the call to your agent."

"Easy for you to say. I've been working my butt off clearing out the house to make sure the sale goes through."

"Bud was murdered."

Courtney stopped moving and stared at Kelly. Then her face crumpled and she started crying. "I know. I know. I can't believe he's gone." She plucked a tissue out of a box and wiped her eyes dry.

"Neither can I," Kelly said. "Look, I won't keep you. But I do have a question I hope you can answer." When Courtney nodded, she continued. "Did your parents hire a private investigator to investigate Miranda after Daniel died?"

Courtney discarded the tissue in the trash bin beneath the counter. "Yeah…yeah, I think so. I remember overhearing my parents talking about it one night when they thought I was asleep."

"Do you remember the PI's name?"

"No, it was so long ago."

"Maybe there's some paperwork, like a report from the PI, at your mom's house?"

"I have no idea. Why are you so interested?"

"My uncle is a suspect, and I know he didn't do it. I need to help clear his name."

"A lot of people had a reason to kill Miranda. She ruined a lot of lives. Including my parents'. Heck, I probably could be a suspect."

Kelly blinked, hesitating a moment. In a split second, she had to decide what to say next. With the police so interested in her uncle, she didn't have much choice.

"Since you brought it up. Did you kill Miranda?" As soon as the words escaped Kelly's lips, she regretted them. Of course Courtney didn't murder anyone.

Courtney looked as if she'd been slapped. "How dare you ask me that question? We're done talking. Get out!"

"I'm so sorry," Kelly said. And she was. "I had to ask."

"Get out!" Courtney pointed to the door. "Now!"

The weight of Courtney's glare on her back made the trek to the door feel like she was walking through waist-high wet sand. Finally, outside the shop, the temptation to go back inside was strong, but she remained right where she was—glued to the sidewalk. Going back in there would only make things worse. It was better to leave things as they were and allow Courtney to cool off. After all, Kelly pretty much accused her of being a murderer. Pepper always said that you had to crack a few eggs to make delicious muffins when baking. Well, to solve a murder, you had to ask some hard questions.

Though, some were harder than others.

Good going, Kell.

She pushed herself forward. Taking the first step was a killer when every instinct in her screamed to go back in the shop and make things right with Courtney.

"Good afternoon, Kelly." Violet Briggs approached, carrying canvas grocery bags. Her curly raven hair framed her oval face, which was tanned and showing signs of aging thanks to her decades on boats. Like her late brother, she felt most comfortable out on the water. She glanced at Courtney's shop. "She closed early. I hope everything is okay."

"She just got some bad news." Kelly realized she probably shouldn't say what the news was, but because of the concerned look on Violet's face, she couldn't leave the woman hanging. "Bud Cavanaugh is dead. He was murdered."

"Oh my goodness. How horrible." Violet's shock morphed into curiosity. "What happened?"

"He was murdered in Courtney's mom's house. Bud was there taking furniture to consign at Walt's shop."

"Wow! This seems so unreal. First Miranda, and now Bud? I'm shocked. And sad. I liked Bud. Everybody liked Bud."

Not everyone, obviously. But Kelly kept that thought to herself. She also decided not to ask Violet the questions she wanted to. So far, whatever tact she thought she possessed seemed to have been imagined because she'd irritated several people so far with her inquiries. The last thing she needed was a scene played out on Main Street. Even though all she wanted to know from Violet was if she'd seen Miranda before her murder and if she harbored any animosity against her brother's widow. They seemed like innocent questions. But why risk it?

"You know, I have to get back to the boutique, but I'd like to talk to you…in private. Would you mind coming over to my apartment tonight?"

"Sure. That shouldn't be a problem. Oh, wait…I have book club tonight at the library. I can swing by after the meeting. Okay?"

"Sounds good. What book are you reading?"

"*The Captain's Daughter.* It's a historical fiction novel about a sea captain and the legacy he left for his family. It's a fascinating read. And more so because of Ariel's skill at leading the group."

Kelly's interest in the book club was piqued. "Ariel will be there?"

"Of course. She runs the book club. Why?"

Kelly gave a casual shrug. "Do you think I could join the book club?"

"I don't see why not. Are you reading the book?" Violet asked.

No, she wasn't, but that wasn't going to stop her from making another attempt to talk with Ariel. "As a matter of fact, I am. What a coincidence, huh? You're right. It's a fascinating read."

"Great. I'll send you a text with the time. See you later." Violet smiled and then continued down the street.

Kelly pulled out her cell phone and tapped on her favorite bookstore app. A few more taps and she was downloading an electronic version of *The Captain's Daughter*. After the purchase was complete, she scanned the hundred-plus reviews. She'd have to read through them quickly and then skim the book so she'd be able to talk about the story. Yeah, it felt like high school all over again.

Before she put her phone away, she sent a quick text to Nate, letting him know she wouldn't be able to make dinner. After sending the text, she shot off another one because she wanted to make sure he didn't think she was blowing him off because he still suspected her uncle in the murder case. She told him she had a chance to meet with Ariel and hoped he understood.

Chapter 13

The rest of the day passed by rather uneventfully, mostly because Kelly hid out in the staff room for most of the afternoon to avoid the latest topic of conversation in town—Bud's death. The few times Breena or Pepper came into the room, they said it was a smart decision for her to stay hidden because there were a lot of questions about the murder. She used the time wisely. She wrapped up admin work and did the payroll. Once those tasks were completed, she skimmed *The Captain's Daughter*. Confident she had enough of a grasp of the novel to make it through one book club meeting, she hurried upstairs after closing the boutique to change for the meeting.

After she fed Howard, she quickly changed into dark jeans and a marled pullover sweater. She pulled out a quilted vest at the hall closet and slipped it on. Her e-reader was already in her purse, and all she had to do was give Howard a pat goodbye before heading out.

The evening was beautifully mild, so she opted to walk to the library. The restaurants were lit up and filled with diners enjoying conversations over delicious meals. The retail shops that had stayed open longer than the boutique were closing, and the library had come into sight.

Inside the library, she made her way to the community room, and at the doorway, she spotted Ariel in the center of the circle of chairs arranged for the meeting. She hadn't noticed Kelly, since her head was down. It looked like she was reading a page in the notebook on her lap. There were a few book club members gathered in the corner in deep conversation.

Kelly squared her shoulders, lifted her chin, and pushed forward. She was going to talk to her friend. She cleared her throat when she reached Ariel's wheelchair, prompting Ariel to look up.

"Hi there. Nice night for a book club meeting." Kelly smiled brightly.

"What are you doing here?" Ariel's expression was unreadable. The gal always had a good poker face.

Kelly lifted her e-reader. "I'm here to talk about *The Captain's Daughter.* Violet told me her book club was discussing the novel."

"You're reading the book?" Ariel's tone made it clear she didn't believe Kelly.

"I hope you don't mind if I stay." Kelly wasn't about to lie to her friend—again.

"No, not at all. I hope you find our discussion interesting."

"I'm sure I will. Just one more thing. Could I have just a few minutes of your time to try and explain what happened?" *Please, please, please.*

"Sure. Go ahead," Ariel said with a shrug.

"Really? Thanks. Okay…um…I never wanted to hurt you." Kelly grabbed a chair, scooched it closer to Ariel, and then sat. "You have to believe me. But my uncle's secret was his to tell. I know I've said that before. And if I were in your place, I would have wanted me to say something. But I couldn't betray him. Just like I wouldn't be able to betray you if you told something to me in confidence. Believe me, he hadn't intended to tell me the secret."

"Then why did he?"

Kelly looked upward and shook her head. "I don't know. He just blurted it out when I pressed him on why he hates me so much."

"I don't understand."

"He said every time he looked at me, he saw you in the hospital bed after the accident." Every word he said during that conversation last spring was etched in her memory. "Then he explained what happened between him and your mother. After that, I was torn between family and friendship."

"Good evening, Ariel!" A plump woman with short auburn hair shuffled toward a chair on the other side of Ariel. She joined the circle and opened her book. Behind her was a group of women, also in good spirits, who broke apart when they reached the circle and then took their seats. "I'm so excited to discuss this book tonight. I'm loving it."

"Happy to hear that," Ariel said, and then she turned back to Kelly. "I'll need some time to think about what you've said."

"Okay. I totally understand." Kelly was cautiously optimistic that Ariel would come around and forgive her.

Violet Briggs scurried in with her book in hand. "So, so sorry I'm late." She dropped onto the only empty chair.

"It's great to see everyone this evening. We even have a new member joining us. Kelly Quinn." Ariel smiled. "To make Kelly feel welcome and a part of our club, I'm going to let her start our discussion."

Kelly's face dropped. What was Ariel doing?

"Much of this novel is about the kind of person someone becomes after learning that a hero in her eyes was really not a hero. Kelly, what did you make of Evangeline's discovery of her father's illegal acts and how she came to the decision that she had to deal with the inconvenient truth?" Ariel asked.

"Ah…well…" Kelly crossed her legs and tapped on her e-reader. "Evangeline, being the strong woman…" Gosh, there might as well have been a neon sign over her head confirming she hadn't read the book. Then she noticed the sly smile twitching on Ariel's lips. She'd asked Kelly the question on purpose, to make her squirm like only a good friend would. It looked like they were on the road to rebuilding their fractured relationship.

"Looks like our new member is shy," the plump woman said. "Let me tell you what I think about Evangeline and her disastrous decision."

Disastrous decision? Kelly hadn't known much about Evangeline, but she could relate to making terrible decisions. Maybe she should actually read the book.

By the end of the meeting, the book club ladies impressed Kelly with their insightful discussion about a work of fiction. Now she really wanted to read the book. Through the lively conversation, members identified with the emotions of the characters. A few even shared some real-life experiences. Though Violet had remained quiet during most of the meeting. Kelly couldn't get a read on her. She wondered if it was the news about Bud that had her so low-keyed.

When the group broke up, two members cornered Ariel, and Kelly overheard them offering suggestions for the next book to read. Disappointed that she wouldn't get to speak with Ariel again, she realized it might be for the best. Her friend needed time to process everything that Kelly had said. And it gave Kelly time to catch Violet before she took off for the evening. She'd spotted Violet at the doorway moments ago, so Kelly dashed out of the room.

"Thanks for letting me know about the meeting tonight. I enjoyed it," Kelly said when she reached Violet just before she made it to the library's exit.

"No problem. I hope you can make it next month." Violet pushed open the door and stepped outside. "The next book is going to be a contemporary novel."

"I'm going to try." And she was. Even though she hadn't read *The Captain's Daughter*, she enjoyed the meeting. The ladies seemed lovely and enthusiastic, and it would be nice to do something that wasn't work related for a change. Oh, wait. That's what her therapist had suggested last month. Better late than never, right? "It's still kind of early. Do you want to stop by my apartment? I can make us a cup of tea."

"Right. You asked me to come by. I'd love to, but I have to be at work early tomorrow. Last-minute staff meeting and I'm exhausted. Can I have a rain check?"

"Sure. No problem." It appeared Kelly would have to ask her questions right there and then. "We can drink tea and talk books another time."

"Sounds great. I have a few favorites I can share with you," Violet offered.

"I'd love that. Hey, do you mind if I ask if you were close to Bud?"

"I guess we were friends, but I wouldn't say we were close. Why do you ask?"

"You seemed distracted this evening. I thought it was because of what happened to him."

"His death makes no sense." Violet zipped her jacket. "I should get a move on. Good night, Kelly."

"Wait, Violet. Before you go, I want to ask you something about your brother."

"Nolen? Whatever about? He's been dead for nineteen years."

"I know. I'm sorry for your loss."

"Wait, this is about Miranda, isn't it?" Violet slung her tote bag over her shoulder. "What do you want to know?"

Kelly hadn't expected this to be so easy.

"I've been hearing that many people thought Daniel Parnell had offshore accounts, and that's where he funneled the money he stole from his clients. Since Nolen was a boat captain who married Daniel's widow, it's been said Nolen was involved somehow."

Violet stopped walking along the path, and under a lamppost, Kelly saw her face twist with anger. "I can't believe you're asking that question. Are you serious? My brother was a thief like Daniel? What my brother had been was foolish enough to fall for Miranda."

"Why?"

"I'm certain his death wasn't an accident on the boat like the police report said. I think she killed him."

"Why would she do such a thing? What was the gain for her?"

"I have no idea. We weren't exactly close. Look, it was no secret she married Daniel for money, and maybe my brother was only a rebound for her. Maybe she got bored with him and didn't want to risk a divorce settlement, or maybe my brother found out where the money was and threatened to tell the police."

"I'm sorry but I have to ask, where were you when Miranda was murdered?" Kelly asked.

"Are you out of your mind? You think I killed her?" Violet wagged a finger at Kelly. "And then, what? I killed Bud? Oh, this is outrageous."

"It probably is, but I had to ask," Kelly said.

"Why? Are you a cop now? Running your grandmother's shop isn't enough for you? You're moonlighting as a detective?"

"Try to understand. My uncle is suspected of murder. I have to do what I can to help him."

"Please. You'll find any reason to worm your way into a murder investigation. Admit it, you enjoy sticking your nose into other people's business. You've got quite a reputation, and you're living up to it." Violet turned and marched away, disappearing when she veered left onto Main Street.

Kelly let out an annoyed breath. She'd made another enemy and had nothing to show for it. Moreover, she didn't know where Violet was at the time of the two murders.

"Making new friends?" Nate asked.

Kelly turned around, surprised to see him there. "What are you doing here?"

"On my way home. I stopped at the Gold Sands. I wanted to get a beer after being stood up."

"What are you talking about? Stood up? I texted you earlier that I wouldn't be able to make dinner."

Nate shook his head.

"You need to double-check because I did send a text." Kelly pulled out her phone and tapped on the text app. She scrolled for Nate's name and pulled up their ongoing conversation. "What the heck?" She looked again. There wasn't a text from her about canceling dinner. "Maybe I sent it to someone else by mistake."

"Find it yet?"

"No. I'm so sorry. I could have sworn I sent the text. You must hate me for making you wait at the restaurant." Kelly put her phone away and frowned.

"I don't hate you." He reached out and pulled her close to him. "I was worried you were upset with me, and that's why you didn't show up."

She raised her hand and caressed his face, which was prickly with day-old stubble. His eyes were hooded and bloodshot. It was apparent he'd been working long days and sacrificing sleep. It was also clear that he was working so hard to make sure the right person was arrested for the murders.

Otherwise, he would have slapped cuffs on Uncle Ralph and hauled him in for arrest. That would have made his job a lot easier.

"I promise you the reason I didn't make dinner tonight wasn't because I'm upset with you." Kelly's heart melted when he covered her hand with his. His touch was warm and comforting. "I was going to call you when I got home and tell you what happened this evening. That was Violet Briggs who just stormed off. Her brother was Miranda's second husband. She suspects that Nolen's death wasn't an accident. In fact, she just told me that she blamed Miranda for his death."

Nate looked off in the direction of where Violet had headed. When his gaze returned to Kelly, it was different from before. He looked at her sternly and pulled back from her. "Didn't we have a conversation about you not inserting yourself in my case?"

"Yes, but—"

"Kelly, listen to me. I cannot tolerate your interference in my investigation."

"Tolerate?" She propped a hand on her hip.

"I know it's not what you want to hear, but it's a fact. I have a job to do, and I don't need your assistance. I've been working as a detective for many years without your help. I've actually closed dozens of cases on my own."

"I'm sure you have. What's so wrong with taking a little help from me?" she asked.

Nate dragged his fingers through his hair as he paced on the sidewalk. He finally came to a stop, and his shoulders slumped.

"You know, this isn't working right now. Maybe we should take a break until this case is solved."

"Break?" The word sent shock waves through Kelly that rattled her right down to her toes.

"Only until I wrap up the case." He leaned forward and kissed her forehead. He offered a small smile before walking away without looking back.

Where was he going? What was happening? She lunged forward to stop him, but something inside stopped her. Sure, she was upset with him for not seeing that her uncle was innocent. Really, how could he believe any member of her family could be a murderer? But she didn't want a break.

She balled her hands into fists.

Darn it. I really, really like him.

Still, maybe a little distance would be a good thing for them. At least she hoped so.

Gosh, I hope I didn't mess this up.

Chapter 14

"Shoot. Shoot. Shoot." Kelly shoved her hand between the sofa cushions, her fingers feeling for the car key. She doubted it'd be there because she never took any of her keys to the sofa. Never. She always kept them in her purse.

"This is ridiculous." Just like Nate suggesting that they take a break last night. Utterly ridiculous.

She replaced the cushions and thought of where the darn key could be. She'd already emptied out her purse and her laptop bag and shook the booties she wore to the book club meeting just in case the key fell in one of them.

She thought back to when she returned home after finding Bud's body at the Travis house. Ah-ha! She had gone to the fridge for a soda.

Kelly darted out of the living room and scurried to the kitchen. Maybe, just maybe, the key was in the refrigerator. Had she been carrying the key when she was pulling out the can?

She replayed the scene in her head, and now it seemed unlikely the key was in there. She remembered that when she went for the soft drink, she had one hand on the door handle and her other hand grabbed the soda.

When she reached the kitchen, she went straight for the refrigerator's handle and yanked the door open with more might than she planned. Thinking about Nate and his stupid break idea was riling her up. He didn't even want to discuss it. He'd just made up his mind and then decided that they'd get back together after he finished the investigation.

Her nostrils flared. Pretty cocky of him to assume she'd be waiting around for him after *she* solved the murders.

Kelly gave herself a mental shake. It was time to stop thinking about Nate and focus on finding her car key. And there it was on the middle shelf next to the peanut butter jar. Looked like her memory wasn't perfect. What the heck was going on with her? She swiped the key and closed the door.

"How on earth did this get in there?"

A loud meow drew her attention toward the doorway, where Howard sat looking all judgy.

"Don't pass judgment on me." She looked at the key in her palm, and then she slipped a look to her cat. "Did you put this in there?"

Howard yawned. Apparently, he was bored with the conversation. He then stood and strutted out of the kitchen.

She glanced at her watch. No time to finish interrogating the cat. She was already running late for her breakfast date with Marvin. After getting out of the shower, she'd chosen a pair of pinstriped trousers, a pale blue button-down shirt, and a coordinating vest for her outing. To finish off the smart look, she slipped on stiletto-heeled booties. Hurrying out of the kitchen, she took out a trench coat from the hall closet and grabbed her purse. Passing the mirror hung between the closet and the door, she double-checked her eye makeup. She'd done her best to hide the puffiness from her cryfest last night. Thanks to plumping eye patches and concealer, she just looked exhausted, not heartbroken.

Kelly arrived at the Lucky Cove Inn ten minutes late, but Marvin didn't seem bothered by her tardiness. Instead, a large smile spread across his face as she approached the table. He stood and kissed her cheek and then pulled out the chair for her. He was always the gentleman.

"I ordered us breakfast. I hope you don't mind." Marvin Childers looked both debonair and comfortable in a pink open-collared shirt and navy blazer. His thinning white hair was neatly combed, and his eyes were alert. When she'd first met him nearly a year ago, he'd been living like a hermit in a messy house with his little white dog, Sparky. Now he was happy, painting again and even preparing for an art show.

"Of course not. Thank you so much for ordering for me." Kelly unfolded her napkin and set it over her lap. "What am I having?" She hoped he ordered her waffles. He gestured, and she looked over her shoulder. Their waitress approached. Kelly stretched her neck to see over the tray, and she smiled. Waffles.

"For you, pumpkin waffles," Marvin said as the waitress set the plate in front of Kelly. "And for me, a western omelet."

"You know me so well." Kelly lifted the syrup pitcher and drizzled a slow stream over the waffles, filling in as many crannies as she could. "And coffee. You're too good to me."

Marvin beamed. “It’s my pleasure. Now eat up. Enjoy.” He cut into his omelet and took a bite. Along with the eggs came toast and hash browns. After he swallowed, he asked, “How are you doing, dear? I heard about that nasty business you’ve found yourself entangled up in. Two people murdered. Were they really dating?”

Kelly nodded as she savored the light, fluffy bite of waffle. Its just-right pumpkin flavor was enhanced with nutmeg and cinnamon. And the drizzle of the maple syrup on top had her in heaven as she ate.

“They were. It’s really sad, isn’t it?” She cut another piece of waffle. “Honestly, I’m not doing too well.”

Marvin dabbed his mouth with his napkin and then set it back on his lap. Concern creased his face. “I’m sorry to hear that. What’s going on?”

She shrugged as she continued eating her breakfast. This was the most enjoyable meal she’d had in days. Last night, she had a frozen meal instead of a lovely dinner with Nate. Her heart squeezed with pain. Now wider awake, food in her belly, her thoughts were clearer and less hostile toward him. She wondered why she had chosen to go to the book club instead of meeting him for dinner. She knew the answer. She wanted to talk with Ariel and also question Violet.

Even though she seemed to have a knack for sleuthing, was it something she should do? Sure, she’d been able to uncover murderers, and those individuals were now serving time for their heinous crimes. On the other hand, risking personal relationships was a considerable cost to bear. If she continued snooping all the time, would she end up a lonely old cat lady?

She set her knife and fork down and took a sip of her coffee to help slow her racing thoughts.

“I’m having trouble sleeping, and I’m forgetting things.” Kelly gave him a rundown of the things she’d forgotten, including leaving the apartment door open, which allowed Howard to sneak downstairs and set off an allergic reaction in Aurora Cavendish of all people.

“Aurora? Oh, dear. She is a persnickety woman. I hear she’s been banned from the senior center,” Marvin said with a mischievous glint in his eyes.

Kelly pressed her lips together so as not to laugh because she had a feeling being Aurora Cavendish meant living a very lonely life. And she kind of felt sorry for the woman.

“Then last night, I know I texted Nate about not being able to make dinner. But when I checked, the text was gone. I guess I didn’t send it. Heck, I’m not even certain I wrote it.” Kelly slumped in her chair. “Pepper suggested that I go back to the therapist.”

"It may not be a bad idea." Marvin reached for his coffee and took a sip. "She seemed to help you before. Though I sense you're hesitant to go back. Why?"

Kelly returned to eating her waffle. No matter how upset she was, that waffle wasn't going to go to waste. "I thought I could handle things on my own. Guess I was wrong about that too."

"Don't be so hard on yourself." Marvin lifted a slice of his toast and took a bite. After he swallowed, he said, "It seems like these problems started when you found Miranda's body."

Kelly set her fork down and thought about what Marvin had just said. He was right. Up until a few days ago, she hadn't lost or forgotten anything or typed ghost texts.

"Perhaps all you need is some time away from the boutique and the murder investigations."

"No, no, no. There's too much to do at the boutique and for the chamber of commerce."

"Nonsense. Pepper and Breena are perfectly capable of running things for a few days, and the chamber of commerce can handle you taking a few days off." He gestured for the waitress and asked for a coffee refill for them. "Why don't you take a long weekend out at the cottage?"

"The one you rented in Montauk? There's no way I can afford that." Kelly added cream to her coffee and stirred.

At the beginning of summer, Marvin rented a cottage at the tip of Montauk to recharge and refill his creative well. He'd been in a significant artistic slump for years but craved to paint again. The getaway had been successful. He'd not only produced new works, but he also got an art show booked at a local gallery. Kelly had watched him bloom from a hermit last winter to a vital, artistic person who had a renewed passion for life.

"You don't have to worry about the cost of the cottage," Marvin said.

Kelly arched a brow. "Why not?"

"Because I bought the cottage."

"No way!" She couldn't fathom how much that had set him back. From time to time, she browsed the real estate websites and always checked out the homes in the Hamptons and Montauk. She'd never be able to afford even a shack in those towns, but it was nice to window-shop.

Marvin smiled. "I felt very at home there, and my creativity sparked like never before. So I talked to the owner, who had been thinking about selling. We came to an agreement, and it's mine. Which means it's yours to use for free whenever you want to."

The temptation to take Marvin up on his offer was strong. A few days away, at the very tip of the island, sounded delightful and peaceful, especially at this time of the year. While there were still a few tourists stretching out the season in Lucky Cove and surrounding towns, Montauk would pretty much be dead. She drained the last of her coffee. While the offer was appealing, it would be nothing more than running away. Ten years ago, after graduating from high school, she couldn't wait to get out of Lucky Cove and away from her mistakes.

"What do you say?"

Kelly checked her watch. It was getting late, and she had to get a move on because there was a meeting with the Shop Small committee at town hall. Plus, there were some stops she needed to make before the meeting.

"Thank you for the offer." Giving Marvin an outright no wouldn't be easy. Maybe she should think about taking a few days off. There wasn't a need to be hasty. The cottage and his offer would still be there later. "I really do appreciate it, and I'll think about it. I promise. I hate to run off, but I do have to be at a meeting."

"I understand, dear. You're a busy businesswoman." His smile was so sincere and full of pride. Even though she wasn't his granddaughter, he loved her like one. "You go on. I'm going to finish my coffee before I head home."

"Be sure to send me the details about your art show." Kelly stood and walked around the table. She leaned down and dotted a kiss on Marvin's cheek. "Thank you. Thank you for everything." Everything included the unconditional love he offered, just like her granny had when she was alive.

He patted her hand. "Take care of yourself, kiddo."

She nodded and then turned, heading for the lobby. When she reached the area, she looked for Renata to ask her about Eve Marlow but didn't see her. Instead, she spotted Jocelyn Bancroft heading in her direction.

"Miss Quinn, I hadn't expected to see you this morning. Then again, this is a small town." Jocelyn removed her oversized black sunglasses. She didn't look like she was about to apologize for accusing Ralph of being in cahoots with Daniel Parnell decades ago. "My offer still stands. The Diana Delacourte case has nothing to do with what is currently happening."

"I haven't given your offer much thought lately. There's been so much going on," Kelly said, still hoping to catch Renata before she left.

"There certainly has. I heard about the second murder. You found Bud Cavanaugh's body, didn't you? I must say, you have a propensity for finding dead bodies. Or you're a very unlucky woman." Jocelyn adjusted the moto-style leather jacket draped over her shoulders. It was the perfect accent piece to the dark blue sheath dress that skimmed her fit body.

"Just think about the people I find dead. How unlucky they are." Kelly took a step forward. Since she'd made no decision about the interview, she had nothing to discuss with Jocelyn. Rather, she had another breakfast meeting to get to. It was a last-minute idea she had on the drive over to the inn, and she wasn't sure what would be accomplished. But she knew if she didn't sit down and ask those nagging questions, she'd regret it.

Jocelyn stared at Kelly. Apparently, she wasn't sure what to say next.

"Look, despite your outrageous allegation about my uncle, I haven't made a decision yet. Though I do have a question for you."

"Do you want my alibi for the second murder?"

Kelly shrugged. "If you're willing to share." She didn't think Jocelyn would share, so she didn't wait for an answer and continued with the question she'd wanted to ask. "What makes you think my uncle was involved with Daniel's embezzlement besides them being friends?"

"Timing. Your uncle's business was struggling because he'd overextended years earlier. Loans were coming due, and he needed money. Then all of a sudden, he was flush with cash and was buying properties left and right."

"Sounds like a lot of theory. Do you have any proof connecting him to the actual crime?" Kelly asked.

Jocelyn's gaze flicked away for a moment. "Let me know what you decide about Diana Delacourte's book." She replaced her sunglasses on her face and then breezed past Kelly, out the sliding doors, and in seconds, she disappeared from view.

"She's got nothing," Kelly muttered to herself. At least she hoped so.

* * * *

Kelly arrived at the Bayside Diner and scanned the restaurant for Paul before claiming a booth by the window. He'd suggested meeting there because he lived nearby. The diner had been a fixture in the area for years, and she'd spent many afternoons there hanging out with friends after school.

"Sorry to keep you waiting."

Paul's deep voice interrupted her thoughts of simpler days. She looked up just as he slid into the booth.

"No need to. I just got here." When she'd called him earlier during her drive over to the inn to meet Marvin, she'd been nervous that he'd decline her invitation. After all, he'd seemed to have said everything he had to say about the deaths of Miranda's husbands the other day.

Paul pushed away the diner's menu, and when the waitress appeared, he ordered a black coffee. She looked at Kelly, who ordered a cup of tea, and then walked away to the counter.

"Thanks for meeting me," Kelly said.

"No problem. I'm actually glad that you reached out to me." Deep lines fanned out from his eyes when he smiled.

"You are? I wasn't sure if you'd want to talk about Miranda Farrell."

"There's not much to talk about. But if there's anything I can tell you that will help you in whatever you're doing, I'm happy to do so."

The waitress reappeared with the hot beverages. Then, with a flash of a smile, she hustled away.

"What can you tell me about the deaths of Miranda's husbands?" Kelly sipped her tea and then leaned back, hopeful she'd hear something useful, like an undisclosed detail from one of the cases. This must have been what it was like for Jocelyn—meeting a law enforcement source, getting info that hadn't been revealed to the public, and then putting together the puzzle of the subject's life and ultimately, death.

Paul raised his cup and took a long sip. Over the rim, he studied Kelly. Feeling the weight of his gaze, she did her best not to react. She remained steady and outwardly unnerved, but on the inside, she felt like he was looking right through her.

"I can tell you there was nothing to indicate either man died an unnatural death. Also, there was nothing indicating that Miranda was involved in the untimely passing of her husbands."

"So, just bad luck? A coincidence that she married two men in Lucky Cove, and they both died shortly after marrying her?"

He nodded. "Sounds like a true crime story, doesn't it? Guess it has all the elements," he mused with a chuckle.

"I read that Daniel died from a heart attack. Aren't there drugs that can mimic that?"

"Yes, to both."

"Miranda could have poisoned Daniel. Slipped him something without him realizing." She wondered if Miranda had been a doting wife. Had she prepared Daniel's coffee in the morning? Had a cocktail waiting for him when he arrived home from work?

"We considered that. However, the autopsy didn't show any signs of unprescribed drugs or an overdose of his prescribed meds. When I interviewed Miranda, she struck me as an appropriately grieving widow."

Kelly cocked her head to the side. *Appropriately grieving widow?* She wondered how he gauged that.

"Even though my gut said she had nothing to do with his death, I did do some investigating. I found no unusual financial transactions—"

"Like if she paid for someone to kill her husband?"

"Exactly. I also found she had no financial incentive to kill her husband. Well, not one that was substantial. According to Daniel's will, she inherited only a hundred thousand." He took another drink of his coffee.

"There were people who thought she was a gold digger. Perhaps they misjudged her," Kelly said.

"I would say so. Six figures are nothing to sneeze at, but it's not exactly what one would expect she'd be left. Then again, we found out Daniel's luxury lifestyle was paid for by other people's money."

"What about Nolen's death?"

"What about it? He slipped and fell." Paul reached into his jacket's pocket and pulled out his cell phone, checking for messages.

"Accidental, then?" When Paul nodded, Kelly lifted her cup to her lips. She couldn't exactly argue with him. He'd been an experienced police detective, and both deaths had sounded pretty cut and dry. Heart attack and accident.

"A lot of people wanted Miranda to be the bad guy in those two deaths. Heck, it would have made my job a lot easier." Paul returned his phone to his pocket.

"What do you mean?"

He scratched his forehead. "I can't tell you how many times I got stopped by people wanting to know when I'd arrest her. The court of public opinion had her tried and convicted. It wasn't pretty."

Then why on earth had she returned to town? Even if she fell head over heels in love with Bud?

"You know, there was someone in Miranda's life that raised my radar."

"Who?"

"Eve Marlow."

Kelly's interest was piqued. According to her uncle, Eve had been a good friend of Miranda's. "What about her?"

"I got the vibe she was one of those jealous people. Miranda was beautiful, and she was the kind of woman who always seemed to land on her feet."

"They'd been friends, but you sensed something else between them?"

He gave her an appraising look. "How do you know they were friends?"

"It's just what I heard." Kelly didn't want to reveal too much about her conversations with her uncle.

"You're a busy person, aren't you, Kelly Quinn? How do you manage to run your shop?"

An excellent question. Honestly, she had no idea how she was managing what she was doing. Maybe that's why she kept forgetting things.

"One more question. Were you involved in Daniel's embezzlement case?"

"No. Why?"

"I was just curious if there had been any talk about him having an accomplice…that wasn't Miranda."

Paul shook his head. "Sorry. The only person suspected of helping Daniel was Miranda."

So maybe Jocelyn made the allegation simply to stir the pot. Why would she do that? One reason could have been that she didn't like having the tables turned on her. Given her long career, she was the one used to asking the questions and looking for alibis.

"Sorry. Before you go. What marina was Nolen's boat docked at?"

"Ah…the Lucky Fishing Boat Marina."

"Thanks. I appreciate your help," she said.

He chuckled as he reached into his back pocket and pulled out his wallet. "My help? I don't think I was much help to you." He dropped a ten-dollar bill on the table and slid out of the booth. "But I did appreciate the company over coffee."

Kelly finished her tea as her mind churned over what she learned from Paul. Admittedly, not too much, though his observation about Eve Marlow was interesting. Now, only if she could find Eve.

Chapter 15

Kelly returned to the boutique long enough to park her Jeep and dash inside to check on Pepper. It appeared everything was under control, and she told Kelly to knock 'em dead at the committee meeting. Kelly intended to wow her peers with her brilliant idea and detailed plan. With her computer bag slung over her shoulder, she headed out. Her next stop was Doug's to buy a coffee. The large black coffee was a bribe to get Breena's permission to look in the shoe shop's basement.

What her uncle said yesterday had stuck out to her—Miranda had refused to let the plumber in the basement. Why? Had her intent just been to be difficult like he assumed? Or, had there been something down there she hadn't wanted anyone to see? It was a crazy thought, but what if she stashed a boatload of money down there? The money her first late husband had embezzled from his clients. Far-fetched? Absolutely. But what if she discovered a big bag of money? Or a lead to where the money actually was? Or another body? She shook off that last thought. No, this time, if she was going to find anything, it should be money.

Kelly reached the shoe boutique and opened the door, careful not to jostle the coffee as she stepped inside. She was surprised that nothing looked changed from the last time she was there. Shoes were displayed, fixtures were polished, and the mirrors smudge-free. Nothing indicated that the shop owner had been murdered. It all looked perfectly normal.

"What are you doing here?" Breena asked from a round glass pedestal display that featured a pair of red stilettos. "Ooh. Coffee? For me?" She held out her hand for the to-go cup.

"Enjoy," Kelly said as she handed over the cup. The pull of the red shoes was overwhelming for her. She couldn't resist. "These are beautiful."

Though, her heart belonged to the pair of black D'Orsay pumps she'd seen in the window the other morning. She wondered if it would be insensitive to ask if she could get them at a discount now that the shop would be closing.

"I do appreciate this. I feel like I'm running on fumes these days." Breena dropped onto an upholstered shoe bench and took a drink of her coffee.

"I know the feeling. I was wondering..." Kelly looked at the shoes again. Asking about a discount would be insensitive. Maybe later. "You've taken on a lot of responsibility that doesn't feel like it should be yours to handle."

"Tell me about it. I have a million things to do. I have to go through all of Miranda's contacts and tell them about Miranda and that the shop will be closing."

"This isn't your business."

"I know. To tell you the truth, I will miss it. I really like the shoe biz." Breena's eyes brightened, and then she took a sip of coffee. "I truly appreciate this."

"You're welcome. I did come to ask a favor. Would you mind if I checked out the basement?"

"The basement?" Breena gave her a quizzical look. "Why? What do you think you'll find down there?" She stood and walked over to the sales counter, where a laptop computer was open. She set her coffee down and then typed on the keyboard.

"I don't know. Probably nothing. I won't be too long."

"Don't go finding another body." Breena chuckled.

"Haha." Kelly walked through the sales area of the shop and entered the back room where there were two doors—one to the small bathroom and one to the basement. She set her tote on the desk and then went to one of the doors, twisted the doorknob, and flicked on the light switch. The light was dim, so she carefully descended the staircase. The wooden steps were worn and creaky. She hated basements. They were dark, musty, and eerie. She propped her hands on her hips when she reached the dirty cement floor and looked around.

There wasn't much to see. Along one wall was a metal shelving unit that housed a few cardboard boxes and old paint cans. To her right was the furnace, and in the corner was the electrical panel.

She stepped forward. There was a folded tarp and an open toolbox on the floor, which was almost empty. She doubted what tools were left would come in handy for any type of repair job.

A rumbling sound that intensified startled her. Instinctively, she jumped and swung around, on high alert. Then she realized the culprit.

"Phew. Just the furnace." She swiveled back around, and something caught her eye. She moved closer to the tarp and bent down. A golden ballet slipper charm. She picked it up and studied the little trinket.

Was it Miranda's?

She tried to remember if Miranda had worn a bracelet. No. She hadn't. Especially not a charm bracelet. Those were hard to miss because they were noisy. Besides, the charm could have been dropped there months or even years ago by anyone.

Before straightening up, she took a quick peek under the tarp. Perhaps there were more charms, or maybe even the bracelet. Or something hidden, like a clue to why or who killed Miranda. She frowned. Her glimpse turned up nothing.

Kelly closed her hand, securing the charm in her palm, and sighed. Other than the jewelry, there was nothing unusual down there. No bags of money, no bodies, and no clues. It seemed Miranda had just wanted to be difficult. Then suddenly, a chill skittered through her along with a feeling she wasn't alone.

"What are you doing down here?"

The voice surprised Kelly, and she jumped, spinning around to see Ernie Baldwin coming off the last tread on the staircase. Dressed in a charcoal-gray suit with polished shoes, he looked like the bank manager he was. In fact, Kelly couldn't recall ever seeing him casually dressed. Then again, she wasn't a member of the country club he belonged to, and that's probably where he let his hair down, so to speak.

"Gosh, Ernie, you startled me." She tightened her hold on the charm. "You know, I could ask the same of you."

"I came by to check on Breena. To see if she needs any help in closing up shop. I know it's a lot to take on. She said you were down here. Why?" He looked around the dark space with interest.

"That's nice of you. I'm sure she could use the help." If she weren't so caught up in the murder investigation and planning the chamber's event, she would have had the time to help Breena. Yet another example of her risking her personal relationships. "My uncle said that Miranda refused to let his plumber come down here the other day. I was curious why and wanted to take a look."

"Find anything?"

"No. I don't see a reason for her to have not wanted someone down here."

"Sounds like she was being herself. Always difficult."

Kelly recalled Miranda's comment at the chamber luncheon: *"Well, he worked his way up the ladder at the bank."* Actually, it was more of how she said it. The tone. Then there had been that glacial stare he directed at Miranda in the hallway outside the reception room.

"How well did you know Miranda?" she asked.

"Not very well."

"But you said she was difficult."

He slid his hands into his pants pockets, brushing back his blazer. "You didn't need to spend too much time with her to know that. Come on, let's go upstairs. It's damp down here."

Kelly nodded. She didn't need to be asked twice to leave the unpleasant space. She walked to the staircase, keeping her hand closed. She didn't know why, but something told her not to show Ernie the charm.

They climbed the stairs in silence, and when they emerged from the basement, Breena looked relieved.

"I honestly don't know where to start. There's inventory to get rid of, orders to cancel, and accounts to close," Breena said.

"I'm sure Miranda's lawyer can assist you. And he should. This is far too much for you to tackle on your own." Kelly walked to the desk and discreetly slipped the charm into her tote. "I'm sure Ernie will do what he can, but you really need to ask Miranda's lawyer for help."

"You're right. I'll call him this afternoon. I guess I can close up for now. Thanks for stopping by, Ernie," Breena said.

"No problem. You know where you can find me if you need anything. Don't hesitate to call, okay?" He lingered for a minute before saying goodbye and leaving the shop.

"Well, that was weird," Breena said from the doorway as she watched him leave the shop.

"What are you talking about?" Kelly asked.

"The bank manager showing up to help me." Breena looked at Kelly. "Why would he do that?"

"Good question. Has he stopped in before?"

Breena shook her head. "I haven't seen him here. But, then again, I only worked part-time."

"Why did he come down to the basement?"

"He said he wanted to check on you. I don't know why. It's not like you could get into any trouble down there." Breena laughed. Probably because she knew Kelly could get into trouble anywhere at any time. She pulled out the charm from her tote and showed it to Breena.

"Did Miranda wear a charm bracelet?"

"I never saw her wear one. It's pretty." Breena walked out to the front of the shop. "Did you find it in the basement?"

"It's probably been down there for a while." Kelly put the charm back in her tote and followed Breena. She didn't know why she was keeping it. "Ready to close up?"

"You know, I'm thinking about staying open for a few hours. Maybe I'll mark down some merch and sell what I can. Do you think it would be tacky?"

"I don't think so. You need to do something with the merchandise. Do you feel comfortable opening?"

"No." Breena sank into a chair. "I'm at a loss for what to do."

"Let Miranda's lawyer handle all this. Come on, let's close and get out of here."

"Sounds good." Breena rose from the chair and walked to the counter. There, she closed the laptop computer and slipped it into a bag.

The front door opened, and a woman in her midsixties entered. Looking uncertain, like she wasn't sure she was in the right shop, she offered a tepid greeting to Breena.

"I'm sorry, we're not open," Breena said.

"I'm not here to buy anything. I'm Eve Marlow. I was a friend of Miranda's." She stepped farther into the shop.

Kelly and Breena shared a glance. While Breena looked nervous, Kelly was intrigued.

"We're so sorry for your loss." Kelly extended her hand. It looked like she wouldn't have to track Ms. Marlow down after all.

"We are?" Breena whispered. It appeared she hadn't known that Miranda and Eve had been friends a lifetime ago.

"Yes, we are." Kelly nodded, hoping Breena would take her lead. "I'm Kelly Quinn. This is Breena Collins. She worked for Miranda."

"You own the consignment shop. I've been in there a few times." Eve took her hand back. She wore a trench coat over black trousers and ballet flats. Her gray-blond hair was styled in a simple bob with bangs fringing her eyebrows. "I'm not sure why I'm here. I was walking by, and something drew me in, I guess. I've been visiting family in Pennsylvania and heard about Miranda, so I decided to come back to Lucky Cove. I usually don't visit until the summer."

"I've heard you and Miranda were good friends," Kelly said.

"You did?" Breena whispered. She clearly wasn't following Kelly's lead.

"We were. Oh, maybe not so close in the last few years. Maybe if we were, she would have listened to me when I warned her that I had a bad feeling about her coming back here."

"You did? Let's have a seat." Kelly gestured to a nearby bench. She and Eve sat while Breena dashed out from behind the counter and pulled over a chair to join them.

Eve pulled out a tissue from her purse and dabbed her eyes dry. "How could something like this happen?"

"Why did you warn Miranda about coming back to Lucky Cove?" Breena settled on the chair and crossed her legs.

"Isn't it obvious? This town was nothing but bad news for her." Eve took a breath. "We met the summer she came here, and we worked together at the Lucky Cove Inn. There she met and fell in love with Daniel Parnell. I know what his uppity friends thought about her. They made her out to be a gold digger."

"She wasn't?" Kelly asked.

"No. She loved him. But he was a hard man to love."

"How so?" Breena leaned forward; curiosity was written all over her face. Kelly liked having a partner in crime.

"I once saw Miranda with a black eye," Eve said.

"Daniel hit her?" Kelly asked.

"Miranda never confirmed it, but I know he did it. Who else would have hit her? It wasn't the last time she had bruises." Eve plucked another tissue from her purse and blew her nose.

"Daniel has been dead for decades. Why did you have a bad feeling about Miranda coming back to town?" Kelly asked.

"There's nothing I can pinpoint. You know, it was just a feeling. The same one I had after Daniel died and then Nolen." Eve chewed on her lower lip, and she seemed to be thinking about what to say next. "There's no proof, but I felt that Miranda was being stalked."

"That's a serious allegation." Based on what Paul had told Kelly, it would have been Eve who would have been doing the stalking. Then again, perhaps the retired detective just wasn't well versed enough in female friendships to understand the depths of emotions or how women cared for each other.

"It's a known fact that stalking can turn deadly. You hear about it all the time on the news. I wish I had more to go on than just a feeling. Perhaps that's why Miranda didn't heed my warning." Eve choked back emotion. She gathered her purse and stood abruptly. "I'm sorry, I have to go. Being here is too much for me." She rushed out of the shop.

Breena let out a deep whoosh as she leaned back and Kelly stared at the door. Then, together, they sat in silence for a few minutes, processing what Eve had said.

If Miranda had a stalker, that could explain why she and Bud were murdered. The stalker could have felt rejected by Miranda. And the stalker could have fatally lashed out at Bud because he was dating Miranda.

But was it feasible for a stalker to resurface after twenty years?

"What are you thinking?" Breena asked.

"Those keys on the counter, are they for the shop or…"

"Miranda's apartment."

Exactly what Kelly had hoped to hear. "I have an idea."

Breena tilted her head. "You do? Oh, you want to snoop around the apartment."

"Only if it's not still considered a part of the police investigation." The last thing Kelly wanted was to be arrested for tampering with a crime scene. She'd already been handcuffed once by the police.

"Could we be arrested if we're caught in the apartment? Like for trespassing?"

"Probably not since you've been tasked with wrapping up Miranda's business details, and she could have brought work home with her." Then again, Kelly wasn't 100 percent sure, but it sounded good, and that's what she'd say if they were caught. "How about we meet at her place after my committee meeting?"

Breena stood. "Text me when you're done, and I'll head over there. I want to finish some things here. Okay?"

Kelly nodded. "Sounds good." She stood and left the shop. There was a pit stop she wanted to make between the committee meeting and going over to Miranda's apartment that she didn't want to mention to Breena.

Chapter 16

Kelly barely made it to town hall on time. As she entered the building's lobby, she was cutting it close to the meeting's start time. She hadn't planned on meeting the one and only friend Miranda Farrell had in Lucky Cove. The unexpected visit gave Kelly a piece of information she hadn't had before. Since Eve had just arrived in town, she wondered if Nate knew Miranda could have had a stalker.

Did taking a break in their relationship mean they wouldn't communicate at all? What was the etiquette for a break? She knew the terms and conditions of breakups. But a break? Maybe she'd binge the *Friends* season where Ross and Rachel took a break to give herself a refresher of how they handled it. Why bother? She had no intention of wasting time worrying what was allowed and what wasn't in this very fuzzy period of their relationship. She'd text Nate after her committee meeting because he should have the information. By the time she came to the decision, Kelly was facing a perturbed-looking Zoe Carlisle, who'd just stepped out of a room.

"I was worried you'd forgotten about the presentation." Zoe tapped her watch. It appeared Gregorio's assistant manager was moonlighting as hall monitor for the committee. "Everything is all set up, and now that you're here, we can start. Come on." Her heels clicked on the terrazzo floor as she led Kelly along the hall, passing by various town offices.

Kelly entered the meeting room behind Zoe. She took a quick inventory of everyone in attendance. She noticed Ariel was seated at the end of the second row with a notepad on her lap. Ariel was probably there in her capacity as a freelance writer, her other part-time job, and was on an assignment. However, she also noticed someone was missing.

"Where's Ricky?" Kelly walked to the front row of chairs.

Zoe looked over her shoulder. "He had a call that he was late for, and he was still on it when I left the store."

"It's a shame. I was looking forward to his feedback on my presentation." Kelly dropped her tote on a chair in the front row.

"Probably, these days, he's not the best person to give feedback." Zoe lifted her agenda from a chair farther down the row. "He's been out of sorts since Miranda Farrell was killed."

"How so?" Zoe had a reputation of being a gossip, so getting information out of her would be easy peasy for Kelly.

"Ricky is punctual. You know, to the point where it's freaking annoying. But lately, he's been late for a lot of things, like the call this morning. It's with one of our suppliers." From Zoe's tone, it sounded like Ricky had committed a cardinal sin. "Come to think of it, the morning Miranda was murdered, he was late for a delivery."

Kelly's ears perked up, and she was about to press Zoe for more information when Liv took her spot at the front of the room and called the meeting to order.

"We're going to get right to business. Kelly, come on up and show us what you've got." Liv flashed a big smile and returned to her chair.

Well, that was a short introduction. Kelly had hoped she'd have a few minutes to set up while Liv talked. She grappled with her tote bag, pulling the computer out and connecting it to the AV system in the meeting room. She blew out a relieved breath when she got it set up.

"Good morning." Kelly tapped on the computer's keyboard and opened her presentation.

The first slide introduced the event. The top and bottom borders were filled with red-and-white reindeers and a sleigh for a festive flair. The center of the slide had two snowflakes anchoring the event's name.

"'Tis the Season to Shop Small in Lucky Cove, NY," she read proudly.

Kelly glanced at her audience. Then, with her confidence bolstered by the pleased looks on their faces, she continued and clicked to the next slide. She shared the data and hoped it reinforced how meaningful every business's participation was.

"As you see here, 39 percent of the respondents from the survey said they celebrate Small Business Saturday. In addition, you'll notice that most of the survey respondents make a point of shopping at local businesses. On the slide, you'll see a breakdown of what people shop locally for. This is all very encouraging."

Kelly paused a moment to give room for any comments. Then, when there weren't any, she continued.

"We've already discussed the importance of spreading the word early to build up excitement for the day." As she spoke, she clicked for the next slide. "We should also consider special business hours on—" A collective gasp interrupted her sentence. She looked out at her audience and now saw confused looks, and whispering had started. Her head swung toward the screen, and she nearly had a freakin' heart attack.

"Is that a family tree?" someone shouted out.

"What's going on, Kelly?" Zoe called out from her seat.

"I...I...don't know." Her heart pounded against her chest as heat rose through her neck to her face. She was frozen in place, staring at the Blake family tree. How on earth did that get into her presentation?

On the top of the tree was her granny, Martha. The next row identified her children—Ralph and Kelly's mom.

Breathe, Kell. Breathe.

Then the tree branched out from Ralph with three women's names. His first wife and the mother of Frankie. His current wife and mother of Juniper, Summer. And Ariel's mother with Ariel's name beneath.

Oh. My. Freakin'. Goodness.

"No. No. No. No. This can't be happening." Kelly lunged for her computer and attempted to close the presentation, but to her horror, she only enlarged the family tree slide. "No!" She willed her fingers to work correctly, but her mind was racing with too many thoughts to think clearly. Finally, she jabbed at enough keys to get the presentation closed.

Out of the corner of her eye, Kelly saw Ariel spinning her wheelchair around and heading for the door.

"No. Wait. Please!" She couldn't let Ariel leave without explaining. Kelly went after Ariel, and as she closed in on her friend, she realized she had no explanation to offer. She had no idea how the family tree got into the presentation. She'd never seen it before. "Wait. Ariel. I can explain. I think."

Ariel's wheelchair came to a halt, but she didn't look back at Kelly. That was okay. It was something, at least. Kelly raced around so she was face-to-face with her friend.

"Please, let me try to explain." Kelly leaned forward, her hands in prayer position. "I am so sorry."

"How could you? Now everyone knows Ralph is my father." Ariel was on the verge of tears.

"I don't know what to say other than I did *not* create that slide. I swear!"

"Oh, come on. It was in your presentation you were so proud to show off. If you didn't create it and add it to the presentation, who did? Tell me! Who did?"

Kelly straightened. She had no idea. But she'd find out.

"Yeah. Thought so." Ariel pressed the power button on her wheelchair and zipped out of the room.

Kelly rubbed her face and sucked in a ragged breath. This couldn't be happening.

"What was that all about?" Liv came up beside Kelly. "Why on earth would you include your family tree in the presentation? Why would you even make a family tree? And Ariel's your cousin? Since when?"

Kelly lowered her hands and rested them on her hips. "It's a long story. But trust me, I didn't make that stupid family tree. I checked the slides last night, and that one wasn't included because I never made it."

"Kind of hard to believe." Liv looked around at the others in the room, who were huddled and whispering. "You really messed up this time." She walked past Kelly and out of the room.

* * * *

Kelly splashed cold water on her face, sucked in a breath, and hit her face with another splash. What just happened was really, really bad. Her mind raced with thoughts, but none of them solved the problem of how she would fix this new mess. Finally, the faucet automatically shut off, and she heard voices coming closer to the restroom door. She scrambled to hide. But where? Not wanting to be seen or talk to anyone, she had only one choice. She darted into the stall at the very end and locked the door shut.

"It's never a dull moment when Kelly Quinn is around. Right? I can't believe she did that. Can you?" The nasal voice sounded like Taylor, the assistant manager of Fashion Essentials, a women's clothing shop. "Let me freshen up my lipstick, and we can go. Guess we shouldn't be surprised. I've heard she's been acting strange lately."

"What's been going on?" asked Davina, the manager of the global gift market just off Main Street.

"For starters, she called the police the other night to report a break-in. Turns out she forgot to lock the back door. Talk about a waste of our precious town resources." Taylor tsk-tsked. "Then somehow her cat got loose in the boutique, and Aurora Cavendish had an allergic reaction."

"Oh, boy. Aurora can be a nightmare," Davina said.

"And now this. What do you make of that family tree slide? Is Ariel really Ralph Blake's daughter? Haven't Ariel's parents been married like forever?"

"Sounds scandalous, doesn't it?" Davina chortled.

Kelly's lips pressed together. Her tummy ached at the thought of the rumors that would be flying around in no time. The Lucky Cove gossip mill loved a good scandal.

"Poor girl. Ariel's been through so much, and now this. You know, if it's true, I can't see how she could forgive Kelly for announcing it to the world like that," Taylor said.

"Why do you think Kelly did it? I thought they were friends," Davina said.

Kelly's eyes watered again, and she fought back the sobs threatening to escape, revealing her presence. She covered her mouth with her hand. She'd not make a sound. They wouldn't know she was there.

"Well, now they're family, and it's a whole different ball game. Seriously, how much do we really like our family members?" Taylor's laugh trailed off. "I know this isn't funny. I'm sincerely worried about Kelly. You know, I heard someone say the other day that she was becoming unhinged."

Unhinged? Kelly dropped her hand, and she was ready to burst out of the stall and make it clear to them that she wasn't disturbed in any way. But she let the scene play out for a moment in her head, and she realized it would make a case for the argument against her.

"Okay, I'm all set. Ready to get out of here?" Taylor asked.

A moment later, Kelly heard steps toward the door, and then the door opened and closed. She waited a few seconds before opening the stall door and poking her head out. The coast was clear.

She scurried to the door and then slowly pulled it open. She looked in all directions to ensure there was no one in the hallway. After her disastrous presentation, she couldn't face any of the other committee members. Luckily, the meeting hadn't lasted much longer after she hightailed it to the restroom. Hiding around the corner, she watched the lingering committee members leaving town hall. Finally, it looked like the coast was clear to go back into the room and get her computer.

Kelly ducked into the meeting room, which just a short time ago was filled with her peers and she was wowing them with her brilliant ideas. Now she was being whispered about and being accused of being unhinged.

In a flurry, she packed up her computer. All the while, she had a feeling of being watched.

She looked over her shoulder a couple of times and swore the portraits of prominent members of Lucky Cove's history that hung on the walls were staring at her. *Paranoia now?* This wasn't the way to prove she wasn't unbalanced. Shaking off the thought of being surveilled, she slipped her computer mouse into a pocket in her bag and then slung it over her shoulder.

Keeping light on her feet to not alert anyone of her presence, Kelly made her way out of town hall without encountering anybody. As she passed by the town offices, she heard voices, but no one came out into the corridor, so she continued forward. A sense of relief surged through her as she stepped outside. All she wanted to do was to go home and hide under her bed covers, but she had plans to visit the marina and then meet Breena at Miranda's apartment.

She was tempted to cancel and hide out, but what would that accomplish? Nothing.

She pulled out her phone and sent Breena a text that she had to make a couple of stops and then would head over to Miranda's apartment.

"Kelly! Hold up!" Courtney stomped toward her with her finger pointed in the air.

Kelly braced herself for another unpleasant interaction with Courtney.

"Looks like I've missed the committee meeting. Want to know why?" It really hadn't sounded like a question she expected Kelly to answer. "Because I was being questioned by Detective Barber. Because of you, I'm now a suspect. What on earth did you tell him? Don't you think my family has been through enough?"

"I'm sorry...."

"Save it. Let me tell you something you don't know. My family lost more than money because of Daniel Parnell. My father committed suicide because he couldn't live with the guilt of bankrupting his family."

The news hit Kelly so hard she felt the air seep out of her lungs. "I had no idea. I'm sorry, I really am. I only want to find the truth, the person who killed Miranda and probably Bud."

"I don't want your apology. I want you to stay out of my business. And my life!" Courtney turned and walked away.

Kelly's bag slipped from her shoulder, and she hunched over, resting her hands on her thighs. Lightheaded with a rapid heart rate and her whole body trembling, she feared she'd collapse right there.

What is happening to me?

She wiped her forehead, which was moist with perspiration. She struggled to straighten up and get her breathing under control. It took all her concentration to force herself to slow her breathing.

A ping of her cell phone brought her back to the here and now. She fumbled to pull the phone out of her purse. It was a text from Breena.

Closed up. I need to pick up a few things for Tori.

Right. She had a date to break into Miranda's apartment and search it.

Heck of a way to spend the rest of her morning after she just blew up Ariel's life.

No problem. Don't rush.

* * * *

Kelly returned to her apartment, sneaking into the building so as not to be seen by Pepper. By the time she unlocked her door, she was certain that news about her debacle at the committee meeting had already spread through town, and she wasn't up for answering questions. Nope. She hoped to be like an ostrich and keep her head buried in sand and wait for it to all blow over.

A girl can dream, she thought, as she did a quick change into khakis and a long-sleeved thermal top with coordinating vest for her visit to the Lucky Fishing Boat Marina.

She made it back out to her Jeep without being stopped by Pepper. Within twenty minutes, she was parking at the marina and emerging from the vehicle to find Ray Collins. The morning had become overcast, gray clouds filled the sky, and the wind was picking up speed. She checked her weather app and it warned that a storm packing a wallop was working its way up the coastline. Perfect way to end one of the worst days of her life.

Walking along the decking, Kelly's sense of balance was solid, thanks to the pair of boat shoes she wore. She glanced down and gave a slight smile, proud of her impulsive yet practical purchase over the summer. The iconic shoes gave excellent traction as she walked along the boat slip, searching for Breena's dad. She spotted him up ahead talking with another man standing on the stern of a boat.

"Kelly Quinn?" Breena's dad's voice boomed. Mr. Collins wore a buttoned flannel shirt over dark jeans. His frame was large, and he was impressively strong from working on boats for over thirty years. And he gave the best bear hugs. "What on earth are you doing here?"

"It's a gorgeous day, so I thought I'd stop by and deliver these." She handed him a pastry box from Doug's Variety Store. Not only did they bake gigantic, delicious muffins, but they also baked the best fudgy brownie. Though, she never shared that opinion with Liv. "Brownies from Doug's."

"I love these. Hey, Mitch, this is Kelly Quinn, Breena's friend and boss." He laughed. "Hard to believe little Kelly Quinn is a boss now. Weren't you just graduating from high school?"

Kelly smiled. "Some days, it feels like that. Nice to meet you, Mitch."

The older man nodded and then excused himself, disappearing down the cabin of his boat, the *Golden Lady.*

"While I'm happy to receive this gift, I don't think you came all the way out here to deliver brownies. How about you tell me what's up." Mr. Collins wrapped an arm around Kelly's shoulders and guided her along the boat slip, heading back to the shop.

"Nothing gets past you." Kelly had known her ruse wouldn't work. Mr. Collins always seemed to know when his daughter and her friends were up to something. "I'm hoping you can fill in some blanks for me about Nolen Briggs."

Chapter 17

"Nolen Briggs? He's been dead for what…nineteen, twenty years? Why are you interested in him?" Mr. Collins paused a moment before he opened the door to the marina shop. "Oh…wait. You're poking around Miranda Farrell's murder. Breena mentioned that over dinner the other night." He set the pastry box on the counter. The shop was bright and organized for maximum efficiency for boaters and crew. "I told her I didn't think it was a good idea. But you girls never did listen. Guess I was wasting my breath."

A black lab trotted out from the back and greeted Kelly, nudging with her snout, and then sat ready for pets. Kelly obliged, patting the dog on her head.

"Molly is the marina's official greeter." Mr. Collins opened the box and took out a brownie. "Nolen loved dogs. Back then, we had Trixie. She loved being out on the water and never passed up a chance to go out with him."

Molly sniffed the air in the direction of the brownie, but when it was clear she wasn't going to get any, she moseyed off and settled on a bed behind the counter.

"What happened to Nolen? I've heard he had an accident, probably slipped and hit his head, killing him."

"Yeah, it was a bad day." A look of melancholy spread over his face. "His boat was docked, and he was doing routine maintenance that day."

"How do you know?" Kelly asked.

"I saw him while doing my usual walk around the marina to check things out after I opened the shop. It was about eight o'clock. I remember it was one of those foggy mornings. Took forever for the fog to burn off." Mr. Collins helped himself to another brownie. "Anyway, a couple hours later, I was helping Paddy with his engine. Paddy's always been a cheap old bird and no way was he buying a new engine. Can't tell you how many times I had to work on that stupid thing. Anyway, something seemed odd on Nolen's boat."

"What was it?"

Mr. Collins shrugged. "I don't know. It was just something that seemed off. Anyway, I boarded the boat and found Nolen. Dead."

"What happened?"

"The best I can figure is that he slipped. Unfortunately, accidents do happen, even to experienced boat captains."

"Other than Paddy, was there anyone else at the marina that morning?" Kelly asked.

Mr. Collins let out a breath and then rubbed his chin. "It was a long time ago, Kelly." He was quiet for a moment, and then his eyes widened as wrinkles crossed his forehead. "Well, I'll be...."

"What? What is it? You remember something, don't you?"

"An engine starting." He looked astonished by the memory.

"A car engine?"

"Yeah. I heard it when I reached Nolen's boat." Mr. Collins sank down onto the stool behind the counter and remained silent, as if to get his thoughts together. "I haven't thought about that morning in years. It was quiet. Early in the season, so we were getting boats ready. Nolen had been working on his for about a week. My wife was busy back there." He gestured to the closed door behind him. "She still does all the bookkeeping and administrative work. I saw Lyle Cunningham. He was the boater I was talking to before I saw Nolen walk past the front of the shop."

Kelly glanced over her shoulder at the large-pane window that gave a view of the docks and fish cleaning station.

"You then went outside to talk to Lyle?"

"Yeah. He was having money problems, and I had someone interested in his boat. I grabbed my jacket and went to tell him. It was damp that morning. The rawness cut right through you." He stared off into space. "There was someone else...walking away from Nolen's boat. Well, I'll be damned. After all this time. How did I not remember that?"

Kelly hung on every word Mr. Collins said. He'd remembered something from the day of Nolen's death. She couldn't help but feel proud that she had played a small role in him recovering a long-ago memory. It could support Violet's claim that her brother's death hadn't been an accident, but rather murder. Too bad Mr. Collins hadn't gotten a good look at the person walking from Nolen's boat. It could have been Miranda. Or someone she paid to kill her husband.

"Did you see the person's face? Was it a man or woman?"

Mr. Collins shook his head. "Sorry, Kelly. I don't know."

The front door opened, and a white-haired man entered. "Hey, Ray, did my order come in yet?"

"Just arrived yesterday afternoon. Let me go get it. Sorry, Kelly, I have to get back to work."

"I understand. If you remember anything else, call me, okay?"

"You got it. Thanks again for the brownies. And be careful, sweetie."

Mr. Collins had always called his daughter's friends "sweetie." She hadn't heard that endearing nickname in a long time. "I will." She spun around and walked to the exit, passing the customer, who opened the door for her. Even though her day had turned into a massive disaster, she slowed down and allowed herself to take in the beauty of the marina. Seagulls swooped overhead and dove into the water for their snacks. The rumble of boat engines filled the air, and the slapping of water against the docks transported her back to her childhood when she and Caroline spent hours watching waves and crabbing.

Her trip down memory lane ended when the door of the boat shop opened, and that white-haired man exited, stepping around her as he headed to his boat. It was time for her to get going. She had to meet Breena at Miranda's apartment.

She hurried to her Jeep, and when she slipped in behind the steering wheel, she sent off a text message to Nate. She hadn't heard back from him about her other text. Either he already knew about Miranda's possible stalking, was too busy to reply, or he was taking the whole break thing seriously and cutting off communication. Her fingers furiously typed before she changed her mind. She worried she was giving him another reason to make their break permanent.

Found out something. Thought you'd want to know. Ray Collins remembers seeing a person walking away from Nolen Briggs's boat before he found Nolen dead. Hopefully, he'll remember more. Just wanted to pass along the info. Hope you're good.

Kelly was about to start the ignition when a Suburban pulled into the space next to her. The driver was the last person she expected to see at the marina. Yolanda Cavanaugh. She'd wanted to talk to Bud's sister, and now it looked like she had her chance.

Kelly opened her car door and stepped out, walking around the front of the Jeep. Yolanda pushed open her door and climbed out of her vehicle. She acknowledged Kelly and then reached in for a stack of file folders. Yolanda was five years older than her brother, though she looked ageless.

Her tanned skin was flawless, her brunette hair was glossy, and her plaid barn jacket couldn't hide her enviable curves.

"Hi, Yolanda. I'm so very sorry for your loss. Bud was a great guy." Kelly couldn't believe she was talking about Bud in the past tense. His death hadn't fully sunk in yet. Though the image of his body on the kitchen floor had been seared into her brain.

"Thank you." Yolanda closed the Suburban's door. Her eyes were puffy and red from crying, and she offered a weak smile. "I miss him so much. I can't believe he's gone. Bud never hurt anyone. It's not fair."

"I agree. Never in a million years did I think when I arrived at the Travis house, I'd find him…well, you know. It seems so senseless."

"That must have been awful for you. It still doesn't seem real." Holding the file folders close to her chest, Yolanda walked toward Kelly. "And honestly, I'm terrified for when it feels real. I don't think I'll be able to handle it."

Kelly reached out and gave Yolanda's arm a reassuring squeeze. "You're strong; you'll be able to handle it. But it won't be easy. Trust me. And if you ever need to talk, I'm always available." Having lost her granny and her cousin within a year had seemed unfair, downright cruel. Though, she was starting to see that those two experiences had given her the ability to help others work through their grief.

Yolanda took in a deep breath. "Thank you. Now, I must get these to my boss. He's been staying on his boat since he left his wife. I wish he'd rent a house. I'm getting tired of traipsing out here to the marina every day. Though, it's keeping me busy and I'm grateful for that."

"Do you mind if I walk with you?" Kelly asked.

"If you want." Yolanda started walking. Her steps were weighed down by sorrow. She slightly tilted her gaze upward. "Looks like a bad storm is rolling in."

"It does. We don't need a nor'easter." A raging storm would be the cherry on top of the miserable day Kelly was having.

"Maybe a storm would knock some sense into my boss, and he'll move back onto land," Yolanda said with a little smile. "I know why I'm here, why are you? Thinking of buying a boat?"

"A boat definitely isn't in my budget. I came to talk to Mr. Collins about Nolen Briggs," Kelly said.

"He's been dead for years." Yolanda climbed the steps to the deck and continued forward to her destination. "What are you up to?"

"I want to find the person responsible for Miranda's and Bud's murders. I think it's connected to the deaths of Nolen and Daniel."

"How are you going to do that? You're not a police officer."

"I'm not, but I do seem to have a talent for tracking down killers. Who knew?"

"I never would have guessed it. Back in high school, you had a talent for attracting the eyes of some pretty hot boys." Yolanda smiled at the memory of those high school days. She had taught algebra, and Kelly had been one of her underwhelming students.

Kelly's cheeks warmed at the memory. "Those days are far behind me. Thank goodness."

"You had a rough senior year. I'm glad you came back to Lucky Cove and reconnected with Ariel," Yolanda said.

Kelly's stomach lurched at the mention of Ariel. She doubted now that they would ever be able to reconnect as friends.

"I'm not sure what you think you can do, but if you could help flush out the person responsible for killing my brother, I'm in. What do you need from me?"

That's what Kelly liked about Yolanda; she had always been straightforward.

"Tell me how Bud met Miranda."

Yolanda stopped in front of a thirty-two-footer boat. Kelly didn't know too much about them, but she knew the basics thanks to growing up in Lucky Cove and knowing Breena. Yolanda's boss owned a very pricey cruiser perfect for day fishing trips or extended outings.

"It'll have to be the short version because I really need to get on there." Yolanda gestured to the vessel. "They met while he was in New Jersey visiting our cousin. You know how hard he always fell for women. This time, it seemed right. They did the long-distance thing for a while until he convinced her to come back to Lucky Cove."

"When they first met, did he know who she was? That she'd been married to Daniel Parnell and Nolen Briggs?"

Yolanda shuffled, adjusting her stance. "He didn't know when they first met, but she told him within a few days. She seemed to be very open about her past. I remember him calling that week and telling me about her. While he really didn't recall those events, I did. Then again, he is…I mean…was five years younger than me." Her chin trembled and her eyes watered. "I told him what I knew, and then he told me about Miranda and what a great woman he thought she was."

"I'm surprised she would have wanted to come back to Lucky Cove. I've heard a lot of people weren't kind to her. Some called her a black widow, while others thought she made off with all the money Daniel had embezzled."

"Bud told me Miranda had been reluctant to come back." Yolanda stopped talking and looked up at the boat's deck. Kelly guessed she was looking for her boss and when she didn't see him, she continued. "Though she came around to the idea. She told me that she wanted to reclaim her life. She'd been living under a cloud of suspicion all these years, even while living in a different state. She wanted to be happy, and Bud made her happy."

Listening to her talk about Miranda, Kelly got a very different version of the dead woman than she had from Erica, Ricky, and even her uncle.

"Did they keep their relationship a secret?" Kelly remembered Walt's comment that he thought Bud had a new girlfriend.

"Not really a secret. Though they weren't advertising it. Miranda wanted to get settled in town and open her shop. Bud wanted to do whatever Miranda needed." Yolanda's gaze drifted. "He had such a kind heart."

"He certainly did. Do you know if he had a problem with anyone?"

Yolanda scoffed. "You knew Bud. He never had a problem with anyone. However, Miranda did. Look, I don't know if she took the money Daniel embezzled. Since it has never been found, it's possible she had it. The Miranda I got to know recently was nothing like the person being portrayed by the likes of Erica Booth or Ricky van Johnson."

"Yolanda!" A male voice called from the boat, and then a clean-shaven man in his midforties appeared. "I have a call with Parkerson in ten."

"Be right there. Sorry, Kelly, I have to go. Thank you again for your condolences." Yolanda hurried away and climbed aboard the boat.

Kelly swung around and headed for her Jeep. The murders weren't the only mysteries. "If the money was never found, what happened to it? Who has it?"

* * * *

"Is it true?" Breena pushed off from the side of her car, where she waited for Kelly's arrival, and scooted forward. "Is Ariel really your uncle's daughter? Your cousin?"

Kelly stared in disbelief. It'd just been a couple of hours since her catastrophic presentation. The town gossips certainly weren't slacking in their duties.

"I don't want to talk about it." Kelly started walking toward the two-family house. The ordinary colonial had a neat border of dwarf shrubs around its front and side. Just enough for some interest, but not too much for maintenance. Though, the garden bed needed a raking. The overhanging oak tree was losing leaves. Which reminded Kelly she needed to schedule the fall cleanup for around the boutique.

Breena followed. "How exactly did a slide of your family tree wind up in your presentation? Why do you even have a slide of your family tree? Are you working on a genealogy project? That would be cool."

"I don't have a slide, I'm not working on a…never mind. Do you have the key?" Kelly stopped and hitched her thumb toward the side door.

"Of course I do." Breena pulled out the keys from her jacket's pocket. "It's understandable if you don't want to talk about Ariel. But I wish you would because I'm dying to know."

Kelly leveled a flat look at her friend.

"What? I'm being honest." Breena unlocked the door. "And honestly, I'm nervous about going into the apartment."

"Don't be. There's no indication this is off limits by the police, so at least we won't be tampering with a crime scene," Kelly said.

One of Breena's brows shot up at the word "tampering." Kelly gave herself a mental kick for poor word choice. She started climbing the stairs. Maybe if she kept Breena moving, she'd have less time to rethink their plan.

When they reached the small landing, Breena unlocked the apartment door and peered in before stepping forward. "It feels weird being here."

"Like you're walking on her grave?" Kelly looked around the living room space. Tall ceilings, plain white walls, and average wood flooring. A typically bland rental. And it made Miranda's furniture pieces look out of place with their modern lines and bold colors. She had a flair for drama, even in her décor.

"Ewww…that's a very creepy image, but accurate." Breena set her backpack on the coffee table.

Kelly's nose wriggled. "Do you smell something? Spicy. Like a man's cologne."

"Faintly." Breena hung back while Kelly moved farther into the room. "What are you looking for?"

"Not sure. Have you been here before?" Kelly browsed the bookshelf between the two front windows. Artificial plants, decorative books, and framed photos filled the shelves. She zeroed in on those three photographs. Miranda was in them all, and she'd been smiling. She looked relaxed and very young in the first two pictures. The men in the photos with her were Daniel, Nolen, and Bud. Her heart squeezed seeing Bud's big grin. She pulled her gaze from the photographs and scanned the room for more. There weren't any.

"Nope. Everything seems normal, doesn't it?" Breena sounded disappointed. "I don't know what I was expecting."

"A nice big clue would be great." Kelly moved from the bookshelf unit, and she stood in the center of the room. "I'm going to check out the rest of the apartment."

"Okay. Don't take too long. I'm not sure what I thought when I agreed to come here. It's creepy." Breena wrapped her arms around herself. Her cell phone pinged, and she grabbed her backpack to pull out her phone.

"You were thinking we might find something to help solve the murders." Kelly walked across the hardwood floor and down the hall. Its walls were bare, and the closed doors were simple and worn by age and use. She opened the first door on her left. It was the kitchen. Next was the bathroom, and on her right was the bedroom. She stepped over the saddle and looked around the room. She smelled that spicy scent again. And now it was more potent.

"Hey, Kell! I have to go. My mom texted and said I need to get home ASAP."

Kelly poked her head out of the bedroom. "What's going on? Is it Tori?"

Breena appeared in the hall. "Tori is okay. Mom's not saying what's up. Are you okay by yourself?"

"Sure. Just leave me the keys."

"They're on the coffee table. Be sure to lock up. I'll text you later." Breena pulled open the door and exited the apartment.

Now alone, Kelly didn't want to linger too long. She wasn't too far into the room when she noticed a framed photo on the floor between the bed and closet. She got closer to the photo, and when she picked it up, she realized it had been smashed. Tiny bits of glass were scattered on the carpet. It was Miranda and Daniel's wedding photograph. He had his arm around her waist, and she was kissing him on the cheek. They looked happy.

Had he really been a monster? Stealing from friends and hitting his wife?

Based on that photograph, Kelly would have guessed no. Another reminder that you can't believe everything you see.

She set the frame on the nightstand, and just as she turned to face the closet, it suddenly opened, and a person lunged forward, knocking her down with force. Kelly screamed as she landed on the floor, her head striking the edge of the nightstand. She barely made out the figure dressed in all black and smelling like the spicy fragrance as they raced out of the room.

She reached for the side of her head and rubbed the tender spot. It took her a couple seconds to process what had just happened, but the sound of the door slamming shut had her bolting upright and chasing after the person.

Kelly sprinted out to the hall and followed the intruder down the stairs, though they were out of sight. But it was the only way out of the house. She wasn't giving any thought of what she'd do if she caught up with the attacker. All she knew was that she wasn't going to be pushed around and then cower. When she reached the first floor, she jerked open the door. Outside, she was greeted by falling temperatures and a sweep of wind that chilled her to the core. She gathered her twill jacket closer to her body and didn't hear the person approaching from behind.

"What are you doing here?" he asked.

Chapter 18

The male voice had Kelly swinging around with her arms up, hands balled into fists. She was ready for whoever it was. "Ah-ha!" Kelly caught herself before throwing a punch at Ricky, who looked stunned. "Why were you hiding in Miranda's bedroom closet?"

"What are you talking about?" Ricky glanced at the side door and then back at Kelly. "I wasn't in the house."

"No? Then why are you out here? Are you following me?" Kelly lowered her hands, but she wasn't lowering her guard against Ricky. As far as she was concerned, there was a big, fat question mark hanging over him.

"I asked you what you're doing here."

"It's none of your business." Kelly wasn't about to admit to snooping upstairs. Especially not to him.

"I'm sure the police will be interested in your trespassing," he countered, looking and sounding smug. Because he sold fancy cheeses and ingredients that were difficult to pronounce, he had a bad habit of believing he was better than other people. He'd shared Summer's opinion of Kelly's boutique; to him it was nothing more than a thrift shop.

"Go ahead. Then you can tell them why you were up in the apartment, hiding."

"Are you crazy? Whoever you're talking about wasn't me. I just got here. Go ahead, feel the hood of my car."

"How long have you been out here?" Kelly looked at his blue BMW parked next to her Jeep. When she arrived, it wasn't there, so it looked like he was telling the truth. "Did you see someone come running out?"

"Only you," he said. "Now, do you care to tell me what's going on?"

"How about you tell me why you're here?" Kelly crossed her arms and waited for an answer.

"Okay, you got it." Ricky returned to his car and opened the passenger side door. He retrieved a shopping bag and returned to Kelly. "I'm here to deliver these groceries to Mrs. Allen. She lives on the first floor. She's on her way back from outpatient surgery, and her daughter asked me to drop these off to her."

"Oh." Kelly sighed. Of course Ricky was there to do a good deed. Wait. To make sure he was telling the truth, she leaned forward and sniffed him. He didn't smell like spiced cologne, but he sure gave her a weird look. "That's very nice of you."

"It's the least I can do. Mrs. Allen was my mother's best friend." He walked past Kelly, heading to the front of the house. There, he left the bag by the door. He walked back to Kelly and shoved his hands into his jacket pockets. "Now it's your turn."

"I came to help Breena look through Miranda's apartment. She's tasked with closing the shop, and Miranda had taken some work home with her." Kelly knew she was telling an outright lie, but she didn't trust him enough to tell the truth.

"Where's Breena? And why did you come running out of the house looking like you were ready for a fight?" He craned his neck and stared at her face. "Are you hurt? You're bruised."

Kelly instinctively touched the side of her face where she'd hit the corner of the nightstand and winced. "It's nothing." But she was sure it was going to hurt like the dickens.

"What happened in the apartment?" Ricky asked. He sounded concerned.

"Breena had to leave, so I stayed to look for any paperwork, and then out of nowhere, someone jumped out of the closet and knocked me over."

"What?" He swung around and looked up at the second-floor windows. "Why was someone hiding up there? You need to report this to the police."

"I will. But before I do, I have to ask you something."

"What is it you want to know?" Ricky returned his gaze to Kelly.

"What did you mean when you told Miranda she'd regret coming back to Lucky Cove?" Looking back, it seemed he'd foreshadowed her death.

He shook his head as he walked toward his vehicle. "Miranda had a lot of enemies in town."

"And possibly a stalker. Was it you, Ricky?" she asked.

"What are you talking about? I never stalked her."

"Where were you the morning she was murdered? Don't say you were at work because you weren't."

Ricky's jaw tightened, and his face clouded. "Who told you that?"

Kelly angled her head and considered what to say next. His demeanor had changed, and she didn't want to answer any more of his questions. What she wanted to do was to get away from him.

"Fine. But don't say you haven't been warned. Stay out of things you have no business getting involved in." He turned and stomped away to his BMW.

She remained standing in her spot until Ricky pulled his car out of the driveway. As Kelly watched the car disappear down the road, she couldn't shake the feeling she was being watched. She lurched forward, looking for any signs of the person who had attacked her in the apartment.

If it wasn't Ricky up in the apartment, who was it? And where had that person gone?

* * * *

Kelly was halfway back to the boutique when she got a frantic call from Breena, and she made a very unlawful U-turn on Main Street to head to the hospital. Breena was so upset, all Kelly could make out was that her dad was in the emergency department because something terrible had happened. She really didn't need to know more. Her friend was scared, and Mr. Collins had been hurt. She tried not to speed, but the adrenaline pumping through her body made it difficult to control her foot on the accelerator. Though, having a lead foot at the moment did get her through a few yellow lights, which meant she got to the hospital sooner rather than later.

Her follow-up calls to Breena on the drive to the hospital went straight to voice mail, leaving Kelly's mind to consider the worst-case scenarios.

She parked in the first space she found and ran into the emergency department. The automatic doors swished open, and she entered, looking for Breena.

There, in the corner of the waiting room, she spotted Breena with her daughter, Tori, seated close to her. Breena stroked her daughter's hair while her eyes were glassy and swollen from crying.

Kelly bolted forward but was intercepted by Gabe. Boy, was she glad he was there. Having a friend who was a police officer came in handy, especially when she wanted information.

"What happened to Mr. Collins? Is he okay?" Kelly asked.

"What we know at this point is that he was attacked from behind." Gabe tossed a look to Breena and her daughter. "It's not good, Kelly. The head injury is significant. Also, we recovered a tire iron from nearby. Whoa." He leaned forward to get a closer look at Kelly's face. "What happened?"

"It's nothing." She should have checked the visor mirror before coming in and added some makeup if necessary. By the look on Gabe's face, it was necessary.

"Nothing? It's a bruise on your face. Did someone hit you?" Gabe's jaw clenched, and his nostrils flared. He'd always been protective of Kelly. After all, they were as close as siblings growing up. Now adults, they still looked out for each other. He reached out and positioned her face so he could get a better look at the injury.

She swatted his hand away. "Not really. Maybe. It all happened so fast. But I'm okay."

Gabe pulled back his hand and folded his arms, ready to hear all the details. And he would want them all. He was a good cop who followed the rules and filled out all the forms. There would be no shortcuts with him. So it was better just to tell him, and then she could get to Breena.

"I was in Miranda Farrell's apartment, and someone came rushing out of the bedroom closet and knocked me down. I hit the side of my face on a nightstand."

"Why were you in her apartment? Who gave you permission to go in there? Did you report the incident?"

Kelly looked at Breena. The last thing she needed was to be implicated in a possible trespassing case. So, Kelly chose not to answer Gabe's first two questions. Of course, he would notice, but that conversation would have to wait for another time.

"I didn't report it. At least, not yet because I got the call to come here. Look, this may sound crazy but I think Ricky van Johnson is following me."

"Following you? Why?" Gabe rubbed the bridge of his nose. It was a little thing he did when he was deciding on how much information he wanted to know. Needless to say, he did it a lot when Kelly was around. "Honestly, I'm not sure I want to know what you've been up to."

"Good to hear because I don't feel like telling you." She patted his arm. "I'm more interested in Mr. Collins. Any leads on who attacked him?"

Gabe shook his head. "Not at this time."

"I just saw him a little while ago at the marina." Kelly thought back to the people she saw when she was there. The white-haired man who held the door for her, Yolanda, and her boss. She doubted any one of them attacked Mr. Collins with a tire iron.

"What were you doing at the marina?" Gabe asked.

"I took him brownies from Doug's, and I asked him a few questions about Nolen Briggs. You know, he remembered something from the day Nolen died. He saw a person by Nolen's boat! That means there's a chance Nolen's death wasn't an accident. He could have been murdered."

"Hold on. Slow down, Kelly." Gabe's phone buzzed, and he held up a finger to indicate he needed a moment. Then, after checking the message, he returned the phone to its pouch on his utility belt.

"It's possible Nolen's killer is still in Lucky Cove, and maybe he killed Miranda and Bud." Kelly's spidey senses were telling her that was the case. She was sure of it.

"Did you tell anyone about this?" Gabe asked.

"Only Nate. I texted him before I left the marina." Her eyes went wide, and her hand flew up and covered her mouth as a new horror settled over her. "I did this, didn't I?"

"No. No, you didn't." Gabe reached out and grabbed hold of Kelly's arms.

"I did. I put him in danger. If anything happens to him, it's my fault. How could I have done that to Breena? She's my friend. And little Tori. That's her grandpa in there." Kelly's chin trembled as her eyes watered.

"This isn't your fault. No one other than Detective Barber knew what Mr. Collins told you."

"But Mr. Collins could have told someone about our conversation after I left. A conversation he wouldn't have had if I hadn't jogged his memory. Or the killer followed me there and got nervous. Or…" Her words stopped when an unpleasant thought crossed her mind. She remembered the spicy fragrance in Miranda's apartment, and Nate favored a similar cologne. And she told him about Mr. Collins's recovered memory. Could Nate be… No. Impossible. Nate was a newcomer to Lucky Cove. He had no connection to Nolen, Miranda, or Daniel. But maybe that would explain why he pushed her away. Thinking that he was involved was crazy, proving the rumors of her becoming unhinged true. She needed to stop being so suspicious. Especially about the man she thought she was falling in love with. It wasn't Nate, but it could have been the guy delivering groceries.

"Ricky! I told you I think he's been following me. How else would he have known I was at Miranda's apartment? He followed me to the marina, saw me talk to Mr. Collins. He always wondered if he'd been seen when he killed Nolen. That has to be it!"

"Whoa. Take a breath and think about it a little more clearly. After the marina, he followed you to Miranda's apartment. How could he be in two places at once? If he followed you, how did he assault Mr. Collins?" Gabe asked.

Leave it to Gabe to throw a wrench in a scenario Kelly conjured up with absolutely no evidence to back it up. Wait. “He wasn’t there when I arrived at the apartment. He may have had enough time to attack Mr. Collins and get to the apartment.”

“But, how did he know you’d be there?” Gabe asked.

Right. Kelly knew he had a good point. “I see your point. Besides, if he followed me from the marina how would he have gotten up to the apartment before me? I don’t know. I can’t think clearly.” She rubbed her temple on the side of her face that wasn’t throbbing.

She noticed the door from the treatment area of the emergency room open, and a doctor emerged. He walked toward Breena, who popped up, nearly toppling Tori. She gave her daughter a quick check and then settled her in the chair.

The doctor looked serious from Kelly’s vantage point, but Breena remained unemotional. Perhaps he was delivering some good news. The doctor stopped talking and then Breena said something, prompting him to pat her on the shoulder. A few more words were exchanged, and then he returned to the interior workings of the department.

“I really need to talk to Breena. Can we finish up in a few minutes?” Kelly didn’t give him the chance to say anything. Instead, she dashed away to her friend. “Gabe filled me in. What’s the update on your dad?”

Breena sucked in a breath, and then her face crumpled as she dissolved into tears. It looked like there wasn’t any good news. Kelly closed the space between them and pulled her friend into a hug.

“He’s in a coma. I don’t understand how this happened. Who would do such a thing?” Breena sniffled between sobs and then pulled back. She reached for her backpack and pulled out a tissue to dry her eyes. “They induced the coma to help reduce the swelling in his brain.”

“What does that mean? Is he going to be okay?”

“If the swelling goes down, yeah, he should be okay. Right now, they’re not sure. But my dad is tough. I know he’ll pull through.” Breena returned to her seat and wrapped an arm around Tori. The little girl looked up at Kelly, and it nearly crushed her heart. Where there should have been a big, bright smile was a deep, uneasy frown. She then nestled closer to her mom for security.

“He’ll pull through. He is one of the strongest men I know,” Kelly said.

Breena kissed the top of Tori’s head and looked back up at Kelly. Her eyes narrowed, and her lips parted as she stared at Kelly’s face. “What happened? You have a bruise.”

Kelly waved away Breena's concern. She didn't want to add to her worries. "It's nothing."

"Don't tell me it's nothing. Gabe!" Breena gestured for him to come over, and when he joined them, she pointed at Kelly's face. "Look at her. She's been hurt."

"I'm fine. You don't have to worry about me." Kelly then gave Gabe a look that said to back her up or else. He knew she had some very unflattering photographs from high school that would embarrass him.

"Right. She's fine," he said flatly.

That hadn't sounded very convincing to Kelly's ears. And by the look on Breena's face, she wasn't convinced either. Time to change the subject.

"Is there anything you need, Breena?" Kelly asked.

After a moment, Breena nodded. "Yes. Would you mind taking Tori to my cousin's house? I don't want her to stay here." She gave her daughter another squeeze.

"Sure, I can take her now. Okay?" Kelly asked, happy to be able to help Breena and her family. After all, she might be the reason why Mr. Collins was in a coma now.

"Great. Thanks. Joanne is expecting her." Breena whispered in Tori's ear while Kelly cozied up to Gabe.

"Will you follow up with Ricky van Johnson?" she asked.

"And I'll be following up with you," Gabe said. "There are a lot of blanks that need to be filled in."

Kelly nodded in agreement. "Tell me about it."

* * * *

After dropping Tori off at Cousin Joanne's house, Kelly made a beeline back to the boutique. She slammed the door shut and cringed. Making a racket wouldn't help anything, but it sure felt good to slam something. Inside the staff room, she walked to her desk and dropped her purse. It landed with a thump. Her foul mood had time to flourish on the drive from Joanne's house to the boutique. Now she was taking it out on inanimate objects. She dropped into her chair and slumped. Everything was a mess, and she was no closer to finding the killer.

Maybe Frankie had been wrong about her *thing*. It appeared she'd failed at that as well as failing as a friend to Ariel and as committee chair. She squeezed her eyes shut at the memory of the meeting.

Her cell phone chimed, alerting her to an incoming text. She reached into her purse and pulled out the phone to read the message. It was from

Jay, the vice president of the chamber of commerce. Her head started to throb again as she read the short and straight-to-the-point text.

Given the incident at the committee meeting, the board had an emergency meeting and decided to remove you as the committee chair.

She tossed the phone on the desk and flung herself back. There had been many low points in her life—Ariel's accident, losing her dream job at Bishop's department store, her granny's death, Becky's murder—but at that moment, she'd never felt so defeated and hopeless. For the next ten minutes, she tried to figure out what to do next, but she didn't see a clear way out of the mess she'd created. There were too many people upset with her, and she might well be losing her mind.

But maybe I'm not.

Kelly straightened and placed her hands on the desk. Drumming her fingers on the wooden surface, her thoughts replayed the last few days since finding Miranda's body. Maybe Marvin had been onto something when he noted that all these troubles started right around Miranda's murder. Sure, she could have misplaced a few things, forgotten to lock doors. She'd admit all those things were possible. What she knew as absolute truth was that she hadn't sabotaged her own presentation to intentionally hurt Ariel's feelings. No way.

Someone else did that. She was certain.

But how?

"Someone hacked my computer," she murmured as she lifted her computer bag from the floor. When she snuck into the boutique to change for her visit to the marina, she had swapped out her tote for her purse.

But how? She had all sorts of security set up. Indeed, an alert would have popped up. Wouldn't it?

The ringing of her phone interrupted her thoughts. She glanced at the caller ID and saw Courtney was calling. Not in the mood to be yelled at again, she shoved the phone away. She tried her best to get back to figuring out how her presentation had been sabotaged, but the unanswered phone grated on her. She grabbed the phone and pressed the button to accept Courtney's call.

"Please don't hang up. I'm sorry." Courtney's words were rushed, and she sounded sincere. "I've had some time to cool off and think about everything."

Not what she expected to hear, but Kelly was relieved to hear she had one less person who hated her.

"There's no need to apologize. I understand why you reacted the way you did. I probably would have done the same thing."

"Thanks for not being angry at me. Look, I'm calling because I came across a file box at my mom's house and in it was the name of the private investigator my parents hired."

"You have his name? What is it?" Kelly scrambled for a piece of paper and pen. "I'm ready."

"Ben McDougal. I checked before calling you, and he's retired, living out on Montauk."

Kelly jotted the name down and the phone number Courtney gave her. "Thank you, thank you, thank you."

"What are you going to do now?"

"I'm not sure. Though I do promise I'm going to make up for all the distress I caused you."

Courtney laughed. "I'm going to hold you to that. Be careful, okay?"

Kelly ended the call. She unzipped her computer bag and pulled out her laptop. After she turned it on and opened the browser, she searched for Ben McDougal. Nothing helpful came up. It looked like she'd be taking a drive out to Montauk to follow up in person with the retired PI.

Chapter 19

A knock at the back door interrupted her online search. She pushed back from the desk and stood. She wondered if Gabe was coming to follow up on their earlier conversation. How on earth would she explain her and Breena trespassing into Miranda's apartment? When she opened the door, those worries vanished. Instead of Gabe, she found Marvin standing on the other side. He had a knack for being there for her when she needed a friendly shoulder to lean on. She threw her arms around him and squeezed him tight.

"This is some greeting. I should show up unannounced more often." Marvin shuffled her inside and closed the door. Unbuttoning his coat, he asked, "What's going on?"

Kelly's head dipped back, and she moaned. Yes, she realized she was being dramatic but it had been a heck of a day.

"Where to start? It's been a horrible, horrible day. Coffee? I could use some coffee." She headed to the kitchenette. "Do you want a cup?"

"No thanks. I cut off caffeine after lunchtime." He followed her, stopping at the table. He became quiet as he appraised her. "What happened to your face? Did you fall?"

"Yes, I did." Technically, it wasn't a lie. "Just a little clumsy." At the counter, she prepared a pot of coffee. After scooping out the grounds, she returned the canister to the upper cupboard. She pressed the On button, and the machine started brewing within seconds. "I'm so glad you stopped by. Though I'm curious why you have." She said a silent prayer that he hadn't heard about what happened at the committee meeting.

"I came to give you this." From his coat pocket, he pulled out a set of house keys. He walked to Kelly and held them up. "For you. And I won't take no for an answer."

Kelly caught her lower lip and considered the offer. The timing couldn't have been more perfect. She'd drive out to Montauk, find the private investigator, and spend the night at the cottage. Sure, Marvin was hoping she'd spend a few days out there to rest and recharge, but there was too much to do. Like, take back her life and her reputation. For the first time in days, she felt energized and clearheaded. She intended to not only get answers from Ben McDougal but also find out who tampered with her presentation. Kelly snatched the keys out of Marvin's hand and smiled.

Marvin looked surprised. But bless his heart, he didn't look one bit suspicious of her. "This was easier than I thought. I expected it would be hard to convince you to go away for the weekend."

She kissed him on the cheek. "I appreciate your concern and your offer to use your cottage. I'd better go tell Pepper and then pack."

"You do that, dear. Let me write down the address for you and then I'll be going. Be sure to call if you need anything." Marvin pulled out a business card from his pocket and walked to the desk for a pen.

Uh-oh. Kelly's computer was open to the search page for the private investigator. If Marvin noticed it, he'd put two and two together and figure out why she was all of a sudden so eager to go out to Montauk. She set her coffee down and rushed to the desk.

"Here, let me get this out of your way." She shifted the computer off to the side, its screen out of Marvin's view.

"There's a list of important numbers at the cottage. But I don't think you'll need them." He set the pen down and gave Kelly a warm smile before leaving the staff room.

Pepper entered just as Marvin left out the back door. "Was that Marvin?"

"Yeah, he stopped by to drop off the keys to his cottage. He's offered it to me for the weekend." Maybe she would stay an extra day. She could take a walk along the rocky point of the island and let her mind and body unwind. Then she'd return home with a fresh perspective to help solve the mysteries at hand.

Pepper clapped her hands together as she grinned happily. "You're going for some R&R? Wonderful news."

She wouldn't be getting much rest, but she didn't want to tell Pepper her plans. Kelly returned to the counter and picked up her coffee.

"I know it's not ideal with Breena's dad being in the hospital. Also, will you check in on Howard? Feed him?"

"Of course, I'll take care of the little guy. And don't worry about the boutique. I can manage. Plus, knowing Breena, she'll want to work a few hours to keep her mind off her dad. It's such a shame. I can't imagine anyone wanting to hurt her dad. He's a big teddy bear." Pepper poured herself a cup of coffee. "When you come back home, maybe you'll talk to your therapist again. Just something to think about. No pressure."

"I'm not some fragile flower."

"Of course you're not." Pepper sipped her coffee. "What I've realized over the years is I cannot force someone to do something. All I can do is share my opinion. What you decide to do is up to you."

It most certainly was, and there was another decision Kelly made in a nanosecond.

And it looked as if she was back to the whole leaping without thinking phase. That was risky. Not in the sense that her life would be endangered. But, instead, a door could be slammed in her face.

* * * *

Kelly could have easily driven past the house without stopping, without making one last-ditch effort to reconcile with Ariel. Standing on the welcome mat, which seemed ironic considering she knew she was far from welcomed, she pressed the doorbell and impatiently waited for the door to open. When it did, Ariel didn't look pleased. So Kelly put out her hand to keep the door from being shut in her face.

"I know I'm the last person you want to see. Please, give me a couple of minutes. And if you're still angry with me, I'll go away." Kelly had to push back on the door to keep it from closing. Her friend was stronger than she expected. "For good. I promise."

"Fine. Start talking, and it better be good." Ariel released her grip on the door and then folded her arms. She looked skeptical that Kelly could say anything that would change her feelings.

"I swear that I didn't put that family tree slide in my presentation."

"Then how did it get in there?" Ariel asked.

"My computer was hacked. I discovered someone has been accessing my computer remotely, but the IP address is blocked." After telling Pepper about her last-minute trip to Montauk, Kelly did some cybersleuthing. But her bare-minimum skills had gotten her only so far.

Ariel's features softened…slightly. "Why would someone do that? It's not like you have state secrets on your computer."

"I know! It's nuts, right? But it explains how that slide got into the presentation. And it got me to thinking about my phone. I think it was cloned." When a confused look crossed Ariel's face, Kelly gave her a quick rundown of what had happened with her text messages.

The skepticism on Ariel's face faded. "Who do you think is responsible?"

"The killer, of course. I figure that the killer is concerned I'll be able to identify them. What better way to discredit me than to sabotage me enough that people will question my credibility and sanity? The police won't believe anything I say. No one would. Heck, even I started to question my sanity."

"That's a pretty big leap, Kell. It's not like you're Hercule Poirot or Miss Marple." A slight smile tugged on Ariel's lips. "Or Jessica Fletcher."

"Are you throwing shade on my sleuthing prowess?" Kelly removed her hand from the door and propped it on her hip. "How many murders have I helped solve? It stands to reason I'm making the killer nervous. And they should be because I'm going to figure out who it is." Kelly caught her lower lip between her teeth. On her drive over, she got a call from Summer. Her uncle, with his attorney, had another meeting with Nate. Her tummy rumbled with dread. Another interview wasn't a good sign.

"How are you going to find the killer?" Ariel asked. "Especially since your computer and possibly your phone, too, have been compromised."

"I left my computer at the boutique along with my phone. I'm going to pick up a burner on my way to Montauk." Burner. She sounded like she belonged in an episode of *Law and Order.*

"Why are you going out there?"

"To track down a private investigator who worked for Courtney's parents. They hired him to investigate Miranda years ago. I want to find out what he knows. Also, Marvin gave me the keys to his cottage so I can stay over."

Ariel blinked and then navigated her wheelchair back into the foyer. "Give me fifteen minutes."

"For what?"

"To pack an overnight bag."

"You want to come with me?"

"This way, you won't have to buy a burner phone. By the way, you're not cool enough to say burner phone." Ariel smiled before turning her wheelchair around, leaving space for Kelly to enter. "I'll be packed in a flash. Why don't you raid the kitchen for some road trip snacks?"

* * * *

Ariel's van bounced over the rutted driveway, which cut through a thick forest of evergreens swaying in the wind. The storm that had been working its way up the northeast coastline was getting closer to Montauk. The Atlantic churned with the energy of the nor'easter, and now the rain had started. Not heavy yet. That would come later in the evening. When Marvin offered her the cottage, the storm had been on track to take a sharp right turn and go out to sea, maybe taking a swipe at Nantucket. When she loaded her bag into Ariel's van, the radio meteorologist broke the news—the model had been wrong. Kelly rolled her eyes. She hadn't been surprised since the weather models had less accuracy than her wonky scale.

"My goodness. Look at it," Ariel said wistfully.

The weathered-shingle cottage with white shutters finally came into view. Set back from the road for privacy, it was easy to drive right past. *Adorable* had been Kelly's first impression of the dwelling. A breezeway connected the cottage to a one-car garage where Marvin parked his beat-up old car. He had been able to afford a getaway in the high-dollar real estate haven of the rich and famous, yet he drove a vehicle that looked like each drive would be its last. He certainly was a quirky old guy.

"It's so cute." Ariel pulled up to the garage and shifted her van into Park.

"Let me open the door." Kelly clicked her seat belt, tugged up her hood, and exited the van. The vehicle had been customized to meet Ariel's needs and was why they opted to take it rather than Kelly's Jeep. Zipping her jacket, she hurried to the garage door and unlocked it. Tucking the key ring back into her pocket, she reached down and grabbed the handle. One would think the pricey pad would have come with an automatic garage door opener. With the garage opened, she dashed back to the van.

"Why don't you go and open up the house? I'll be right behind you," Ariel said.

"Okay." Knowing her friend was fiercely independent and didn't need assistance, Kelly wouldn't argue with her. Their friendship was on the mend, and arguing was the last thing she wanted to do. She closed the door and then opened the back door, grabbing both overnight bags. Then, with one anchored on each shoulder, she rushed across the soggy grass to the front door.

The light spritzes of rain that had been simply annoying were now turning into big plops, and they landed hard on her head and shoulders. She pulled open the screen door. Her fingers grasped the keys in her pocket, and with a bit of jiggling, she got the door open. Again, pricey pad with old locks. She couldn't help but wonder if Marvin used a real estate agent or just wrote a check.

The solid wood door finally opened, and she stepped inside, dropping the bags on the floor. While adorable had been her first impression of the cottage, now inside, her impression was *wow*.

The open-concept space lured her in. From the gleaming hardwood floors to the large windows, sliders, and skylights to the wood-burning fireplace. Kelly immediately felt welcomed.

No wonder Marvin had found inspiration here.

There was a knock at the door that connected the kitchen to the breezeway. She hurried toward the door and unlocked it, letting Ariel inside the cottage.

"This is amazing." Ariel sounded as wowed as Kelly had felt when she stepped inside. "I can see why Marvin fell in love with this place. It's so isolated. Maybe we can watch a scary movie tonight."

A chill worked its way through Kelly. She hated scary movies. And given what was going on in her life and the two dead bodies she found, she was more in the mood for a rom-com.

"Come on. I promise I'll choose one without much gore. Maybe we can find an old black-and-white one," Ariel said.

"Maybe." Kelly walked back to her bag and pulled out the burner phone she picked up at a convenience store outside Montauk. Even though Ariel offered her phone to use, Kelly wanted to make sure neither of them was without a phone. "I have some sleuthing to do."

"Well, I'm starving. How about I go and get us a pizza?" Ariel suggested.

Kelly wasn't keen on the idea of her friend driving out in the nor'easter.

"Let me put these bags in the bedrooms and I'll go with you."

"Don't worry. I'll be fine. It's only a few raindrops, not a hurricane." Ariel wasn't waiting for Kelly's agreement. She was on her way to the breezeway door. "Be back soon."

The door closed behind Ariel, leaving Kelly to start worrying. She wanted to think it was because she was nervous about her friend driving in the inclement weather, but there was an uneasiness she couldn't shake.

And being alone in the secluded cottage ramped up that feeling.

Maybe if she did something to distract herself, the unease gripping her body would disappear. She could start with the reason why she came out to Montauk—contact the private investigator and arrange a meeting with him. Considering the weather, it probably would have to wait until tomorrow.

With her cell phone in hand, and the notebook she'd started jotting in on the drive out to Montauk with her thoughts about the murders, she found the PI's phone number. But when she tapped on the phone, she noticed the bars were low. So she walked around the living area, trying to get a better signal.

She even tried the bedrooms and the one bathroom in the cottage to no avail. There wasn't a better signal anywhere. Then, back out in the living room, she realized that no cell service was a downside to living way out on the island. And possibly why there was a landline on the kitchen's peninsula. She walked across the room and settled on a stool. She dialed and waited for the PI to pick up.

"McDougal," a gruff voice said.

"Hello, Mr. McDougal. My name is Kelly Quinn."

"Not interested in what you're selling."

"I'm not selling anything. I'm calling about a case you worked twenty years ago. Miranda Farrell."

"Why the hell are you interested in her? Haven't you heard she's dead?"

Kelly rolled her eyes. "I know. I found her body."

"Sorry to hear that." Though his voice lacked sympathy. "Why are you calling me, then?"

"Annabeth Travis's daughter gave me your name. Her parents hired you to find out if Miranda had been involved with her first husband's embezzlement. Do you remember?"

"Of course I do. I remember every one of my cases. Some more than others…let me tell you, those are the ones I'd like to forget."

"I'd like to meet with you to discuss the case. Are you free tomorrow?"

"I'm retired, so I'm free every day." He paused. It sounded like he took a drink of something. "But it won't be necessary to get together. I came up with zilch that she'd been involved in Daniel Parnell's crimes. And to boot, I found nothing to indicate she'd been unfaithful during her marriage. Though she'd cozied up to Nolen Briggs quickly after she buried the first husband. Mr. and Mrs. Travis weren't thrilled with my report. But I couldn't help finding what I found, which was not much."

"I can understand why they weren't happy with your findings." Kelly believed they wanted to blame a living, breathing person for their financial loss and the effect it had on their lives. All they got was a confirmation that they'd hired the wrong financial advisor.

"Why are you so interested in Miranda Farrell?"

Because my uncle is a primary suspect.

Because I believe the killer is messing with me.

Because I can't help myself.

"Thank you for your time." Kelly returned the receiver to the cradle and wrote a summary of her call with the PI. One word wrapped up the call—disappointed.

Kelly grabbed the notebook and pressed it close to her chest, carrying it to the living area. The PI had been a dead end. In hindsight, she probably shouldn't have expected much from the conversation. If he had found something way back then, Miranda would have been arrested and charged and possibly still be in prison. It was starting to look like Miranda had been a young bride who married the wrong man.

Dropping down on the sofa, Kelly eyed the overnight bags and considered unpacking, but what she wanted to do was sit with her thoughts and her notes.

She rested her head against the comfy sofa and let her gaze drift around the room. Little touches reminded her of Marvin—like the painting over the mantel. The seascape was breathtaking. Marvin had not skimped on using striking colors to create a powerful piece of art. He captured the roughness, unforgiveness, and loneliness of the ocean in a way that captivated the observer, drawing her into the work with no desire to leave. Known for his illustrations for decades, Marvin definitely had broadened his artistic wings over the summer. Coming full circle, her gaze landed on a framed photograph of Marvin and his family. She recognized his grandson, Barlow. The business shark had accused her of wanting to weasel money out of his grandfather last spring when she'd needed funds to replace the boutique's roof. In that picture, Barlow looked so young. And sweet. "Well, he definitely grew out of that phase," she muttered. She hadn't seen him in months and wanted to keep it that way.

The man between Marvin and Barlow must have been Marvin's son. The family photograph reminded her of the ones around her parents' home and those she didn't have in her apartment. She glanced at her phone. Well, her temporary phone. All her photos were stored in some cloud. Her gaze flicked back to Marvin's family photo, and a decision was made—she'd have the most important photographs on her phone printed and framed. She cocked her head sideways. The Childers family portrait reminded her of another photo she'd seen recently—the one at Courtney's mom's house. The one with Miranda and a man.

Kelly unfurled her legs and straightened up. She was sure it had been Miranda in the photograph because she'd seen pictures of her in the *Weekly* and her wedding portraits. But the man Miranda was with was a mystery.

She popped up from the sofa and moved to the peninsula and redialed the PI's number, but her call went to voice mail.

Shoot.

She dropped onto a stool and squeezed her eyes shut, trying to place the man's face onto the face of someone twenty years later.

He wasn't Ralph. She was 100 percent certain of that. The mystery man didn't have Ricky's square jaw, and he also looked older than Nolen would have been at the time.

Who is he?

The mystery man would have been around her uncle's age today.

Think, Kelly, think.

There was Walt, but he was at least ten years older than Ralph and Ricky. And the face shape didn't seem to match. Who else? She tapped her fingernails on the countertop as her mind did a mental inventory of older men in Lucky Cove. Men who could have known and possibly killed Miranda and poor Bud. Since she believed the killer was the one who hacked her computer and phone, whoever it was had to have some tech proficiency. But was that mystery man in the photograph the killer?

A name finally popped into her head.

"No…it couldn't be him," she said, shaking her head. "Could it? He's been around lately."

Chapter 20

With his name bouncing around in her head, Kelly opened her notebook and started writing all the places she'd run into him lately.

Just before we found Miranda and Uncle Ralph standing over her body.

He was at the Lucky Cove Inn the day of the chamber luncheon.

He's been in the boutique.

I've spotted him on Main Street a few times but never gave it a second thought. Why would I have?

Kelly set her pen down and stared at her list.

Could the mystery man in the photograph have been Paul Sloan? The retired police detective who'd investigated the deaths of Miranda's two husbands? The same former cop she sat down with for coffee and asked questions about his investigations?

Things finally started to fall into place. She remembered what Pepper had said about Paul's late wife's father being abusive. And that he had been killed by a hit-and-run driver who had never been found.

"She always liked what I picked out."

He rescued her. He dressed her. He controlled her.

"A police officer would have the ability to cover up a murder. Especially if he had been the one in charge of the investigation."

Chills skittered up, down, and sideways on her skin as her stomach constricted with dread. She reached for her cell phone and tapped it on. Still no bars. Shoot. She grabbed the landline phone and dialed.

"Please, please, please pick up."

"Hello?" Pepper's voice sounded cautious. She probably expected there to be a robocaller on the other end of the unknown phone number.

"Hey, Pepper, it's me," Kelly said.

"Thank goodness. I thought you were some robocall trying to sell me an extended warranty or threaten to haul me off to jail."

"I get it." Kelly laughed and it felt good, though a bout of somberness quickly displaced the lighthearted moment and she asked, "Any updates on Mr. Collins?"

"Nothing has changed. I talked to Breena a little while ago. She's so worried, and I don't blame her. Hey, why aren't you calling from your cell phone?"

"No signal, so I have to use the landline in Marvin's cottage." It wasn't a lie. She just left out the part about her not having her cell phone with her. Yet, she still felt a clutch in her chest for not being completely honest.

"Huh." That little sound was as potent as Pepper's infamous glare.

Oh, boy.

"I guess you wouldn't get a signal since your phone is here in the boutique. What are you up to, Kelly? And don't tell me nothing."

Busted!

"I left my phone there because I believe someone hacked into it and has been spoofing messages. So, I picked up a cheap phone on the way out to Montauk. And that isn't getting a signal here."

"Hacked your phone? What are you talking about?" Doubt was laced in Pepper's voice, and Kelly couldn't blame her. While the older woman had embraced a more youthful way of dressing and styling her hair, technology wasn't her thing. Spoofing, cloning, and hacking were concepts she had difficulty wrapping her head around. And honestly, so did Kelly.

"I can explain more when I get back home. I'm calling because I have a question for you. What do you know about Miranda and Daniel's marriage? Any recall of him possibly beating her?"

"Talk about a doozy of a question. Why are you asking? Wait…never mind…I don't know…."

Then the line went silent.

"Hello? Hello? Pepper?" Kelly grunted. Not having phone service wasn't a good thing. She stood and walked to the window beside the front door. Hard sheets of rain now pelted the house, but so far, it appeared the wind hadn't kicked into overdrive.

So why was the phone dead?

She moved back from the window and wrapped her arms around herself. Ariel would be back soon, and then she'd toss the overnight bags into the van, and they'd hightail it out of Montauk.

All she could do now was wait.

And try to finish putting the puzzle together.

She returned to her notebook at the peninsula.

Could the highly decorated retired detective be a killer?

If so, why?

Kelly let her mind wander freely with all thoughts, hoping for a reason not to suspect Paul. As her mind turned over ideas, her gaze wandered. On an open shelf in the kitchen was a platter with a pretty floral pattern.

Flowers.

She remembered seeing Bud carrying a bouquet of roses. And the following day, when Miranda's body had been discovered, the bouquet had been pulled apart, and the rose petals had been crushed. Up until now, she hadn't given much thought to them.

For the moment, she allowed herself to assume her uncle had killed Miranda and tried to think of a reason why he would have destroyed the roses. It made sense the vase would have been knocked over during a struggle. But why crush the petals? That seemed to be a more intimate act done in a fit of jealousy rather than an angry rage over real estate.

A gust of wind slapped the house, and her head swiveled to the window by the door. Next, a boom of thunder sent her jumping. Then a flash of something outside the window sent her for a closer look. She thought she saw a figure pass by. Now all she saw was a dense grove of trees swaying in the intense winds.

Perfect for a vacation getaway, bad for being alone with a killer on the loose.

A creak from inside the house perked her ears up. She gave a sideways look to the breezeway door that led from the kitchen to the garage. Maybe Ariel hadn't secured it after taking off to get the pizza.

Keep it together, Kell.

A click from the breezeway door had her doing a complete turn so she faced the kitchen. She gulped. Ariel hadn't returned. She would have heard the van pull up to the house.

So who was entering?

She stepped away from the window, not taking her gaze off the door as it opened.

First, a sliver.

Her heartbeat kicked up into HIIT-on-steroids-level territory.

Then a little wider.

"Get out! I've called the police! They're on their way!" Even if she had called the police, it was unknown how long it would take for their arrival. Montauk wasn't Manhattan. And she was isolated out there on the end of the island.

Finally, he pushed the door completely open and stood there with a grin on his face. Paul Sloan knew the police weren't on their way.

"I said get out!"

"Spunky. I like it. Though I think your spunk may have gotten you in over your head."

Kelly looked around for a weapon. Anything that would fend off Paul would work. Like a knife. But he was standing in the kitchen, where the knife block was. She needed something else. Anything.

"Usually, people find my spunk endearing." She did her best to keep her tone light. She had a thought. A crazy one. But given she was alone with a killer and no way to get help, crazy or not, she went with what she had. Maybe, just maybe, she could convince him she didn't think he was a cold-blooded killer and buy herself some time. "I have to admit, seeing you let yourself in was a little nerve-racking. Being here alone had my mind wandering with all sorts of thoughts, and then you showed up. Bah!" She flashed jazz hands, hoping to lighten the mood.

"I really wish things could have turned out differently." He didn't look like he was buying her act. Instead, he eyed the knife block as he gave a dark laugh. "In fact, I said those exact words to Miranda before I strangled her."

Kelly gulped. Her plan had failed. So it was time to start piecing another one together. ASAP.

Paul pulled a knife from the wooden block. He raised it up and studied it. "This should do nicely."

Kelly's eyes enlarged, and a wave of fear swept through her, but she struggled to maintain some clarity. There was a way out of this. She was sure of that. She just had to figure out what it was. Until then, she had to try and talk some sense into the murderer. "You don't have to kill me, Paul."

He smirked. "Yes, I do. Because you simply cannot mind your own business. I tried so hard, but you kept pushing and pushing. You're a tenacious little—"

"Why did you kill Miranda?" Knowing she couldn't overpower Paul easily, she'd keep him talking until she could get a surprise advantage over him. Then she'd worry about the next step when she got there. Her plan was obviously fluid.

"You want to understand me? What makes me tick?" His voice teased, taunting her. "What makes me kill?"

Kelly's stomach lurched, almost tossing up the snack she ate on the drive out to Montauk. But instead, she forced herself to keep it together. "Yes."

He stepped forward, slamming the knife on the peninsula, leaving his fingers covering the handle, ready to grip it at a moment's notice.

"I've been in love with her since the first time I saw her. I'd just been promoted to detective and was celebrating with some buddies at the Lucky Cove Inn, and Miranda was our waitress. By the end of the evening, I got up the nerve to ask her out. She turned me down."

"Why? What did she say?"

"She was already seeing someone. I found out she'd started dating Daniel Parnell. Guess it made sense. He was wealthy and a widower who swept her off her feet." He pounded his fist on the peninsula. "I would have worshipped her!"

Kelly flinched. "Of…of course you would have. Daniel probably just looked at her like she was a prize to win. Men like him usually do that." She started piecing together the bits of information about Paul she'd learned. He'd been a good cop, believed in law and order. He'd married a woman who had been abused by her father, who had been killed. He'd fallen in love with a woman who chose a man based on his wealthy status only to become a victim. Paul had been a rescuer. That's how Jocelyn Bancroft described the next-door neighbor in *Danger Next Door.*

"The honeymoon didn't last long. Daniel started hitting Miranda."

"How do you know that? Did she report it?"

He shook his head. "I saw him do it."

"You stalked her when she was married to Daniel?" Kelly slowly inched back. What her next move would be was unknown. She just needed more space from Paul Sloan.

"I had to make sure she was safe. Near the end of Daniel's life, things got worse for Miranda. I think he was struggling to keep his embezzlement a secret, and it made him drink more, and he took his anger out on Miranda. I had to save her before he killed her."

Kelly didn't miss the irony in his statement.

"What did you do?"

The corner of his lip tugged upward, and he looked so proud. "I helped him along with his heart attack. But, really, it was only a matter of time before he had one. Overweight, drinking too much, and under so much stress."

"You drugged him, didn't you? Then, as the detective on the case, you made sure what you did wasn't revealed."

He shrugged. "Why let my promotion go to waste?"

"Did you really think Miranda would fall into your arms?"

"A guy can dream." The cockiness he'd shown only moments ago vanished. Now he looked like a heartsick teenage boy. "If it weren't for that Nolen Briggs, yeah, she would have fallen into my arms."

"Had they been having an affair?"

"No. But I saw how Briggs looked at her. Once she gave the signal, he pounced. He only wanted her money. Like everyone else, he believed she'd gotten her hands on the money Daniel stole. I knew as soon as he realized there was no big payout, he'd dump her, breaking her heart."

"That's why you killed him? Because you thought he only wanted her money?"

Paul nodded. "I wasn't going to let him hurt her."

"It was you Mr. Collins saw at the marina that morning!"

Paul nodded again.

The confirmation wasn't surprising. But what she hadn't expected were the next puzzle pieces to fall into place. And it had her reaching for the top of the side chair to steady herself.

"It was you who attacked Mr. Collins!"

Paul shrugged. "I couldn't take the chance he'd remember something else that could place me at the marina that morning."

"How could you? Don't you have a conscience?" Kelly spat.

"I have a heart of gold." He opened his arms up wide. "I protect those I love and will destroy those who threaten my loved ones. Like you."

Kelly recoiled, but there wasn't anywhere for her to go. She was cornered. She concentrated on steadying her nerves. There wasn't any choice; she had to shove down every ounce of fear. Her life depended upon it. Being calm and clearheaded was the only way she'd get out of that cottage alive.

Despite what Paul Sloan proclaimed, he hadn't been in love with Miranda. Instead, he'd been obsessed with her. Now he had nothing to lose.

"Why did you kill Miranda?" Kelly asked. "You said you've loved her since the first time you saw her."

Paul swept up the knife and then bolted out from behind the peninsula, stopping short. A slow, menacing smile crept onto his lips as he leaned back against the counter.

"I hoped we'd have another chance when she returned to Lucky Cove. My wife had just died and Miranda was back. It was as if we were meant to be together." He looked at Kelly reflectively, and she couldn't help but wonder how delusional the man was. How had nobody ever realized he was a danger? No—that he was a killer.

"She came back here to be with Bud. How could you think you stood a shot with her?"

His lips pressed together, and now anger seeped from every pore, making Kelly rethink her strategy. Who was she kidding? At the moment, she had no strategy.

"Because she needed me! Stupid, stupid woman! I called her. I wanted to talk to her. Convince her that Bud wasn't the right man for her. He couldn't protect her like I had. But she refused to take my calls."

"You were at her shop the morning she was killed. That's where you were coming from when I bumped into you!"

"I begged…begged her to dump Bud. Do you know what she did? Do you?!"

Kelly shook her head. The steadiness of her nerves she'd been able to maintain was faltering. The sight of him tightening his grip on the knife made her lightheaded.

"She laughed at me. Laughed!"

"That wasn't very nice." On the other hand, agitating him wasn't helping the situation, so maybe placating him would.

"Well, she stopped laughing when I told her what I did for her twenty years ago. Then the way she looked at me…like I horrified her."

Kelly could understand the feeling.

"I told her I did it all for her. The woman was ungrateful, right to the very end. She told me that she never asked for my help. She didn't have to ask. What choice did I have? I had to save her."

"Like you had to save Dorie from her father."

He nodded.

"Why did you kill Bud? Was it to punish him for dating Miranda?"

Paul shook his head. "He called me and told me he knew I'd been watching Miranda—he called it stalking—and was going to tell the police. You can see why I couldn't let him do that."

"Don't you think it's time to tell the truth? The police are looking at my uncle as a suspect. You know he's innocent. Why don't we talk to Detective Barber together?"

"Let's be real, Kelly. Your uncle isn't a very nice guy. Come on, he refused to acknowledge his own daughter all these years. Not exactly a stand-up guy, wouldn't you agree? That morning I hadn't planned on him finding Miranda or that you and your friends would then find him standing over the body. It was lucky for me, right? Though, bumping into you had been a mistake. A bad one. The last thing I needed was for you to put two and two together."

"You've been the one gaslighting me all this time." Kelly's body rocked with anger; her hands balled into fists so tight that her nails bit into her flesh. "You made me question everything—my judgment, my memory, my actions."

"I didn't have much of a choice. I figured the best way to handle you without resorting to murder was to discredit you. It really wasn't too hard. You had a rough year, your breakup with that lawyer fellow and your cousin's murder, I figured it wouldn't be hard to make you appear unreliable. Then who would believe you?"

Kelly regained control of her emotions. She needed to stay levelheaded if she wanted to get out of there alive. "How did you do it?"

"Not that hard. Over the years, I've picked up some skills. Maybe a few not so legal. Like entering premises without being detected. Like planting a listening device in that pretty new plant by your desk."

"That's how you heard everything. Ariel's secret. My plan to come out to Montauk."

"I made a point not to let my little gray cells waste away in my golden years, so I've kept up on technology."

"Hacking into computers and spoofing and deleting text messages."

"Too bad you won't have the opportunity to experience self-improvement in your golden years." He pushed off the peninsula. "Time to get this over with before your friend gets back. I'd hate for her to come in and see me here. I don't want to have to hurt her."

Kelly didn't want that either.

He motioned to Kelly with the knife. "Let's get this over with."

Chapter 21

Kelly sucked in a deep breath as she squared her shoulders. *Yes, let's get this over with.* After being attacked in Miranda's apartment, which clearly had been Paul, she vowed not to cower. And she wasn't about to start now. This was her chance. Her one chance to make a move to throw the deranged detective off his game. She had to strike his Achilles' heel.

"I understand why you feel you need to do this. But you've never killed a..." she purposefully let her voice trail off.

"Killed a what?"

"A woman." Her lower lip trembled, and she hoped he saw it. She needed for his unhealthy obsession to be a protector to kick in. It would be the only way she'd stay alive. "At least not intentionally. Paul, you've spent your whole life protecting women. I bet Dorie wasn't the first woman you helped. You were that guy in high school. The big brother who kept an eye out for the girls who seemed...vulnerable. Now, here we are. It's one thing to kill a man who had abused someone you loved, and what happened with Miranda was fueled by hurt, but how will it feel to kill me, a young woman who is loved by her family and friends, in cold blood?"

He snickered. "Nice try. But your attempt at reverse psychology isn't going to work."

She lifted her shoulders. "Can't blame a gal for trying."

"Spunky right to the very end." He sprang forward.

Kelly zigged to the side, half her body landing on the love seat.

Paul's balance faltered, but being in shape and nimble, he righted himself quickly and pivoted toward Kelly, closing the space between them.

She raised her leg and kicked him in the groin, pushing him backward, ignoring his string of curse words. His balance wavered enough, and he landed on the floor, the knife falling from his grip, clanking when it landed away from his body.

Kelly hopped up and tried to run past him, but he grabbed her ankle, yanking her down.

She tried to resist, break the hold, but he was too strong.

She landed on the floor hard. The impact of her chest hitting the hardwood knocked the breath out of her, leaving her body feeling like a rag doll when Paul tossed her over on her back.

He straddled her and gripped her throat with his fingers and squeezed.

She gasped for air, clawing at his hands, and her feet kicking. Her eyes watered; her screams caught in her throat as his grip tightened.

The energy in her legs faded, and her fingers weakened, one by one letting go of his hands.

Her eyelids fluttered closed.

Her hands fell to her side.

Darkness overtook her.

Silence.

Then a scream and a rush of air in her throat jolted Kelly's body.

Another gulp of air worked its way through to her chest as the screaming continued. She opened her eyes and found Paul's body convulsing, and then he slid off her to the side.

With the weight of Paul off her, Kelly scrambled to sit up and figure out what the heck had happened. She dragged in deep breaths, filling her chest and reminding her brain that her near-death experience was just that—near death.

"Are you okay?"

Kelly's head lifted in the direction of the familiar voice.

Ariel?

When did she come in? How…what exactly happened? Kelly's thinking was muddled thanks to almost being choked to death. Ariel must have come in through the breezeway. Since Kelly had been fighting for her life, she hadn't heard the door open or Ariel wheel in.

Kelly pulled her gaze from Paul's body and looked at Ariel, who was lowering her weapon.

"You have a taser?"

"Lucky for you I do." Ariel navigated her wheelchair toward Kelly, swerving around Paul's body. She tossed Kelly her cell phone. "He's the killer, isn't he?"

"Yes, he is. My cell doesn't have service here." Kelly was about to throw it back to Ariel.

"Mine does. It has all the bars. Call for help on our way out to the van," Ariel said. "I don't want to be in here when he gets up."

Kelly got to her feet, swaying a bit as she got her balance back. "I agree." She tapped on the phone as she followed Ariel out of the house. Passing the kitchen, her nose wriggled from the aroma of the freshly baked pizza pie. She would have loved to grab a slice on the way out. Fighting for your life worked up an appetite.

"I'll buy us another pie. Come on!" Ariel led them through the breezeway to the garage where her van was parked.

Locked inside the vehicle, they waited for the police to arrive. Kelly wondered if Paul had started stirring yet. How long would the effects of being hit by the taser incapacitate him? Still holding on to Ariel's phone, she tapped on the internet app and started a search for information.

"What are you looking for?" Ariel peered over from the driver's seat.

"How long Paul will be out of commission for." Kelly tapped a link and then tapped out of an annoying pop-up ad. "I wonder how much longer we'll have to wait for the police?"

"I'm sure the storm is a part of the delay. Then again, being way out here doesn't help." Ariel's gaze returned to the windshield. There was barely any visibility. "It's getting worse. But don't worry, I can drive in it if we have to get out of here."

"How long did you hold the taser on him?"

Ariel shrugged. "A few seconds?"

"He can be immobilized for up to fifteen minutes. That's not a lot of time."

"It's not." Ariel checked her watch. "We have a few minutes. If the police aren't here, we're leaving."

Kelly closed out of the website and looked at her friend. "Thank you. You saved my life."

"Me and Blue Belle."

"Blue Belle? You named it?"

"Of course I did." Ariel laughed, and then she turned stone-cold serious in a blink of an eye. "I couldn't believe what I was seeing. He was choking you. He was going to kill you."

Kelly closed her eyes, bracing herself as her insides quivered. "I felt myself slipping away." She wiped away tears and then reached out for Ariel's hand and squeezed tightly.

"I'm glad you're okay. I couldn't let you die. I needed to make sure you know that I forgive you." Her voice choked. "And I forgive my parents and Ralph. After the car accident, I realized I couldn't hold on to anger if I wanted ever to be happy again. I think it was the shock of the news that caused me to forget that lesson. I have so much to be grateful for. For starters, I have a bigger family. And you're my cousin!"

Kelly bowed her head. Hearing Ariel say she forgave her melted her heart and threatened to completely undo her. Approaching sirens had her looking up out the windshield and saved her from dissolving into a hot mess of emotion.

"Any tips for giving my statement?"

Kelly gave Ariel a side look.

Ariel smiled. "What? You are the expert in the area."

Chapter 22

Kelly reached the front door of her uncle's house and paused a moment before welcoming the last guest to arrive. She did a quick check in the mirror over the accent cabinet. She smoothed her hair, which was swept into a low updo with a slight bouffant—a nod to a traditional style with a modern twist. Then she ran a hand down her formfitting sweater dress. The self-tied dress had a modest V-neck and an over-the-knee split skirt. It was the perfect shade of orange for the holiday. The doorbell rang again, jarring Kelly from her self-inspection. But she wanted to look perfect.

"Are you going to answer the door, Kell?" Frankie called out from the family room. She'd left him in there with Juniper and Ariel. Ignoring her cousin, she stepped to the door and opened it.

A smile slid across her lips as she tilted her head slightly to the side and took in the sight of Nate. He looked darn good. And very autumnal in a rugby sweater over a coordinating gingham button-down. His look was finished with a pair of corduroy pants and black loafers.

"Wow. You look amazing," he said, holding a bouquet and a bottle of wine. The smile plastered on his face wasn't sweet at all, and Kelly felt herself blushing.

"You don't look so bad yourself." It was the only comeback she could think of because he'd flustered her. Though, she had the presence of mind to open the door wider and let him enter. "Let me take those."

Nate handed off the gifts and then closed the door behind him. Before she turned away, he reached for her arm and closed the small gap between them. He kissed her gently on the cheek, and her body swooned, leaning closer into him. "Thank you for inviting me to your family's holiday."

"You couldn't very well spend the day by yourself."

Nate's gaze drifted over Kelly's shoulder. "How does your uncle feel about me being here?"

She hemmed for a moment. "Maybe we won't discuss the murders over dinner."

"Hey there, Nate!" Frankie emerged from the family room and made his way to greet their guest. "Glad you could make it." Frankie opted for a pair of jeans that weren't torn and a navy fisherman's sweater for their Thanksgiving feast.

"Yay! Nate's here!" Ariel followed from the family room. A day after the almost fatal trip out to Montauk, Ralph had called Ariel and invited her to Thanksgiving dinner. Hesitant at first, because she didn't want to disappoint her parents, she eventually accepted the invite. Spending the day with the Blakes would allow her to get to know her new family better. And it was a perfect day to celebrate all they had to be grateful for. "Does this mean we can eat soon? I'm starving."

Kelly laughed. "Yes. Everyone is here. I'm going to take these into the kitchen," she said, looking at the flowers and wine. "Ariel, why don't you take Nate into the family room and show him where the drinks are. Frankie, come with me."

"Sure thing." Ariel turned her wheelchair around. "Appetizers are also set up with the drinks. They're delish."

Kelly nodded to Nate to go, and once he and Ariel disappeared, she caught up with Frankie, who was already on his way to the kitchen.

"What do you think?" she whispered as they entered the kitchen.

"I'm glad they're both here today. I wasn't sure if Ariel would accept Dad's invitation."

"Neither was I. She said her parents are coming by for dessert." Kelly dashed into the pantry and set the gifts on the counter. Back in the kitchen, she inhaled the tantalizing aroma of roasting turkey, hot rolls out of the oven, and freshly baked pumpkin pie. It was almost too much of an overload on her sense of smell, but she'd handle it. "Caroline is also coming later. Big sis had to go to her fiancé's family for dinner. Looks like we got a big old family get-together." She shouldered Frankie.

"A big old family that's hungry. Come on, let's get the food out. Where did you put the wine?" Frankie asked.

Kelly pointed to the pantry.

"I think we'll serve it with dinner. It'll be a nice gesture to Nate." He grabbed the bottle. "Put the flowers in a vase, and I'll set them on the buffet." Frankie disappeared out of the kitchen.

Kelly went into the pantry and grabbed a vase from an open shelf. She unwrapped the flowers, fluffing them out as she placed them in the vase.

"So he showed up." Her uncle appeared in the doorway holding a scotch glass.

"Be nice." Kelly crumpled the floral paper and tossed it in the trash bin.

"He was going to arrest me."

"Not necessarily." She slid a glance at her uncle as she filled the vase with water and then added the packet of plant food. He didn't look convinced. "If he thought you were guilty, he would have arrested you right after the first murder. Besides, it was over a month ago." She wanted to add that since she'd gotten over Nate's brusque handling of their relationship during the investigation, he needed to move on too.

Ralph grumbled.

She sighed. "It's only for one day. You can be civil." When there was no reply, she looked at him. "Can't you?"

Ralph downed the rest of his scotch and then walked away.

She shook her head. The man was never easy. She gave the flowers one last check. "I guess every family needs a Ralph."

* * * *

After dinner, hand in hand, Kelly and Nate walked out onto the patio off the family room. She cozied up to him for his body warmth since she hadn't grabbed her coat on the way outside. Their stroll out to the early evening chilled air was spur of the moment. They both wanted some private alone time.

"There's something I have to say." Nate's tone sounded serious, and nerves jittered in Kelly's stomach. She braced herself for a goodbye, an apology that things hadn't worked out, a reaffirming *it's not you, it's me* speech. Breaking up on Thanksgiving seemed a horrible way to end the day. Still, it was better than letting their failed relationship linger on. "I'm sorry."

Yep, he was going with the *sorry it's not you, it's me.*

"You don't have to apologize." Like it or not, she was a bit much to handle at times, and she understood it would take an extraordinary person to be able to deal with her. She'd thought Nate would be that person.

"I do. I should have handled things better. It was a mistake to have pushed you away like I did."

"You had a job to do."

"I did, but I still could have done my job without putting distance between us."

Kelly wasn't sure where the conversation was going. She searched his eyes for an inkling, but all she could see was how sad they looked. It broke her heart. He truly was sorry.

"Why did you?" Even though it had been weeks since the murders of Miranda and Bud were solved, she and Nate had only been out a handful of times. The busy retail season meant longer work hours for Kelly, and a detective out on leave meant an extra caseload for Nate. When they had gone out for dinner, they kept the conversation light, not going deep into why a wedge had been driven between them earlier. Looking back, Kelly knew why she hadn't brought up the subject—she was scared it would open the door to a conversation about breaking up. And she didn't want that.

He laced their fingers together and then squeezed her hand. "Eight years ago, I was engaged."

"Oh." That was a piece of information she hadn't known about.

"Her name was Anna. She was a police officer." A tiny smile twitched on his lips. "Like you, she was headstrong and so independent."

"What happened? Why did you break up?"

"We didn't break up. Anna was a good cop. Excellent detective. When she was working a case, nothing got in her way. Nothing." He swallowed. "She'd been working a serial killer case."

A creeping feeling of dread spread throughout her body, and Kelly braced herself for a bad ending to Nate's story.

"Anna was his last victim."

That was indeed a bad ending. On the tip of her tongue was another question, but she decided to keep it to herself. In time, Nate would tell her more about Anna and if he'd been the one who found her body.

"I'm so sorry. Please tell me you got the guy."

Nate nodded.

That was some consolation, but from personal experience, she knew it would never be enough. "I can't imagine what that was like for you."

"No, you can't. And seeing you get entangled in my murder investigation scared me to death."

"It did?" She sensed there was something else he wanted to say. She hoped she knew what it was, and she waited patiently for him to speak again.

His gaze leveled up and locked on her as he let go of her hand and caressed her cheek. "I'm falling in love with you, Kelly Quinn. Heck, I'm already there. I love you." He leaned in for a kiss.

She happily wrapped her arms around him and kissed him back. Her heart burst with joy. Pure joy.

He loves me.

Nate pulled back, and she bit her buzzing lower lip. She hadn't wanted their kiss to end.

"I should have talked to you. I know that now. But it was easier to put up a wall than it was to talk about my feelings."

"You were trying to protect yourself."

"All I wanted to do was to protect you, but you're a stubborn woman." He cracked a smile.

"Among other qualities," she joked.

"When I got the call about you out there in Montauk with the killer...I didn't know what to think. My mind raced with all sorts of thoughts. What if he killed you and Ariel?"

"But he didn't. We survived thanks to Ariel's expertise with her taser. You know, I need one of those."

"Maybe Santa will leave one in your stocking."

She raised her hand and stroked his face. "I'm sorry I worried you. I understand why you behaved the way you did. But I can't promise you I won't get tangled up in another murder. Hopefully, there won't be a next time. What I can promise is that I'll always tell you the truth. I'll be extra careful, and I won't go looking for trouble. How's that?"

"I think I can live with that."

"Good. Because Detective Nate Barber, I love you too." She was leaning in for another kiss when the patio door swooshed open, and Frankie popped his head out.

"Hey, what are you two doing out here? It's freakin' cold. Brrr." Frankie rubbed his hands together.

Kelly dropped her head onto Nate's chest and laughed. Leave it to her cousin to crash one of the most important moments of her life. "We better go back in there."

"Yep." Nate nodded and spun Kelly around. Together, they headed to the door.

"Is there pumpkin pie yet?" she asked Frankie.

"It was just set out. There's also apple pie and a plate of brownies." Frankie had been busy for days preparing their Thanksgiving feast. He'd even delivered hot meals for Kelly this past week, like a meal delivery service. It was his way of thanking her for helping clear his father's name. She'd never thought of charging for her sleuthing services. Though, she wasn't ready to hang out her amateur detective shingle just yet.

Chapter 23

Kelly lifted the two large to-go cups from the Holly Jolly Hot Cocoa stand. The cups' warmth seeped through her gloved hands on the cold, snowy Saturday morning after Thanksgiving. The pop-up hot beverage shop had been drawing a crowd on the corner of Main Street and Seabright Lane since it opened. A mural of a gingerbread family enjoying mugs of hot chocolate delighted customers as they waited in line to place their orders.

"You know, when I suggested doing this, I had no idea I'd be so busy. I had to send the hubby out for more supplies." Gemma Baker's cheeks were rosy from the nip in the November air. She wiped down the counter, preparing to pour three more cups. Kelly caught a glimpse of the woman behind her leaning forward with three raised fingers.

Kelly then pivoted and looked over her shoulder. The line had increased by more than half just in the few minutes since she got there. Pride bloomed in her. She couldn't help but be delighted in the success of 'Tis the Season to Shop Small in Lucky Cove.

After returning from Montauk and Paul being charged with two counts of homicide and plenty of other charges, like Kelly's attempted murder, stalking, and something to do with unlawful electronic surveillance, she'd been contacted by the president of the chamber of commerce. She was asked to chair the Shop Small committee again, and she graciously accepted the offer to rejoin. Though, she did wait a week before diving into the committee's work. Putting a condition on returning to the volunteer job was the first step in regaining control of her life.

After the call with the chamber's president, she called her therapist. Thankfully, her therapist didn't start the conversation with, "about time you called." Instead, Dr. Woodhall was kind and supportive and had an opening available.

Two days later, their forty-five-minute appointment left Kelly with the feeling of a weight being lifted from her shoulders. She knew she'd been gaslighted by Paul. But what came out of the session was that because she hadn't fully dealt with Becky's murder, she'd left herself vulnerable to his manipulation. That was something she could never allow to happen again.

The session gave her the chance to vent and then attempt to come to a place of forgiveness with those closest and dearest to her for believing she had been losing her mind. The venting had been successful. However, the forgiveness hadn't been, so another appointment was made.

"I'm glad it's going so well, Gemma. I'll check back later." Making a mental note to do that, Kelly stepped away from the cart and headed toward the Shoe Fashionista, formerly the Miranda & James shoe shop.

A dusting of snow overnight added to the festive mood, and she had no doubt that it helped energize the mass of tourists and locals that strolled along Main Street. She passed dozens of people who chattered in good spirits, navigated the crowded sidewalk with overflowing shopping bags, and pointed to the next shop they wanted to explore. The sight of happy shoppers did her heart good. The one-day event looked like it was on the road to being a success and a Lucky Cove tradition.

She reached the Shoe Fashionista and opened the door; a gust of cold air swept in, and two women nearest the entry shivered. She entered the crowded shop, scanning the sales floor and happily seeing stacks of shoeboxes piled next to several women who were trying on shoes. It looked like they were doing a little holiday shopping for themselves. Whatever their shopping motivation, it was nice to see that there was a chance the shop could end up in the black by the end of the year.

As part owner of the Shoe Fashionista, that thought was very reassuring.

Following her first appointment back with her therapist, Kelly sat down with Breena for a meeting where she was presented with a business plan. The pitch was professional, and Breena was passionate. Two factors that had made Kelly's decision easy.

Breena explained that while working at Kelly's boutique, she fell in love with retail, and working for a few weeks with Miranda, she realized she loved selling shoes. Though, the business proposal took Kelly by surprise. She had no idea her friend was interested in owning a shop. Nor that she considered Kelly's experience so valuable that she wanted Kelly in as a partner.

She'd never thought of owning a second retail business. Then again, she never considered owning her granny's consignment shop. Breena's enthusiasm had been contagious, and Kelly loved all the ideas for the shop. So much so, she almost said yes on the spot. But she caught herself and explained she needed time to think through the proposal. Her upcoming New Year's resolution was not to make rash decisions, and she figured it wouldn't hurt to start a little early.

Breena had looked a little deflated when Kelly hadn't immediately jumped at the chance, but she said she understood. She hadn't left her friend hanging for too long. Forty-eight hours later, Kelly called with the news that she was in. Together, they worked through tightening up the business plan and, with the help of Ernie Baldwin at the bank, got all the financing in place. Even Ralph agreed not to break the lease, though Kelly knew it wasn't completely selfless on his part. After the murders, Bitsy London decided to stay in the Hamptons. So he needed a tenant.

"For me?" Breena eyed the cup in Kelly's hand and didn't wait for an answer before she reached out for it. Dressed in a pair of knit pants and an emerald-green tunic, she looked comfortable and relaxed. She didn't look one bit rattled by the stream of customers in and out of the shop. "Hot cocoa? Yum. From the Holly Jolly stand? Gemma did an amazing job with it. So stinkin' cute." She turned and walked back to the counter. "How's it going out there? Is everyone as busy as I am?"

"I'm happy to say yes." Kelly sipped her hot cocoa. "How's your dad?"

A week before Thanksgiving, Mr. Collins came out of his coma. He was miraculously on the road to a full recovery. Even still, Kelly liked to keep tabs on his recuperation. Among the issues she was dealing with with her therapist was the guilt that gnawed at her for getting Mr. Collins hurt.

"He's good. We're counting down the days to his release." Breena set her cup down. "Angela is working out great. Look at her. She's a natural."

Kelly turned to have a look at the shop's first hire. The college student had an outgoing personality and an obsession with footwear. Those two qualities made her perfect for the shop. Kelly admired the redhead's block-heeled ankle boots with crisscrossed stud-embellished belts around the ankles. She turned back to Breena.

"Too bad she's only here until after the New Year."

Breena sulked. "I know. She really connects with people. Oh, here comes another sale." She pushed her cup aside and readied herself for the woman approaching with three boxes in hand.

"I should get back to the boutique. I'll check in later." Kelly made another mental note.

Her check-in list was growing long.

"Sure thing, partner." Breena giggled.

Kelly smiled. She was still getting used to having a business partner. She sidestepped an indecisive shopper on her way to the door and couldn't help but give a little style advice. "Those kitten heel pumps are timeless. But if you go up just a little with the heel height, you're elongating your body. Try those." She pointed to a pair of classic pumps and then continued out of the shop.

Another cold wind whipped by, and Kelly tightened her hold on her cup of hot cocoa. She was grateful she pulled on her cuddly plush hat before she headed out to survey the activity on Main Street and check in with retailers. She swallowed another sip of the hot beverage, and it warmed her insides. This was what she missed when she returned to Lucky Cove. In New York City, she enjoyed window-shopping on Black Friday. The crowds, the ringing of bells by sidewalk Santas, and the smell of roasted chestnuts were heaven for her. Now, she had a little slice of that right there in Lucky Cove.

"Kelly!" Jocelyn Bancroft came to a halt. Over her shoulder, she carried a large shopper tote that looked full, and in her hands, she held several shopping bags. "It's good to run into you. I was going to stop in the boutique."

"I hope you will. We have so many good things." Reaching out to Jocelyn had been on Kelly's to-do list. Though, with everything going on, she had planned on waiting until after the holidays.

"I heard what happened, and I can't believe it. Paul Sloan is a master manipulator. He covered up those murders, and no one suspected a thing. Until now."

Kelly's heartbeat quickened. Jocelyn's comments dragged her right back to the cottage and her face-to-face with Paul. In a blink of an eye, her throat constricted. She forced herself to swallow and focus on the here and now.

"Given the circumstances, I can understand if you don't want to be interviewed for my book. Though I can't say I won't be disappointed."

"You know, I would like to be interviewed. It's important to tell the stories of women like Diana Delacourte and Miranda Farrell. Maybe their stories could help someone else."

Jocelyn beamed. "Are you sure? My interviews are in depth. It won't be easy reliving what happened."

Been there and living through that right now.

"I'm certain. Call me to set up a time and place. I have to get back to the boutique. Enjoy your shopping." With that, Kelly pushed off and did not overthink what she'd just agreed to do.

"Hey, Kelly!" Erica Booth called out from the doorway of her bookshop. She dashed out onto the sidewalk. "I can't tell you how busy I've been! It's a Christmas miracle."

"I'm so happy to hear that. Everyone else seems to be saying the same thing." Kelly hadn't had the opportunity to speak with Erica since Paul Sloan's arrest. Actually, she really didn't try to take the time to see Erica. "I see your shop is packed!"

"I really should get back in there. I just wanted to tell you that I'm sorry for how I treated you. Looking back, I know you were only trying to do the right thing for Miranda and Bud. I hope there are no hard feelings."

Kelly shook her head. If Ariel could forgive her, she could do the same in regard to Erica for overreacting to a few simple questions about a murder. "None. See you at the next chamber meeting."

"Absolutely. You know, I really thought we might have learned what happened to all the money Daniel had stolen from his clients. It would have been nice to have some restitution for them."

Kelly nodded in agreement. It seemed likely that with Daniel, Nolen, and Miranda all dead, the whereabouts of the money would remain a mystery.

"There's a line at the counter." Kelly pointed at the interior of the shop. Erica's head whipped around, and then she hurried off to ring up those sales.

Kelly continued down Main Street, soaking in the festive spirit and knowing that justice had been served, and she had played a small role in it.

* * * *

By the time another dusting of snow fell, and nightfall set over Lucky Cove, Shop Small Saturday had come to an end. The shops along Main Street closed for the day, and Kelly was finally able to enjoy some downtime. However, there was one thing she had to take care of before she could chill on the sofa. She'd lured both Frankie and Pepper to her apartment once the workday was over. They hadn't talked since their argument, and it was time for them to clear the air. And Kelly hoped they agreed with her.

"Go on." Kelly shoved Frankie toward Pepper and stood resolute as he glared at her over his shoulder. She gestured for him to turn around and do the right thing. His reply was a thinning of his lips and flaring nostrils.

So dramatic.

"There's something Frankie wants to say to you, Pepper." Kelly crossed her arms, ready to witness Frankie apologize, grovel, do whatever it took to make things right with Pepper. Boy, she wished she had popcorn.

"Does he?" The way Pepper dragged out those two short words indicated she wouldn't forgive quickly.

"He does. Right, Frankie?" Kelly prompted.

Say something, you dramatic jerk.

Frankie turned his attention back to Pepper and cleared his throat. He shoved his hands in his jeans pockets. He was drawing this out and testing Kelly's patience.

"Kell's right. I do have something to say to you. I'm sorry for what I said about you not being family. I was wrong, and it was a hurtful thing to say. While it's not an excuse, I want you to know at the time I was upset and worried about my dad."

Pepper stared at Frankie, and Kelly saw him squirm a bit.

Frankie cleared his throat again. "Actually, I was worried Kelly would listen to you and not do her thing to help clear my dad because you are family. She values your opinion and advice."

"She does?" Pepper asked.

Oh, boy, Frankie. What are you doing to me?

"She does. I hope you can find it in your heart to forgive me." He tilted his head the way he always had since he was a little boy. Kelly remembered the smooth move and how he always got out of trouble by using it.

"Of course I forgive you. We're family, after all." Pepper opened her arms and welcomed him in for a hug. "All is forgotten."

Kelly's body relaxed. She was happy to see Pepper and Frankie make up and move past the stupid comment. Now, she just had to get her uncle and Ariel to hug it out. Which was more challenging because their issue wasn't just a callous remark made in the heat of the moment. No, it was a lifetime of lies and deceit. Yeah, much harder to forgive. Though, they'd made some headway on Thanksgiving. Baby steps, Kelly guessed.

"I'm so glad you two are good now. How about some hot apple cider? Frankie brought over a container, and we can warm it up," Kelly suggested.

"We?" Frankie shot a look at his cousin.

"I can handle heating up apple cider. I'm not that much of a disaster in the kitchen." Kelly turned and started walking to the hall.

"Remember last year when she tried to make those Christmas cookies?" Frankie asked Pepper.

Pepper laughed. "Lucky the whole building didn't burn down."

"Hey, it was just a little smoke," Kelly said, defending herself. While her baking skills were no match for Frankie's, she'd been using the pressure cooker she received as a Christmas gift last year. So far, all those horror stories her mother had shared years ago hadn't happened. "Liv should be here soon once her shift at the bakery is over. Then we can watch the movie."

They finished their cups of hot apple cider, and then Pepper said good night. She wanted to go home and take a hot bath to ease her aching muscles from a busy day at the boutique. Just after Pepper left, Liv arrived ready for a movie and popcorn. Frankie announced he was going to whip up some appetizers and disappeared into the kitchen to work his culinary magic while Kelly and Liv hung out in the living room.

A nudge on her leg had Kelly's attention drawn from the console table to the floor, where Howard meowed. She bent over and scooped him up. It had been a whole year since she became his new mom. To celebrate, she'd served him a plate of tuna fish and went a little wild in the pet shop, buying him a basket full of toys that were now scattered throughout the apartment.

The console table was a gift to herself to commemorate her first full year of living back in Lucky Cove and owning the boutique. She'd seen it in the window of Walt's antique shop. With the Black Friday sale and a generous discount for local business owners, she had been able to afford it. There was a spot in the living room, between the two windows, perfect for the piece of furniture. Once it was in place, she'd then set out to do what she promised herself she would do when she was in Marvin's cottage before almost being killed by Paul Sloan—she printed out photos from her phone.

She splurged on lovely frames from the gift shop, not from the big-box store off the highway. Then she set the photographs out on the tabletop. While there were only five now, she planned on filling the space with more snapshots that captured the memories she wanted to keep forever.

Leading the lineup was a photo of her, Liv, and Gabe at a summer beach party. Then there was one with her, Pepper, and her granny two years ago at Christmas. The third framed photo was of her, her sister, and her parents at Easter. The next in the lineup was of her, Frankie, Juniper, and Ariel. It was their first family photo together. The last one was a photo taken five years ago of her and her cousin Becky. Each photograph represented what she held most dear in life—her family and friends.

"I've been looking forward to relaxing and this movie night all day. The bakery was so busy." Liv sprang up from the dining table, taking the big bowl of buttery popcorn with her. "The movie is ready. Where are those appetizers?"

Howard fidgeted in Kelly's arms and then leaped to the table, toppling the neatly arranged photographs.

"Bad cat!" Kelly shooed Howard off the table and got a death glare from the feline before he leaped up to the sofa. "He's the reason why I can't have anything nice."

Liv laughed as she joined Howard on the sofa. "He's just being a cat." She stroked his head.

"Don't coddle him!" Kelly rearranged the photographs. "He's a terror."

"This sweet boy?" Liv teased.

"Yes, that sweet boy." Kelly stepped back and inspected the lineup. Perfect.

"I really like the photos. They make this place a home." Liv tossed a kernel of popcorn in her mouth. "You know, you need one of you and Nate K-I-S-S-I-N-G." She giggled.

Kelly rolled her eyes. "What are you, thirteen?" She definitely didn't need a photo. Every kiss with Nate was seared into her brain. She stepped back and admired her display.

Frankie sauntered into the living room with a platter of buffalo chicken egg rolls and dipping sauce.

"Oooh, they look delicious!" Liv leaned forward and snatched one off the tray along with a napkin.

"They are." Smiling, Frankie set the tray on the coffee table and then dropped onto the sofa. "Try one, Kell."

Kelly nodded. She knew they'd taste divine. Frankie's food always did. She gave another look to the photo frames.

"I think you're right, Liv, about how these photos make the apartment feel." She moved to the sofa and dropped down on the cushion, wedging in between Liv and Frankie. Howard climbed over and curled up on her lap. He closed his eyes and purred. "For the first time since coming back to Lucky Cove, I really feel like this is where I'm supposed to be forever. I'm never going to leave because I'm home."

About the Author

Debra Sennefelder is an avid reader who reads across a range of genres, but mystery fiction is her obsession. Her interest in people and relationships is channeled into her novels against a backdrop of crime and mystery. When she's not reading, she enjoys cooking and baking and as a former food blogger, she is constantly taking photographs of her food. *Yeah, she's that person.* Born and raised in New York City, where she majored in her hobby of fashion buying, she now lives and writes in Connecticut with her family. She's worked in retail and publishing before becoming a full-time author. Her writing companion is her adorable and slightly spoiled Shih-Tzu, Connie.

You can learn more about Debra at www.DebraSennefelder.com

Printed in the United States
by Baker & Taylor Publisher Services